Anonymous

Life, Trial, and Extraordinary Adventures of John H. Surratt, the Conspirator

A correct account and highly interesting narrative of his doings and

adventures from childhood to the present time

Anonymous

Life, Trial, and Extraordinary Adventures of John H. Surratt, the Conspirator
*A correct account and highly interesting narrative of his doings and adventures
from childhood to the present time*

ISBN/EAN: 9783337182601

Printed in Europe, USA, Canada, Australia, Japan

Cover: Foto ©Raphael Reischuk / pixelio.de

More available books at **www.hansebooks.com**

LIFE, TRIAL

AND

EXTRAORDINARY ADVENTURES

OF

JOHN H. SURRATT,

THE CONSPIRATOR.

A

CORRECT ACCOUNT

AND

HIGHLY INTERESTING NARRATIVE

OF HIS DOINGS AND ADVENTURES FROM CHILDHOOD TO THE
PRESENT TIME

———•———

PHILADELPHIA:
PUBLISHED BY BARCLAY & CO.
602 ARCH STREET.

LIFE OF JOHN H. SURRATT.

This individual, who bears a fearful name, is now endowed with a terrible celebrity, and ranks with Fieschi, Louvel, Bellingham, and the assassins and bravos of the Middle Ages. The plot devised and concocted against the life of the Executive was the first of the kind ever compassed in the United States. The Americans and English are not a blood thirsty or murderous people ; men may be slain, but it will generally be in a fair and open fight ; the Anglo-Saxon character is too manly and generous for any other course. Whether or not John H. Surratt was connected in any other manner with the conspiracy, which resulted so fatally to all concerned, the reader will judge for himself.

The South since the Declaration of Independence has been divided into three classes :

1. The rich planter who spent money lavishly, lived elegantly, and had many ideas in common with the English aristocracy ; he was exceedingly irritable on the slavery question, and would bear no allusion to its wrongs or the iniquities which the North alleged were constantly inflicted on the negroes.

2. The poor whites, who were considered as of less value than the blacks ; these people resided in small meanly furnished houses, were treated with the most undisguised contempt by their more opulent neighbors, and were seldom addressed unless when it was absolutely necessary. This class earned a meagre subsistence by trading with the negroes, occasionally kept hounds to track fugitives, and did not hesitate for a bribe to betray the ill-fated wretch who trusted to their honor, or sought their hospitality.

3. The slaves, who had no rights at all.

Such was the condition of affairs at the time of John Surratt's birth, who is now about twenty-four. His parents belonged to the second class we have described. His father was a man who was disposed to be meek and conciliatory. His mother, a determined virago, who was resolved on all occasions to have her own way, who hated the Yankees, as she denominated all who came from the non-slaveholding States. Unlike her husband, she had received some little education ; was a devoted catholic, and held in some estimation by the Jesuits, and the clergy of Washington. She was not wanting in a certain tact, soon saw the advantages that would accrue to her son from some mental training, and accordingly placed John at an academy kept at the village, where she and her husband had opened a small public house.

John was a moody, fretful boy, who had been exceedingly indulged ; three little negroes about the house, were his playfellows, slaves and victims. One boy who was about six years old was particularly timid; he was an exceedingly light mulatto, with bright eyes, and straight hair, he had been bought from a trader, and a smile never was seen on his melancholy countenance. John Surratt particularly delighted in teasing Charlie ; the poor boy never had a moment's rest.

"Charlie, you black imp, bring me this ; Charlie, you confounded hound, bring me the other. One day John Surratt missed a dog whip, which was a particular favorite, and after making a search all over concluded that the mulatto had stolen it, and accused him of the theft. The unfortunate boy stoutly denied that he had even seen the article, except in the hands of his young master, and touchingly concluded by saying:

"You know, little massa, I never tells lies."

"You lie, you confounded yellow villain, when wont a nigger both lie and steal ?"

" Charlie never steals."

"You lie again ; tell me where that whip is, or I'll take the skin off your back. I'll settle up with you."

" I hain't got it, and I does'nt know where it is."

"You lie, you do ; tell me at once."

"Massa, I can't tell what I don't know."

"Then you shall take a hiding, by God. I'll take your yellow hide off you, and then

21

perhaps you'll tell the truth. Here Jim, Jack, tie him up."

The luckless child, trembling in every limb, glanced at the two stalwart boys of fourteen who advanced deprecatingly; his eyes filled with tears, and he looked pitifully at the boy tyrant, and the two minions who prepared to execute his mandates. The child was stripped to his waist, fastened to a post, and the whip vigorously applied. Poor Charlie made the apartment resound with his cries, but still persisted in his denial. At last Mrs. Surratt entered the room, and inquired what was the matter.

"The infernal yellow villain has stolen my dog whip, and wont tell where it is," said John.

"Tell this moment, you dog, or I'll cut the life out of you," said Mrs. Surratt, eyeing the boy malevolently.

"Missis," said Charlie, imploringly, "I can't tell what I doesn't know."

"Aunt, aunt," exclaimed a little girl, rushing in, "you are wanted. But what's the matter? Oh, John, what a wicked boy; why do you whip poor Charlie, he tries so hard to please you."

The speaker, was a little girl of about ten, whose countenance denoted an amiable and gentle disposition, and to whom Charlie had been particularly attentive; she hated cruelty.

"Because," said John Surratt. "I choose to whip him, and it is no business of yours."

"But tell me what he has done?"

"He has stolen my pretty whip?"

"No, he has not. I saw it in the stable last night, and I'll go and bring it."

"She tripped away, returned in a few moments, and laid the coveted article on the table."

"There, you see that you were wrong, and that Charlie did not take it at all."

"Now let him go, and here is a ten cent piece for him; it is all I have, but he can buy cakes with it," said the little heroine, extending all her worldly wealth to Charlie, who with a broken voice, refused the proferred gift, saying:

"I do not want it."

"John," said Mrs. Surratt, "be more careful in future. Come with me Edith."

Charlie was untied, and Surratt thought no more about it, but Charlie had not forgotten the unmerited and brutal chastisement to which he had been subjected, and studied plans of revenge. John Surratt, like a celebrated French revolutionist, was fond of birds, and prided himself on raising the choicest canaries. He had eight young birds, of the finest color and purest breed.

He went as was his daily custom to feed his pets, but they were all gone, the cage door was open, and no one had done the mischief; a similar fate befell a fine mocking bird, and macaw, and the offender could not be detected. The dogs were poisoned, the cats disappeared, and all by the same invisible hand. Edith who also had her favorites, sympathized with her cousin, but her darlings escaped. The freshest and sweetest mulberry leaves were always placed before her silk worms. Her cages, and fountains were always cleaned, the chickweed, plantains, berries and green food of all kinds, were brought in such profusion, that Edith once said, "If I did not know, that such things could not be, I would think that the fairies had come back again; some one is very good to me."

Mrs. Surratt did not fare better than John, the same invisible phantom tormented her, bread, cake, and pies, all found their way to the pig pen; her wardrobe was torn to pieces. One night it happened that she left her watch on the table; remembering what had latterly transpired in the house, Mrs. Surratt hastily went down stairs, but the trinket was no longer there. Two days after the fragments were put in a conspicuous place. Mrs. Surratt interrogated separately all the members of the family, black and white, but vainly; no one either could or would solve the mystery. John Surratt tried his best to induce Charlie to tell if he knew any thing about it, but always received the answer:

"You thought that you catched me once, and you was wrong. Now Massa John, if I tell you the truth, you wont never believe me."

All his efforts were useless, and the author of all this mischief was never detected.

The academy which John Surratt attended was under the charge of Mr. Anderson, from Connecticut, an excellent teacher, but a thorough disciplinarian. John Surratt was an idle and mischievous boy, who was rarely known to commit his lessons; he was always imperfect in his recitations; he was not deficient in capacity, but was incorrigibly indolent. This defect the principal had long noticed, and was resolved to correct.

"You must commit these lines to memory, and recite them perfectly to-morrow after the school opens. At ten o'clock I will grant you an hour's grace, but you must be perfect; and remember, that if you are not, I shall punish you without fail."

The boy looked sullenly at the principal but made no reply. The next morning, true to his promise, the principal as the clock struck ten called, "John Surratt, come and recite the poem I told you to prepare."

The boy stood before his teacher, stammered through three or four lines, and then remained silent.

"You are incorrect, sir. What reason can you give? I will hear what you have to allege in your defence."

The boy was silent.

"Have you nothing to say?"

No reply.

"You will now go to your seat; in an hour I shall call you up again."

Surratt returned to his desk, maddened by the looks and whispered taunts of his companions, with whom he was not popular. The hour elapsed, Surratt was again summoned to recite his task, and a second time was imperfect.

"John Surratt," said Mr. Anderson, "you are trifling with me, take your seat, you shall remain without your dinner; the others may now go."

The boy saw that the teacher was inflexible, he hated to accomplish the task, as "he did not want to please old Anderson," but well knew that whatever the New Englander said that he would do, he would not fail to execute. He was the more confirmed in this idea by what Mr. Anderson said to Charlie, who came to know why Massa John did not come home to dinner.

"Tell Mrs. Surratt that, I desired her son to commit to memory, or stay. You cannot remember all this. I will write a note, and seating himself, Mr. Anderson produced the following epistle, which was found in Mrs. Surratt's bureau after her arrest."

MADAME.—I desired your son John to commit to memory a few lines of easy poetry, and told him that if he were not ready, when I called him, that I should certainly punish him. He has not done his duty, and shall remain with me till the lines are known. I have repeatedly excused him for indolence, but am now resolved to carry out my threat. He shall stay without his dinner.

Persuasion will be useless. The discipline of the school requires it, and I must be rigidly impartial. Should you send any food, I shall not permit him to use it.

Respectfully yours
STEPHEN ANDERSON.

The note was then read to John, and dispatched. Mr. Anderson said nothing, the exercises of the school proceeded as usual, and about five o'clock, John Surratt stood before the principal's desk, and announced himself ready. The lines were recited without a fault, and John was dismissed with the injunction to be more careful in future, or severe punishments would be in store for him when school was over. The boy clustered around Surratt.

"Well, Johnny, I told you that old Anderson would be too much for you, and that you would have to do as you were told," said one.

"Hold your tongue, and mind your business," was the reply in a savage tone.

"Johnny," said another, a tall boy of fourteen, who was the wit of the school, "I read in a book the other day an old Scotch proverb, 'He needs a long spoon, not to come off second best, who sops kale with the de'il.' You are the man, who wanted the cabbage, and I leave you to guess, who is the old gentleman, with the hoofs and horns, who has his hair tied with an ox's chain."

"Shut up," said Surratt, looking like a fiend.

"I guess you can't make me do that, Johnny, pet. It takes Anderson to manage you, and I advise you, as a friend, to keep on his right side."

"What can he do?"

"What an innocent baby you are to ask me such a question; you know well enough."

"Well, what will he do?"

"Why he'll wallop you like thunder."

"I'd like to see him do it."

"Don't trust him too far, and don't brag too much, or he'll be sure to lamb you; good bye."

These taunts and sarcasms wounded Surratt, who glanced at his companions, and saw at once if he made an attack that he would be overpowered, he contented himself with saying, "Take care, don't go too far."

"Why, what can you do against us all?"

This was a home thrust that could not be parried, and Surratt answering in general terms said:

"You will see what I'll do; I'll make old Anderson repent this the longest day he has to live." Without waiting any further reply, Surratt turned on his heel, quitted the ground, and was soon at home, where he recounted the adventures of the day.

Mrs. Surratt apparently sympathized with her son, but well knew that he required some correction, and was too prudent to interfere. Three weeks elapsed, and Surratt was more diligent than before; the threats of his teacher and the sneers of his companions had not been without their effect, and his mother imagined that all had been forgotten; she was deceived.

Surratt had never forgiven Mr. Anderson, and was determined to be revenged. Secretly possessing himself of a pistol, he waylaid Mr. Anderson and shot him, the ball lodged in the fleshy part of the thigh and fortunately did no harm. A person in the vicinity, saw the whole transaction, assisted the teacher, and summoning aid arrested the would be assassin, but the teacher generously declined prosecuting, and though the whole matter was known through the country, it never came officially before the courts.

Mr. Anderson, when restored to health, quitted that section of the country, and "a new pedagogue reigned in his stead;" the trustees of the academy, however, thought proper to inform Mrs. Surratt, that it was better that she should not send her son as a pupil to the institution under their charge. Mrs. Surratt next placed her son at the old and time honored college of Georgetown, where he was noted for his insubordination and idleness : but warned by the difficulty with Mr. Anderson, John Surratt was wise enough to have no personal contact with the superiors, and after a sojourn of about three years, he quitted that abode of learning to enter into more active pursuits. Mrs. Surratt, meanwhile, had still been engrossed with her business, and report affirms had been so far successful as to invest a few thousands ; animated by the desire of seeing her son rise, she proposed that he should enter the navy, but met a decided refusal. The army was then offered, but with no better success, and the disappointed mother was compelled to allow her son to follow his own inclinations. Her husband had been dead for some years, and she was too proud to acknowledge that she had been deceived in this her favorite child : John Surratt, therefore pursued no gainful calling : occasionally he acted as a real estate broker, and for a short time was an under clerk in one of the departments. His sympathies were always southern and pro-slavery, and he hated the North with an intense bitterness, which he did not attempt to disguise ; thus time passed, till the opening of the rebellion, in the latter part of Buchanan's administration.

For this, neither Mrs. Surratt nor her son, was wholly unprepared, the matter had long been discussed in all the slaveholding states, and the District of Columbia, long before it actually transpired ; as a matter of course, Mrs. Surratt, and all her family were ardent partisans, and warm supporters of the *soidisant* confederacy ; the boarding house, which she then kept, was the rallying point of all the secessionists in Washington, and the adjacent parts of Maryland and Virginia ; shortly before, Booth, who has earned such an infamous celebrity as the murderer of the President, played an engagement at Wash-

ington, and Mrs. Surratt was given to understand that the *artiste* favored the independence of the South ; this was enough, John Surratt easily made the actor's acquaintance : and they soon became intimate : we cannot here affirm positively, but, from the circumstances under our notice, are strongly led to believe that John H. Surratt was a member of the golden circle, which played so distinguished a part in the late war, but one thing is very plain, that John H. Surratt was exceedingly intimate with all the rebel chiefs, and from his position was enabled to furnish some valuable information.

The rebellion broke on the North like a clap of thunder, but at the end of four years, the raw recruits were converted into disciplined soldiers. The hopes of European intervention gradually became weaker, and weaker, and the North was stronger. The South, though unwilling to confess it, was sorely disheartened, and some of the leaders in the conflict entertained the idea, that if the President, Vice President, and other individuals at the head of the government, were removed, that the nation would be plunged in a state of anarchy, and the South at full liberty to march on Washington, and seize the public treasure. The conspirators, Booth, Harold, Payne, Azteroth, met at Mrs. Surratt's, and she was perfectly cognizant of all the plans of the South, in the event of success. Her son, though not directly criminated on the trial, still by his suspicious absence, led the public to suppose that he also was deeply involved in the plot, which deprived the Republic of her Chief Magistrate.

When the news of the death of Mr. Lincoln was conveyed to Mrs. Surratt. She closed her shutters, and calmly awaited the result, but justice, though sometimes likened to a hobbling beldame, cast aside her staff, and arming herself with her sword, quickly grasped the criminals. Nor did she rest, till all had atoned for their crimes with their lives.

Safety alone consisted in flight ; the scaffold loomed distinctly in the distance ; the President would be inexorable, no voice, save that of their legal defenders, would be raised in behalf of any implicated in the foul deed. The police were active, and every corner of the Republic would be searched to deliver these great criminals to the just vengeance of the law.

John Surratt knew that he was a marked man, and concealed himself all day after his mother's arrest in a wretched hovel in the outskirts of Washington, which had been shunned, even by the homeless beggar, since its last occupant had died of small-pox, and

when night came, hid his features with a handkerchief bound over his forehead, he presented himself at the residence of a certain priest, who had been one of his college classmates. The clergyman opened the door in person, as he was going out, but shrunk back when he saw the well known figure.

"You will not betray me," gasped Surratt. "On my soul, I did not raise my hand against any one."

"No matter, whether guilty or innocent, you have sought my hospitality, and I shall not betray you, but you must leave Washington."

"Such is my intention, and I am well furnished with gold and greenbacks, but a disguise is absolutely necessary."

"Go up stairs, lock yourself in the first room you see, and do not open it till you hear my knock; I shall return as speedily as possible."

Left to himself, Surratt entered the apartment and gazed on the books, plain furniture, and few pictures; all breathed peace and repose. Here was a man, who devoted himself to the good of others, while he, besought was insupportable, and to while away the time, a book was selected from the shelves on the wall. The volume chanced to be Hood's Poems, and it opened at the graphic description of Eugene Aram's crime, and his conversation with his pupil.

Surratt threw the volume aside, and walked to and fro, till he heard the welcome rap, and his friend entered.

"I returned as soon as I could ?"

"You have no time to lose ?"

"You must escape or your life will be forfeited?"

"But how, every one knows me in Washington."

"You must assume a clerical dress, and green spectacles. In that wardrobe you will find all that you require."

Surratt hastily threw aside the suit, in which he was then clad, and donning the habiliments in the wardrobe, would easily have been taken for a catholic priest. A breviary and green spectacles completed the transformation; the coat was worn.

"I thank you a thousand times," said Surratt.

"I have not forgotten the service you rendered me. Farewell, may God prosper you, be silent and quiet; above all avoid the society of priests, they will be sure to detect you, if you have done evil. May God forgive you, if you are innocent he will surely deliver you from all snares."

"But," said Surratt, "I have taken your clothes and spectacles; allow me—"

"Not a cent, not a cent," said the priest, hurriedly. A close embrace, and they parted perhaps never to meet again.

The door was locked, as soon as it closed on his departing guest; and the priest then taking the clothes left by Surratt, tore them to shreds and cast them singly into a large fire kindled for the purpose. Then filling a pipe with strong tobacco, its fumes soon overpowered the scent of burning wool, and every trace of his visitor thus disappeared.

"If I have been wrong," said the good man to himself, "may our blessed Saviour pardon me; perhaps John is not guilty, and it is not for us to judge each other."

Surratt, when he found himself again in the street, proceeded at once to the railroad station, and took a ticket for Baltimore, where he was compelled to remain till ten o'clock the following day: he did not leave the depot where he obtained some slight refreshment, till he took his seat in the cars for Philadelphia, where thoroughly exhausted, he repaired at once to an obscure hotel in the northern part of the city, and paying for a room in advance, threw himself on the bed, and was soon wrapped in a deep slumber.

He was aroused by the tea bell, and descending to the table, took the first regular meal he had eaten for three days; he then retired to his chamber, the next day went to a store, made some purchases, and penned the following letter:

"So far I am safe; use the enclosed to make the cloth which I shall send you, take the rest for charity."

A hundred dollar note accompanied this epistle; four days after, Surratt had crossed the border, and was safe in Canada, at least for the present.

What was to be done next: there he could not stay, he would be sure of detection, and though Montreal and Quebec were full of rebel refugees, he could not remain at either place, and determined to visit Europe, assuming another name, he sailed for the Old World, and safely landed in England, whence he sought the Contenent. Before he left Canada, he made the acquaintance of a certain Bishop, who gave him a general letter to all the religious houses on the Continent; his clerical friend in Washington received the letter and a package, he knew whence they both came, but his lips were sealed by honor and charity.

Surratt did not sojourn long in the United Kingdoms, but repaired at once to Paris. While in that gay capital, he attended a ball at the opera house in the costume of a Spanish cavalier. Nature has gifted this individual with an exceedingly attractive exterior, and when he choose, his address is exceedingly winning: a young and graceful woman, dressed as a sultana, who courteously accepted the homage paid to her charms, attracted Surratt's attention, who accosted her. The *incognita's* conversation equalled her personal charms, and the pair were soon whirling in the giddy waltz; an alcove tempted the dancers to repose, and the table was spread with the choisest refreshments. Surratt unmasked, and his companion did likewise, and glanced over the table.

"Do you want any thing?" asked Surratt.

"I should like a few grapes."

An attendant was summoned who soon brought the required delicacies, and placed a small plate with a peach before Surratt, who hanged color, but said nothing. He handed the fruit to his companion, and while she was looking over the grapes, took the peach under which he found a slip of paper, with these words:

"You must leave Paris in three days, or I shall denounce you."

Surratt crushed the note in his hand, chatted gaily with his companion, who, as the clock struck twelve, rose and bade him good night.

"Permit me, at least, Madame, to see you to your carriage."

"I appreciate your courtesy, but you will hold me excused. On this point I am rigid; adieu.

"One word—pray give me your address; shall we ever meet again?"

"I cannot tell what is in store for either of us: do not follow me."

The lady closely masked, and her form concealed in a black silk cloak, left the building, and accepting the arm of a common looking man, walked a square, where a carriage was awaiting her. Before she parted with her escort, she said, "You may tell the person who sent you here, that the warning has been given."

When Surratt was alone, he paced the saloons hurriedly, and at last went to the superintendent of the refreshment saloon, and asked who had brought the fruit he had ordered.

"I cannot tell; but if Monsieur will have the goodness to wait, he shall see all who have been here to-night."

Three o'clock struck, the vast saloons were emptied, and Surratt presented himself again to the chief, who, mindful of his promise, assembled all his employees, but Surratt did not see the man who had waited on him and his companion. But the warning was too important to be neglected, and Surratt quitted

the French capital, after a delay of twenty-four hours, and reached Italy.

Shortly after his arrival in Rome, Surratt entered an ecclesiastical seminary, and presented himself to the superior with the letter from the Canadian prelate. But such an institution did not suit his habits, and we next meet him in the costume of a Papal Zouave.

The remainder of this strange, eventful tale, will be found in the annexed official report, which details briefly, the method of Surratt's capture, escape, and re-arrest.

Late in October, the United States minister to Rome, General Rufus King, received intelligence through various channels, that a man named Watson, serving as a private in the Papal Zouaves, was no other than Surratt, one of the accomplices in Mr. Lincoln's assassination. From information subsequently obtained, it appeared that this fact was well known to some of Surratt's brothers-in-arms. And that others also in Rome, were aware of his participation in the plot, and that he bore an assumed name. Notwithstanding this, he was always made comfortable wherever he went. Supplied with money by sympathizers, and admitted to the companionship of well known residents of Rome.

General King, knowing that there was no extradition treaty between the United States and the Papal government, understood at once that there would be some difficulty in securing the criminal. He went at once to Cardinal Antonelli, stated the case, and in return received the promise of his eminence, that should sufficient proof be received of Surratt's identification, under the extraordinary circumstances of the case, the legal right would be waived, and the prisoner surrendered. General King wrote for instructions from Washington, and busied himself in obtaining the requisite testimony.

On the seventh of November, late at night, he received a message, from Cardinal Antonelli, containing the information that Surratt, whom the Papal authorities had secured of their own free will, awaiting General King's demand for his arrest, had left the Pontifical States. It appears, that as soon as the Pope was informed of the case, he directed that, to prevent all doubts as to his desire to see justice done, that Surratt should be imprisoned until General King should be in a position to claim him on proof of his identity. This was done without the knowledge or request of the representative of the United States, and evinces a sincere desire on the part of the papal authorities, to waive technicalities, where justice and right demand satisfaction.

Surratt was imprisoned in a high tower on the edge of a very steep precipice, where a narrow ledge twenty-eight feet below the room in which he was incarcerated, was the only break to an almost perpendicular drop of two hundred feet. It seems that he must have gained an inkling of the reason for his sudden arrest and imprisonment, and determined to effect his escape. To do this, he requested permission after a good dinner and a smoke, (the fellow was very comfortably kept,) to retire to the water-closet.

He was thus out of sight of the two sentries in his room, and had time to spring out of the window upon the ledge overhanging the precipice. It is now stated, with what truth I cannot say, that two men with an outstretched blanket broke the fall; at all events in jumping out, he severely bruised his back and shoulders, but got away. The colonel of the regiment, which furnished the detachment on guard in the castle, has sent in a certificate, that within five minutes of the discovery of his escape, or say ten minutes from the time he first entered the water-closet, fifty men, and some officers were dispatched in pursuit, but fruitlessly.

The escape was made on a dark night, and Surratt knew every inch of the ground. The frontier was close at hand, and it was out of the question for the Papal guards to follow him beyond it.

On receipt of this information from the Cardinal, General King telegraphed to Mr. Marsh at Rome, the information of Surratt's escape, described his dress, (he was still in uniform,) and requested all United States consuls in Italian ports might be informed of the matter, and take all proper measures for the culprit's arrest.

This was done. General King then received information, that a person answering Surratt's description had been seen at Sonelli. Mr. Hunter, secretary of legation, went there, but only in time to ascertain that Surratt had passed, through still in uniform, on his way to Naples ; this information was telegraphed to Rome, Florence and Naples, and Mr. Hunter returned.

The American consul to Naples, next informed General King, that Surratt had sailed for Alexandria. He had been four days at Naples, three of which were passed in prison, where he was detained on suspicion, and was not set at liberty, till *he asserted that he was a British subject, and was released at the desire of the English consul,* who with some residents of Naples got up a subscription, enabling him to pay his passage to Alexandria : these parties alleged ignorance of his antecedents :

while in Naples, Surratt stated that he was a Canadian, who had served in the Papal Zouaves for ten months, been imprisoned for insubordination, and escaped from confinement; the bruises on his back, and his uniform confirmed his story, and he met with much sympathy.

The Tripoli, a Peninsular and Oriental Coal Company's steamer, on which Surratt had taken his passage, was to coal at Malta, and remain there for twenty-four hours. General King and the United consul both telegraphed to the consul at Malta to arrest Surratt on the arrival of the Tripoli in the harbor at Malta. This official applied to the British authorities to arrest Surratt, and informed them of all the circumstances. But notwithstanding the urgency of the matter, and the impossibility of finding necessary proof within the time required, his application for Surratt's surrender was *refused on the ground of illegality;* a strange contrast to the conduct of the papal authorities.

Meanwhile General King was informed of all that had transpired, and immediately telegraphed to the consul at Alexandria instructions to secure the prisoner immediately on his arrival at that port. An answer was returned from the telegraph company that the cable was broken between Alexandria and Malta, but that the message would be forwarded from the island by the first steamer. The consul at Malta also transmitted information to his colleague at Alexandria in such a manner that the letter was delivered before any one was permitted to land at that city. It is somewhat extraordinary that General King's message requesting Surratt's detention came by the same vessel as the man himself. Before any passengers landed, Mr. Hale, the American consul at Alexandria, came on board with the necessary authority for Surratt's arrest, secured and put him in jail, where he is now safely guarded, awaiting the arrival of a United States gunboat, on which he will be transported to Civita Vecchia, and thence to Rome for identification. Thus, after an extra ordinary combination of events, all tending to facilitate Surratt's escape, after his release from confinement and good fortune at Naples, and in spite of the difficulties thrown in the way of justice by the English authorities at Malta, and the inopportune breaking of the telegraphic cable, the conspirator is at the mercy of the United States authorities, and ere this be read, will be on the way to the United States.

All represent Surratt as a young man of fine abilities, excellent manners, good appearance, talent, and vivacity,

He came to Rome with letters of introduction from one of the Canadian prelates, studied for a month in an academy, and then enlisted in the Papal Zouaves. He was always well supplied with money by persons in Rome, who knew his previous history.

The information which led to his capture was communicated to General King by St. Marie, a French Canadian, who had served in one of the Union regiments during the war. St. Marie, who is rather a queer character, knew Surratt in Maryland, and recognized him immediately when he enlisted in the papal service.

Surratt never disguised the fact, that he had been engaged in the conspiracy; on the contrary he spoke very freely to St. Marie, and told him that Mr. Lincoln's assassination was a preconcerted plot, and that he (Surratt) *carried direct from Davis's cabinet in Richmond,* the principal details of the plot to Washington, and that the murder was committed, not only in accordance with the desires of the rebel ministry, but by the express commands and directions.

St. Marie, positively asserts that all this was communicated to him by Surratt. But as he is a person, on whom but little reliance can be placed, the information must be taken, *cum grano salis.*

A woman, as is usual, was at the bottom of all this. St. Marie was led to betray Surratt, through jealousy, the latter having been successful in a love affair at Washington, in which both were competitors for the affection of the same person. The affair of the capture, escape, and subsequent arrest, occasioned an immense sensation at Rome, Florence and Naples.

TRIAL

OF

JOHN H. SURRATT,

CONSPIRATOR, FOR THE

MURDER OF ABRAHAM LINCOLN.

THE trial of John Surratt, indicted for the murder, and for entering into a conspiracy to murder, the late President Lincoln, was fixed for May 27, in the Criminal Court of the district; Judge Fisher presiding. The indictment against Surratt was found on Feburary 4, 1867. On Febuary 19, a bench warrant was isued for the arrest of the accused. On Febuay 23, he was arraigned and pleaded not guilty. On April 18, a motion was made by the defendant to fix a day for trial, and on the same day the District Attorney made a motion for continuance. On April 23, the motion for continuance was overruled, and on the same day the defendant's counsel gave notice that they would be ready to proceed to trial on May 27.

The case has excited more interest than anything that has occurred in Washington, since the trial of Henry Wirz, and the court was well filled with spectators before 10 o'clock, the time for assembling of the court. At 10 o'clock the court was formally opened by the crier, the counsel for the defence, Messrs. R. T. Merrick, J. H. Bradly, Sr., and J. H. Bradly. Jr., being present.

A few minutes thereafter the counsel for the prosecution, Hon. E. C. Carrington, district attorney, Nathaniel Wilson, assistant district attorney; and G. A. Riddle, Esq., and judge Edward Pierrepont of New York, appeared and took their seats. Judge Pierrepont was on motion of Mr. Carrington, formally admitted and qualified as a member of the bar of this District. The names on the regular panel were called, and all excepting three answered to their names.

Judge Fisher said this was the day set for the trial of John H. Surratt, under an indictment for murder, and he asked if the counsel were ready.

The attorney for the defence responded affirmatively.

District Attorney Carrington said he regretted exceedingly that, upon consultation, several difficulties were presented in the way of proceeding to the trial at the present time. In the first place, the probabilities were that the case would run into the next term of the court, which commenced on the third Monday in June, and the question suggested itself whether, if the trial was proceeded with now and not concluded, the court could proceed with and continue the trial at the succeeding term.

This is one objection, but there is another and a very serious one. As soon as this day was fixed for the trial the prosecuting counsel used all diligence to get witnesses here, but failed to secure the attendance of the most important witnesses. These witnesses may possibly appear at any day. New testimony and new facts have also been recently discovered. New developments have also been made; and in a case of this importance the prosecution would not undertake to go to trial unless perfectly ready and prepared.

Judge Fisher asked if there was not a

statue disposing of Mr. Carrington's first objection?

Mr. Merrick replied that there was, and it was distinctly stated that a case pending at the close of a term could go over, and be continued.

Mr. Bradley asked, and the court directed that the prisoner be brought into court before the argument was further proceeded with.

At quarter of eleven o'clock the prisoner was brought into court and seated in the prisoner's box but he was subsequently assigned a seat beside his counsel. The prisoner looks pale and careworn. He is not in good health, and has for some time been obliged to partake of wine as a tonic.

After the prisoner had been seated, Mr. Merrick said he understood that the District Attorney submitted a motion for the continuance of the case.

Mr. Carrington said he did not move for a continuance. He simply stated that he was not ready to proceed to trial on account of the difficulties that had been suggested.

Mr. Merrick said then there was no motion at all before the court.

After a pause, Mr. Carrington said he simply rose to say he was not ready to proceed to trial for the reasons stated.

Judge Fisher said the regular order of business was either to proceed with the trial or make a motion to dispose of the case in some way or other. If no motion, the trial must be proceeded with.

Mr. Bradley said the defence were ready and could proceed at any time,

The court suggested that the names of the witnesses be called, in order that it might be ascertained who were absent.

Judge Fisher stated that in view of this statement, and under the circumstances, he did not see that anything could be done other than to postpone the case until the 10th of June, and he would necessarily postpone it until that time.

Mr. Bradley made a suggestion as to the payment of witnesses for defence, and the court ordered that they should be paid, and that the expense of bringing others here should also be met. The prisoner was then remanded to the custody of the Marshal, and was taken back to jail.

June 10.—The Surratt trial was the all absorbing topic of conversation, and quite a crowd had assembled in and about the Criminal Court-room, long before the hour

announced for the opening of the court at ten o'clock. Speculations were rife as to whether or not the trial would take place. Many who were not disposed to endure the inconvenience of the crowd, and who simply desired to gratify their curiosity by seeing the prisoner, gathered about the City Hall steps and in Judiciary Square, and patiently awaited the hour when the prisoner should be brought from jail.

At 9.30 A. M. Judge Fisher entered the court-room and took a seat upon the bench. The court was formally opened at 10 o'clock.

The attorneys for the defence, Mr. Merrick and the Messrs. Bradley, being present, the District Attorney and Mr. Pierrepont, counsel for the prosecution, having subsequently entered the room, the jurors were called, and all excepting four answered to their names.

At half past 10 o'clock the prisoner was brought into court by Marshal Gooding. The prisoner was handcuffed. He appears as he did the other day, with a clean-shaven face, excepting a moustache and goatee, and wears his hair long, and hanging about his neck. He was dressed in a dark suit. After being in court a few moments the handcuffs were removed, and he was assigned a seat beside his counsel. Surratt's face is very pale, and he wears a careworn, troubled look, but faintly smiled occasionally as he received a nod of recognition from his friends. After sitting in the court-room for some time he engaged in a lively conversation with his counsel, Mr. Merrick, and was evidently much amused at what was said, as he laughed heartily,

After all the preliminaries had been arranged, Judge Fisher asked if counsel were ready to proceed with the trial of John H. Surratt.

Mr. Bradley. The prisoner is ready, and has been so for weeks.

District Attorney Carrington said he was happy to proceed with the trial of John H. Surratt, charged with the murder of the late President of the United States, Abraham Lincoln, on the 14th of April, 1862.

By 11 o'clock the court-room was literally crowded, and every seat within the bar was occupied.

In answer to a question by Mr. Bradley, Sr., Mr. Douglass said that he had filed away a paper containing the names of the jurors, and had searched for it, but had not been able to find it.

Mr. Douglass then retired from the stand, and Mr. Pierrepont asked that the court take a recess.

The court granted the application for a recess until to-morrow morning at 10 o'clock, and the court then adjourned until that hour.

The prisoner was then remanded to the custody of the marshal and taken back to jail, a large crowd hastening into Judiciary Square for the purpose of getting a good look at him.

JUNE 11.—The trial of Surratt, was re-sumed this morning in the Criminal Court, Judge Fisher presiding.

The crowd in attendance was again very large. Among those in attendance in the court-room at an early hour were three or four ladies, who, however, soon disappeared.

The court was formally opened at 10 o'clock, and the names of the jurors were called.

The jury was composed of the following gentlemen.

Wm. R. Todd, James Y. Davis, J. R. Barr, Col. Alexander, Robert Ball, Wm. McLean, George A. Bohrer, B. F. Parsell, Thomas Berry, B. E. Gettings, C. C. Schneader, Wm. W. Birth.

Mr Merrick. We now propose that the jury be allowed to separate until Monday. The prisoner through his counsel askes this privilege for the jury. Messrs. Pierrepont and Carrington do not object.

The Court. By consent of counsel on both sides, the jury will be permitted to separate. The clerk will enter this upon the records, and to the jury the Court said ; Be here gentlemen, on Monday morning at 10 o'clock. I do not know that I shall then have the pleasure of seeing you. You are admonished to avoid conversation with any-body on the subject of this cause. If you are thus approached, you should regard it as a personal indignity. I am inclined to think that, under the act of Congress, this term is extended. I shall not, therefore, order the Court adjourned in course, but adjourn until Monday morning at 10 o'clock.

The Court was accordingly adjourned.

JUNE 17.—The Criminal Court room was unusually well crowded this morning before the opening of the Court.

At 10 o'clock Judge Fisher, having some-what recovered from his sickness, entered the court room and took his seat upon the bench, and the court was formally opened.

Surratt was brought into court and took a seat beside his counsel. He looks about the same as last week, and appears at all times to be very cheerful.

Mr. Nathaniel Wilson, assistant district attorney, then addressed the jury, and said all were aware that in criminal cases the custom is for the prosecution at the beginning of a case to make known the subject of in-quiry, and to state in outline what proof would be brought forward to support the charges contained in the indictment.

The grand jury of the District of Columbia have indicted John H. Surratt, the prisoner at the bar, for the murder of Abraham Lincoln, late President of the United States. The duty of the jury is to ascertain whether the accused is guilty or not guilty, and an inquiry of a more solemn character was never submitted to human intelligence. They are in fact to turn back the leaves of history, to shut the red page on which are written the awful incidents of that April night, and to inquire as to the blow that was then and there struck, not only at human life alone, but a blow against the perpetuity of this Government and against liberty itself. They would scarcely need witnesses to describe the terrible scenes of that awful night.

A vast audience was then assembled at a public place, whose hearts were filled with the joy of peace, and among that audience was he who had presided over the country through years of sorrow, but who was now recognized as a victor. A victor he was, in-deed, but a victor in whose heart there was no emotion but of kindness. To him death came in the most sudden and terrible form. Witnesses who will come here will tell you that upon that night John Wilkes Booth left the front of the theatre and went back to the box occupied by the President.

Mr. Wilson then rehearsed the circum-stances of the shooting of the President, of Booth's leaping from the box to the stage, and of his subsequent flight. Mr. Wilson then continued, and said the prosecu-tion would prove, as no case was often proved, that the prisoner at the bar was present, aiding and abetting the murder, and that a few moments before the shot was fired he was present in front of the theatre, in consultation with Booth. You will see him as from the light of the lamp that shone full in his face. He shall be known also as the friend and companion of Booth, and as the director of the bullet that pierced the brain of the

President, and of the bloody knife that fell with such terrible force upon the person of the Secretary of state.

It will be fully proven that he was present with Booth, directing the murder; and that the act was not the result of a moment's thought only, but was a premeditated plot, and the prisoner at the bar was the chief and main mover in the matter. It will be proven that he was a traitor to his country, and a spy upon the action of the Government, and who travelled regularly between Washington and Canada, all the time weaving a net, and plotting the destruction of the Government, and the overthrow and slaughter of the armies of the United States; and as an indication of the motive that possessed his mind, the jury shall hear how he boasted that he had shot down unarmed Union soldiers while they were escaping from rebel prisons.

It shall be shown how the prisoner made his home in this city the rendezvous for the perfection of their bloody work, and that it was he who left at Surrattsville the arms which Booth took possession of in his flight, and one of which was taken from him after his death. It will be shown that in April, 1862, Surratt went from Richmond to Canada, and that while in Montreal he, on the 10th of April, received a letter from Booth, commanding his presence in this city.

He came home, and it will be shown exactly by what route; and the prosecution will prove by testimony as clear as noonday sun that Surratt was here on that fatal Friday, and was walking through Pennsylvania avenue, booted and spurred, and that but two hours before the fatal shot was fired he purchased the disguise which the assassins were to use in their flight, and that when the last blow was struck he set forth upon his shuddering flight.

That flight will be traced, because in law flight is criminal's confession, and because during the flight the prisoner, in the fancied security of friendship, makes acknowledgments which fix upon him the guilt. It will be shown that after the assassination the prisoner went to Canada, and his whereabouts in Montreal will be shown. It will be shown how long he remained there, and where he was secreted, and how he was there in disguise during the time the trial was in progress at the arsenal, when he could have thrown much light upon the trial and done much to establish the guilt or innocence of those then charged.

From Canada he crossed the Alantic, and it will be shown that when in mid-ocean he spoke freely of his connection with the conspiracy, and when he landed upon a foreign shore he raised his impious hand and expressed a wish that he could return and serve Andrew Johnson as Abraham Lincoln had been served.

In England he found sympathy; but conscience still haunted him, and he fled again, this time to Rome, and hid himself in the Papal army, and enlisted as a private soldier. He might have felt himself secure there if anywhere; but he was recognized and discovered by the companion of his youth, who pierced through all his disguises; and when he found denial was useless, he acknowledged his identity, and gave utterance to the memoral words, " I have done the Yankees as much harm as I could, We have killed Lincoln, the negroes' friend."

The man to whom Surratt was revealed as in duty bound, made the fact known to the American minister at Rome. We had, it is said, no treaty of extradition with that country, but so horrible was the prisoner's crime, and so notorious was his name, that the Pope and Cardinal Antonelli surrendered him. He escaped again by leaping from a precipice—a leap which would have been impossible to any one except one who had fully realized his guilt, and knew his life was worthless. He fled to Egypt, and was pursued—not by the bloodhounds of the law, as the counsel for the defence seemed to think, but the very elements conspired to point him out—and from Alexandria his face was turned homeward, to the land he had polluted with murder.

He is here now for trial, and when all these things are proved, as proven they will be, and all shall be made clear, as it will be in spite of the subterfuges that will be resorted to, it will be the duty of the jury, in the name of civilization, which Surratt has disgraced, to do full and impartial justice, and retribution shall be meted out to the shedder of innocent blood.

The counsel for the defence enjoy a great privilege over the United States. By an act of Congress they are permitted to take deposition of witnesses in criminal cases, and they can send to any part of the United States to take them. On the other hand, the United States cannot examine any witnesses if they are not personally in attendance. It was admitted by the defence that this is not technically a charge of treason. The indictment charged the prisoner with the murder of an American citizen. The prosecution expected to show that it was a case of murder, aggravated by circumstances of great atrocity, and the object, not only to take the life of the President, but to overthrow the Government.

Mr. Bradley, Sr., said the defense would reserve the opening remarks to the jury.

Sergeon General Barnes was the first witness examined by the United States. He was acquainted with the late President Lincoln, and was called to attend him professionally on the night of the 14th of April, 1865, at the house of Mr. Peterson, on Tenth street, and remained with him until he died ; he examined the character of the wound, and the bullet was the cause of his death ; the President lived until twenty minutes past seven on the morning of the 25th ; he was not conscious at any time from the shooting until the hour of his death ; he did not speak at all ; there were present Drs. Stone, Ford, Lieber, and others, with some of the members of the cabinet ; the death resulted from what is called a gunshot wound.

James M. Wright sworn.—At present am chief clerk in the Bureau of Military Justice. The counsel for the United States handed him a package which he was requested to examine, and which, in his official capacity, had been placed in his possession by Mr. Holt. After looking at the contents he said : "This is the ball."

Mr. Carrington. Let me see it.

The witness handed to him the ball.

The witness. And here is the pistol.

By Mr. Bradley. All the papers are open, just as they were placed in my hands by Mr. Holt.

William T. Kent sworn.—Was at Ford's Theatre on the night of the assassination, and testified as to the shooting of President Lincoln ; he, after Mr. Lincoln was removed from the theatre, picked up the pistol in the box which had been occupied by the deceased, and on asking what he should do with it, some one said, "Hand it to Mr. Godright, the agent of the Associated Press," who was vouched for as a responsible gentleman, and this he did.

Lieutenant Colonel Henry R. Rathbun,

of Albany, sworn.— Was well acquainted with President Lincoln, and accompanied him and Mrs. Lincoln and Miss Harris to the theatre on the night of the 14th of April, 1865. He explained the positions occupied by the company in the private box. When they entered the box the actors stopped playing, and the band struck up " Hail to the Chief," and the President was received with three cheers ; in the second scene of the third act, while the witness was intently looking at the stage, he heard the report of a pistol ; looking round he saw in the dimness of the smoke the form of a man standing between the President and the door : he heard the man shriek out some such word as "freedom ;" witness immediately sprang toward him and seized him ; the man wrested himself from his grasp and made a thrust at him with a large knife ; witness raised his arm to parry the blow, but received a flesh wound between the arm and the shoulder ; the man sprang toward the front of the box ; witness rushed after him, and succeeded only in catching his clothes as he got over the box ; witness thought he tore the man's clothes ; the witness cried out "stop that man ;" he then looked toward the President who had not changed his position, with the exception that his head was bowed forward, and his eyes were closed ; witness rushed toward the door for the purpose of procuring medical aid, but he found the door barred with a heavy piece of plank ; the people outside were beating against the door ; with some difficulty witness removed the bar, and those outside came in ; when he returned to the box he found that the President was being examined, but the wound had not then been found ; the body, with some assistance was removed from the theatre ; witness accompanied Mrs. Lincoln to the house opposite the theatre, whither Mr. Lincoln had been removed.

Col. Joseph B. Stewart was sworn, and testified that he was at Ford's Theatre on the night of April 14, 1865 ; went in company with three ladies, and the party occupied four seats directly in front of the orchestra, on the right hand of the aisle, of what are known as the orchestra seats, and was just in a position to see everything on the stage, and at an angle could see the occupants of the Presidential box ; at a time when there was a pause in the play, witness heard the report of a pistol ; at the same moment he saw a man coming over the bal-

SURRATT AS A PAPAL ZOUAVE.

SURRATT'S FRIGHTFUL LEAP FROM A PRECIPICE WHILE ESCAPING FROM
HIS GUARD.

ustrade, and saw a curl of smoke, and as he cleared the balustrade the man exclaimed " SIC SEMPER TYRANNIS ;" the man came on the stage with his back to the audience, and immediately turned to face the audience ; the man had a large knife in his hand, and witness at once leaped upon the stage and followed the man ; he heard a door slam ; five persons were standing in the passage-way ; they were very much excited, and witness' progress was obstructed ; near the back door witness saw a man standing, who turned to look at witness, and when witness got to the door he caught at the hind side, and heard the the tramp of feet, as of a horse, and as witness passed out of the door, a person also passed out, and the action of that person seemed to be as of one much surprised ; witness' attention was particularly fixed upon the man mounting the horse ; witness saw that he was imperfectly mounted, and that the horse was restive, and he made an effort to grasp the bridle, when the rider wheeled the horse around and forced witness against the wall, and the rider then hastened down the alley ; at the moment the horse turned, witness told the man, who was John Wilkes Booth, to stop, and at that instant some one ran rapidly out of the alley ; witness then heard two sharp clicks of something, and then a shrill whistle, after which the rider rode furiously up the alley ; witness was so near the horse that the first two or three strides splashed the mud on his face and upon his bosom ; witness then heard the horse go, apparently in the direction of the Patent Office ; the man witness saw leap upon the stage was John Wilkes Booth.

Joseph Dye was next called and examined by the prosecution. Witness is a recruiting sergeant in the United States army : is now stationed in Philadelphia ; in April 1865, he belonged to Battery C. Pennsylvania Artillery, and was stationed at Camp Barry : the camp is about two miles from Ford's Theatre ; witness and Sergeant Robert Cooper were in town the night of the murder ; at the time of the murder witness was in an oyster saloon : went into the oyster saloon from Ford's Theatre at 9.30 ; Sergeant Cooper was in company ; witness was sitting upon some planks in front of the theatre, and saw Mr. Lincoln's carriage there ; the street in front of the theatre was lighted by a lamp ; while witness was sitting there Cooper was walking up and down ; while witness was there parties came out of the theatre and

went into the saloon ; before they came down witness overheard conversation there ; witness knew John Wilkes Booth ; Booth was one of the persons entering into that conversation.

Question by Mr. Pierrepont. What was that conversation ?

Witness said the, first that appeared was John Wilks Booth, conversing with a low, villainous-looking person at the end of the passage ; it was but a moment before another person joined them and entered into the conversation ; this person was neatly dressed ; the crowd then came from the theatre, and Booth remarked, "I suppose he will come out now," as witness supposed, referring to the President : the parties in conversation ranged themselves where the President was to pass, and watched eagerly for his appearance ; he did not come, and one of the parties went and examined the carriage, and Booth went into the restaurant and remained there long enough to take a drink, and came out and stepped from the street into the passage leading to the stage ; he appeared in a moment again ; the party above mentioned as neatly dressed then stepped up and called the time to Booth from a clock in the vestibule ; as soon as he called the time he moved up Tenth street to H street ; he did not remain long, but came down again and stopped in front of the theatre, looked at the clock and called the time again, looking directly at Booth and his companion, and being somewhat excited : he turned on his heel and went back towards H street ; it was then witness thought something was wrong ; witness carried a revolver and had a handkerchief wrapped around it, and his suspicions were so aroused that he unwound the handkerchief from about h s revolver ; it was not long until the well-dressed man came again from the direction of H street ; the man stood in front of the theatre and the light shone full on his face ; there was pictured on his countenance great excitement and exceeding paleness, and he told them for the third time the time ; that it was ten minutes past ten o'clock.

Question by Mr. Pierrepont. Did you see the man distinctly ?

Answer. Very distinctly.

Question. Do you see him now ?

Answer. I do, sir (pointing to Surratt) ; there he sits - 1 have seen his face frequently in my sleep ; it was so very pale I could never forget it ; I did not see him since until lately, and now I know the man I then saw was John H. Surratt; the prisoner at the bar, Surratt, then moved up toward H street; Booth then entered the front of the theatre; George Cooper and I then went to an oyster saloon; we had not time to eat our oysters when we heard of the murder, and we went immediately up to H street towards Camp Barry; on our way out a lady hoisted a window and asked us what was wrong down town; I told her that President Lincoln had been shot; she asked who had done it; I told her Booth; she asked how I knew that, and I told her a man who knew him saw him; on that night the moon was light enough to see objects distinctly: I believe the moon was up, but I cannot say if it was at its full: the woman was an elderly lady, but I could not say whether she was stout or otherwise, but she resembled the lady (Mrs. Surratt) who was tried at the arsenal: I have seen the house since; the house is No. 541 H street, on the right hand side of the street going towards Camp Barry. The witness then described the house; it was known as the Surratt house; the woman asked questions in an ordinary tone, but the witness does not recollect that the woman was much excited; when the witness saw Booth, Surratt, and the other party at the theatre, neither of them were disguised.

Cross-examined by Mr. Merrick. The witness is twenty-three years of age, and testified that he was from Washington county, Pa., where he resided before the war, going to school and working at his trade as a printer. He left Washington, Pa. in 1861, and entered the army in 1862. At Camp Barry the witness was first sergeant of his company, and during his absence the next sergeant in line called the roll. The witness did not have a pass on the night of the assassination; he had formerly been quartermaster sergeant of his company, and had a pass while in that position, but he had no right to use it as first sergeant. In answer to questions about his being in town without leave that night, the witness said that nearly all the camp was in town to witness the torchlight procession. It was a frequent occurrence for him to come to town, but he admitted that by so doing he did not altogether justify the confidence which the captain of the company reposed in him. The witness repeated the evidence

4

given yesterday relative to the position he occupied, sitting on the planks in front of the theatre.

Q. To whom did you first communicate what you saw that night?

A. To my father.

Q. To whom next?

A. Well to no one in particular, I mentioned my suspicions to Sergeant Cooper that night.

Q. Who did you first tell what you could prove on this subject?

A. I told no one what I could prove; I only told what I had seen; the first time I knew that my evidence was known I was summoned to appear here to testify at the assassination conspiracy; when I arrived in Washington I went first to the provost marshal's office, and was then taken to the Old Capitol to see if I could identify the man mentioned as "a villainous man;" at the provost marshal's office I was questioned by the officer who had a right to question me.

The witness was in Washington before, in March last, when the trial was postponed, and also on Monday last. After coming to Washington witness spoke about the case to Mr. Carrington and Mr. Wilson, but to no one else.

Q. In answering questions put by the prosecution, why did you describe the third party as a neatly-dressed man and not mention his name, as you knew him to be Surratt?

A. Because I did not think it was necessary until I was asked the question.

Q. Why did you use Booth's name and not Surratt's?

A. Because I did not deem it necessary to mention Surratt's name.

Q. Were you not told not to name him until asked?

A. No, sir, I was not.

He did not know where the neatly-dressed party came from, but he came from the direction of H street; the three parties stood together, and were engaged in conversation at the time; the remark was made by Booth "I think he will come now;" the three parties were standing together below the door, and looking into the space the President must pass, if he came down. The villainous-looking man stood next to the theatre, Booth next, and John H. Surratt next. The suspicions of the witness were first excited by seeing so gentlemanly a looking man as Booth talk to so villainous a looking man as the other appeared to be.

Surratt did not whisper the time to Booth and his companion, but called it out loud. He apeared to have business to attend to also, up at H street, and there was some one up there to whom he had to communicate the time, and the witness believed that Surratt was regulating the whole conspiracy.

Q. Then he was a general commander?

A. Yes, sir.

Q. Did you dream that also?

A. No, sir. [Laughter.] When Surratt moved up Tenth street the witness could not see him cross F street; he appeared to be in hurry, and had not time to whisper, as it was evident he had business up H street, or in that direction. Whenever he came from H street he came in a great hurry, walking as fast as he could. After calling for the third time Surratt moved hurriedly up to H street; his lips and countenance were very pale: the witness could see this as Surratt stood looking at the clock.

Surratt's face was the picture of excitement and nervousness: saw Surratt in March last, at the jail here: he was admitted by General Carrington, to see if he could identify him as the man who was under the gaslight that night, and recognized him immediately.

Q. And this is the man (pointing to Surratt)?

A. Yes, sir: that is the face.

Q. Would you have known that face if you had seen it elsewhere?

A. Yes, sir; it is a face that once seen is not easily forgotten.

Question by Mr. Gittings a juror. Witness saw, at times, all of Surratt's face, on the night referred to, and sometimes only three-quarters of his face.

Question by Mr. Alexander a juror. Surratt was then dressed in a drab hat and black coat; did not see the other part of his dress.

Peter Taltavul sworn and examined by Mr. Pierrepont.—Witness kept a restaurant next to Ford's theatre; was in the restaurant when the murder was committed; witness knew Booth; he frequently came in; he came in that night and called for whiskey; I gave it to him; Booth was alone and drank the whiskey, and then called for water, paid and went out: I saw nothing unusual in his dress: he was not disguised: from eight to ten minutes afterwards I heard the President was assassinated: I had seen

Booth before that time: he came in with gentlemen, and sometimes with Harold: on the afternoon of April 14, Harold came in and asked if I had seen Booth: I told him I had not: Harold then went out and away: it was about 4 P.M. witness saw nothing to awaken suspicion.

No questions were asked by the defence.

David C. Reed sworn and examined by Mr. Pierrepont. I have lived in Washington about thirty years.

The prisoner at the bar was then asked to stand up, and the witness was asked if he knew him. He replied that he did, and had known the prisoner by sight since he was a boy: witness was in Washington on the day of the murder of the President: I believe I saw the prisoner in Washington on that day on Pennsylvania avenue, opposite the National Hotel: it was about 2.30 P.M. His dress on that occasion attracted my attention: I remarked his clothing very particularly; his dress looked to be of country manufacture, and was got up in very good style: he had upon his feet a new pair of brass spurs with large blue rowels, and they evidently bran new: he wore a felt hat not very low crowned, but rather wide brim.

Cross-examined by Mr. Bradley.—Witness was attracted by the dress, because it was exceedingly genteel, and was peculiar: it was such a dress as would attract attention: Surratt always dressed genteely, but his dress was somewhat different from what he had been in the habit of wearing.

Susan Ann Jackson, colored, sworn, and examined by Mr. Pierrepont.—Witness' maiden name was Mahoney. She was married two weeks after Mr. Lincolon's assassination. On the 14th of April (Friday) Mrs. Surratt went down to the country, between 11 and 12 o'clock, with Mr. Weichman. He was a boarder at the house. He and Mrs. Surratt returned between 8 and 9 o'clock. Witness saw John H. Surratt in the dining-room after that, talking to his mother. Witness had never seen John H. Surratt before. She had only been living at the house three weeks. Mrs. Surratt said it was her son who was present. Mrs. Surratt asked witness if Surratt did not look like his sister Anna. Witness went into the room to take in a pot of tea, and it was then that Mr. Surratt and his mother were there.

The prisoner was asked to stand up.

Q. Is that the man you saw with Mrs. Surratt?

Yes sir; that is the man; the time was after nine o'clock; I took in a dish of tea, and Mrs. Surratt asked me to bring in an extra dish; I knew Anna Surratt; was living in the same house with her.

Cross-examined by Mr. Bradley.—I saw John Surratt that night, but I have never seen him before or since until last week, when he was brought out here: I had only been living at Mrs. Surratt's three weeks before that time: I never saw the prisoner at Mrs. Surratt's until the night the president was assassinated: that was the night I saw the prisoner there: never saw the prisoner before that time, and it was on the night of the assassination.

Witness persisted that it was the night of the assassination.

The Court said the same answer had been given at least a dozen times.

Mr. Bradley said he wanted no reflections from the Court.

The Court said any one of the dullest comprehension could have understood the answer.

Mr. Bradley said his comprehension was as sharp as that of the Court, and he wanted no reflections.

James Sangston sworn, and examined by Mr. Pierrepont.—Witness was in 1865, and is yet book-keeper at the St. Lawrence Hall, a hotel in Montreal, Canada.

Witness was shown the arrival book or register at the hotel, the book of bills paid, and a leaf from the departure book showing the time when travellers left, and the route they took. In the book of arrivals under date of April 6, 1865, witness found the name "John Harrison," and the same name under date of April 18. The first arrival was at 10.30 a m. and the second arrival at 12.30 m.

Mr. Bradley, Sr., said the defence would admit that Surratt was in Montreal on the 6th and 18th of April, 1862: that he registered the name of John Harrison. They admitted the names were in Surratt's handwriting.

Mr. Pierrepont said the prosecution was then saved much evidence.

A coat was exhibited and identified as one similar to that worn by Harrison.

The court then took a recess until 10 o'clock on Wednesday morning.

JUNE 19.—The trial of John H. Surratt was resumed this morning in the Criminal Court, before Judge Fisher.

The court-room was, as usual, crowded. For the first time since the trial commenced, a few ladies occupied seats within the bar as spectators.

The prisoner was brought into court at ten o'clock, when the court was immediately opened.

M. Carroll Hobart was sworn, and examined by Mr. Pierrepont. The witness is a conductor of a train on the Vermont Central Railroad: runs from White-River Junction to St. Albans, on the direct line from Boston to Montreal; between April 19, and 20, 1865, the witness was conductor on this road, and got passengers from the first trip of the boat up the lake in April: witness' train left White-River Junction at 11 35 p. m., and went directly to St. Albans.

The prisoner was asked to stand up.

Question. Will you now tell what happened that morning.

Answer. I got to Essex Junction at five o'clock on Tuesday morning, with passengers from Burlington, on the boats of Lake Champlain; as I went through the train, between the passenger car and sleeping car, I found two men on the platform of the passenger car; I asked the men for their tickets or money, and they said they had no money: that they had been unfortunate; one of the men was tall, and had on a close-fitting skull cap, short coat, and a scarf over his collar and starch on his vest: the other man was short, thick-set, sandy-complexioned, and had whiskers around his face: he was a rough-looking man: I can't state how he was dressed: he wore a slouched hat: I spoke with him to come in the car, and he came in and said they had been unfortunate: that three of them had been to New York, and the third one with them got up in the night and took all the money, leaving them destitute: they said they were anxious to get to Canada: I told them I could not carry them through: that I would leave them at Milton, the next station: at the next station I forgot them, and in passing through, the car I saw them again, and they said they must get to Franklin; Franklin is fourteen miles north-west of St. Albans and four miles from the Canada line; the tall man did all the talking; in the beginning of the talk the tall man would imitate broken English, as though he was a Canadian, but when he became animated he spoke in very square English; the tall man's hands were white and delicate, and were not at all like a laboring man's hands; at St. Albans Mr. Locklin was standing at the depot, and I said to Mr. Locklin, " I think those men have beat me ;" the men did not hear this ; they then went out into the streets, and I do not recollect seeing them afterwards: the train from St. Albans would arrive at Montreal at 9.30 a. m.

Q. Have you seen any one in the courthouse who looks like the tall man you speak of ?

A. The man who stood up (the prisoner) looks very much like him in build and appearance ; he wore a skull cap and moustache, but no whiskers : I cannot tell from his face, but he looks very much like him in general appearance.

Cross-examined by Mr. Bradley.—The witness was not sure of the date of the first trip of the steamer in April, 1865 ; it was on a Tuesday, but does not recollect the date ; the witness runs from St. Albans to Rouse Point every alternate morning ; does not recollect that the tall man referred to had a beard ; the tall man did not look particularly fair ; he looked rusty, and as though he had been without sleep ; at that time the passengers from Troy and Albany, in the morning train, did not lie over at Rutland.

By Mr. Pierrepont.—In the beginning of navigation the boats were irregular, and the time referred to above was upon the arrival of the first boat that season.

Mr. Charles H. Blinn was next sworn and examined by Mr. Pierrepont.

The witness is a clerk in the Welden House at St. Albans, Vt. ; between April 10 and 15, 1865, he was employed as a night watchman at the depot of the Vermont Central Railroad, at Burlington : the first trip made by the boat that season was Monday, April 17 ; it was four hours late ; it arrived at 12 o'clock midnight ; he was on watch in the depot ; that night two men came in the depot, one tall and the other short, and asked to stay there until the train left for Montreal at 4 a. m. ; the boat was from White Hall, with passengers from New York ; the tall man asked to sleep in the depot ; he did so, and I called him at 4 o'clock a. m. on Tuesday, April 18 : after the man went out I picked up something where the tall man was lying [a white cambric handkerchief was shown and examined]. The witness recognized the handkerchief as the one he picked up where the tall man was lying ; the handkerchief bears the name of

"J, H. Surratt ;" that name was on the handkerchief when it was picked up : after I picked up the handkerchief and discovered the name I showed it to the agent of the railroad company : I do not know that the agent communicated the fact at St. Albans ; I never saw the two men afterwards. No cross-examination.

Mr. Scipio Grillon was next called and examined by Mr. Pierrepont, He was living near the navy yard in 1865 : kept a restaurant in Ford's Theatre, and knew J, W. Booth by sight : he knew Booth five or six years before ; he knew David Harold and Atzerott : he saw Harold at five o'clock on the day of the assassination, and he saw Atzerott ten minutes after that ; Harold and witness walked together, and saw Atzerott at the Kirkwood House : I was coming down Tenth street : Harold met me and asked if I had seen J. W. Booth ; I said I had at 11 o'clock a. m., at the theatre : I had also seen Booth at 4 o'clock on horseback : he rode a small, gray horse : then Harold said, "You know General Lee is in town ?" I replied I had not heard it ; Harold said, "Yes he is at Willard's and if you will walk with me we shall no doubt see something about it." As we were passing Kirkwood's, Atzerott was sitting on the steps, and Harold stopped to speak with him. Harold and the witness then walked up to Willard's, and Harold talked to two young men there. The witness could not hear the conversation, but when Harold parted with the men he said, "You will be there to-night ?" He then walked toward Grover's Theatre, and I noticed that Harold walked lame, when near the theatre Harold pulled up his pants, and I saw a long dagger-handle protruding from his boot-leg ; I asked him what he was going to do with that : he said he was going to the country that night, and such things were handy there.

Do you see any one in the court who looks like the man to whom Harold said " Will you be there to-night ?"

The witness answered by pointing out the prisoner: he looked very much like the man, but the witness could not say whether he was the man or not ; he wore no beard, but had a slight moustache.

Cross-examined by Mr. Bradley—The witness is acquainted with Mr. Glifford and Mr. Hess, who were at Ford's Theatre ; he did not see either of them in front of the theatre that night, and does not recollect whether any soldiers were sitting in front of the theatre: there was a great crowd there; he was in the restaurant when the president was shot: the clock at the theatre is in the centre of the passage-way, opposite the door.

The court took a recess.

Upon the reassembling of the court John T. Tippet was sworn and examined by Mr. Carrington. Witness resided in Prince George county, Maryland, but is now residing here, and is a blacksmith by trade. He came to Washington on December 10, 1865; was a member of the 1st District of Columbia Cavalry; in 1853, or during a part of the year, was a mail carrier from Washington to Charlotte Hall; knows John H. Surratt: has known him for ten or eleven years: has seen him frequently in that time: knew his mother also; have seen the mother and son together: have heard them conversing but very little together: John had very little to say to me, but I heard Mrs. Surratt say in John Surratt's presence, that she would give one thousand dollars to any one who would kill Lincoln: does not recollect hearing anything more, except abuse of the president; have not heard much that passed after that but occasionally heard abuse cannot recollect the precise words; whenever there was a victory won, I have heard John Surratt say, "Damn the Northern army and the leader thereof: they ought to be sent to hell;" does not recollect whether Surratt did or did not mention the name of Mr. Lincoln; do not know who he meant by "leader of the Northern army;" never recollect of hearing Surratt say that more than once: don't recollect whether his mother was then present; when she said she would give one thousand dollars, no one was present but John Surratt.

Cross-examined by Mr. Bradley.—Witness carried the mail in February and March, 1863; carried a daily mail and delivered it at Surrattville: it was in March witness heard the above conversation: do not recollect what other converation occurred: they would always ask me what news I had: I heard Mrs. Surratt say she would give $1,000 to whoever would kill Lincoln: don't recollect anything else about the conversation.

Robert H. Cooper was sworn, and examined by Mr. Pierrepont. Witness is not now in the army: was discharged in June, 1865: was in the volunteer service from Beaver, Pa.: I live there now, and am clerk in a store: entered the army in 1862: was in Captain Thompson's Independent Penn-

sylvania Battery: in April, 1865, was stationed at Camp Barry, and was a line sergeant: I remember the event of the president's assassination; on that day I came into town after dress parade, at sundown: Camp Barry is about two miles from Ford's Theatre: I came to town with Sergeant Dye, and we went down Pennsylvania avenue, and from there to Ford's Theatre: we were on our way to camp, and stopped at Ford's Theatre: at the theatre Sergeant Dye sat down on a platform in front of the theatre; I do not know whether I sat down at any time or not: I walked up and down toward F street, and came down on the other side opposite the theatre and crossed over: when I came to where Dye was sitting I spoke to him; do not recollect speaking to any other person; I observed the president's carriage there; the driver was sitting on the carriage, and while we were there a gentleman came and looked in the rear of the carriage; the man who looked in the carriage was young and genteely dressed, and that is all I remember about him: he was five feet eight or ten inches high: I observed a rough-looking man near the wall of the theatre; he was not as tall as the one who looked in the carriage; saw a gentleman go into the drinking-room below the theatre.

I heard a man come up and heard a man call out "Ten minutes past ten;" I was not in a postion to see the face of the man who called the time; Sergeant Dye and I then went to an oyster saloon; I can't say that anything particular excited my suspicions; at the oyster saloon we called for oysters; before we received them a man came in and said the President was shot: we eat some of our oysters and started for camp: while passing out of H street a lady raised a window and asked what was going on down town: we replied the President was shot: she asked who shot him, and we replied Booth; we then passed on; the house we referred to had high steps; have seen a house since that looks much like it; it is number 541; we then passed out to camp.

Cross-examined by Mr. Bradley.—Witness does not recollect what oyster saloon he went to; when the man came in the oyster saloon he said the President was shot, and Booth had shot him; it was but a short time after the oysters were ordered that the man came and announced the killing of the President: does not recollect in what direction from the theatre the oyster saloon was: no one racently pointed out the house on H street to witness; was requested to go up there and see if he could identify the house, and did so; recollect the house because there was an alley beside it; I think the moon was shining that night, and the night was clear: I am as confident of that as I am of anything: when the man spoken of called the time I noticed two or three other persons, but do not remember them distinctly: I was not armed that night: the principal thing we came to town for that night was to witness a torchlight procession

JUNE 20.—The trial of John H. Surratt was resumed this morning in the Criminal Court, Judge Fisher presiding. There was an increased attendance on the part of the spectators. The number of ladies in attendance has increased. They occupy seats within the bar.

The prisoner was brought in at 10 o'clock, and the roll of jurors was then called.

Mr Merrick submitted a motion asking that the witnesses Carroll Hobart, Charles H. Blinn, and Joseph H. Dye be recalled, for the purpose of cross-examination upon points which have come to the knowledge of the defence since the other examination closed.

M. Carrington felt it his duty to object.

Mr. Merrick said it was a matter within the sound discretion of the Court, and the recalling was necessary to a just trial of the case.

Messrs. Pierrepont and Merrick were both addressing the Court at the same time, when the Court interrupted them by saying: you must proceed in regular order. When one side has examined a witness in chief the other can cross-examine them, and VICE VERSA. Otherwise there would be no end to the trial.

Edward L. Smith was sworn and examined by the prosecution.—He had, since 1860, resided about a mile from Surrattville; had known the prisoner very well for three or four years; recollected that he stayed at his house in January or February, 1865, and went away next morning; they on that occasion conversed about different things; the prisoner joked about going to Richmond, but never acknowledged to have been there; he, however laughed, and said if the Yankees knew what he had done they would stretch his neck; witness did not recollect what reply he himself made to this.

Cross-examined by the defence.—He came to Washington last Sunday, having been summoned to appear before the District Attorney; he told that officer what he had just stated here; he had been examined by Judge Hall, and what he said was written down; none others went up there besides himself; the witness had said to Mr. Townley B. Robey that being away from home would be a great loss to him, when Robey said he would guarantee ten dollars a day if witness would do what was right; besides this his hotel bill was paid; Mr. Robey said he had seen Mr. Wilson, the Assistant District Attorney, and made it all right.

Mr. Carrington. Have you not been in Mr. Merrick's office?

Witness. Yes; once.

Mr. Merrick. He told me all about it.

The Witness. Mr. Merrick said he was after me with a sharp stick.

James M. Wright, chief clerk, of the Bureau of Military Justice, was recalled, and identified certain papers as having been placed in his custody; these papers were Jacob Thompson's account with the Ontario Bank of Montreal, a draft on that bank, and Booth's bank book.

Robert A. Campbell, teller of the Ontario Bank, Montreal, was sworn, and gave testimony concerning the papers which Mr. Wright had identified.

Mr. Bradley objected to an examination about Jacob Thompson's bank account in Canada.

The court said it deemed that the testimony should be heard for the time being, but if the prosecution failed to convict the prisoner it should be ruled out.

The witness then testified as to the condition of the separate accounts of Booth and Thompson with the Ontario Bank, showing, among other things, that on the 27th of October, 1864, a bill of exchange was drawn for Booth of £61 10s. 10d., and that on the 6th of April, 1865, Thompson drew a check on the bank for $7,098, and the bank gave him, in the course of the transactions, a certificate of deposit for $180 000. This was placed against his account; he having a large balance all the time to his credit, probably $200,000. The witness also testified to the fact that Jacob Thompson was an American. John Lee was sworn and examined by Mr. Carrington.

Witness now lived in Mississippi, between Meridian and Vicksburg; previous to that time lived in Washington: had been sergeant of Company E, 95th New York Volunteers; was ordered to Washington in 1862 for duty as a detective in Colonel Baker's force; in his business became familiar with people in this city; had seen John H. Surrratt; recognized the prisoner at the bar as Surratt; in April, 1865. was on duty at the quarters of Col. J. R. O'Beirne, and went down to the depot to look after deserters; on returning, and when at ——— street and Pennsylvania-avenue stopped to talk to an acquaintance; then went on up Pennsylvania avenue to Willard's, and when opposite the hat store of Mr. Stinemetz passed a man whom I took to be John H. Surratt; to the best of witness' knowledge the prisoner at the bar was the man he met; Surratt was walking at an ordinary gait; I was walking fast; April 15 I went to the Kirkwood House; Major O'Beirne got an order to bring all his men to the Kirkwood House to protect M. Johnson; I went upon the roof to see that all was safe, and that no one could come in through the building; the impression was that somebody would try to kill Mr. Johnson; after getting the men all fixed I went down to the clerk's office; acting upon certain information, I went to room No. 126, and could not find the key; after consultation with Mr. Sprague, I burst the door open and went into the room; a coat was hanging on the wall, and in a pocket I found a spur and a book, [Book produced. Witness recognized it as the book he found in the coat pocket.] I got the book and three pocket handkerchiefs, and a half stick of black liquorice; I then went to the bed and lifted the covering off until I got between the sheet and the mattress, and I picked up there a large Bowie knife with a red case over it; I then hunted for letters but found none; I then took the articles down stairs to the parlor next to Mr. Johnson's room and gave them to Mr. O'Beirne, who showed them to Mr. Johnson and then returned them to me, and I locked them up; Vice President Johnson's room was on the floor below room No. 126; next morning Mr. O'Beirne gave me an order to take the bundle to Secretary Stanton's house; I gave him the things, and he examined all except the pistol: he did not care about looking at that, and I then wrapped them up again and kept them until I was ordered to take them to the office of Judge Holt, and I then gave them to Judge Advocate Burnett, at his office, corner of Eighteenth street and Pensylvania avenue,

Wm. E. Cleaver was sworn and examined by Mr. Pierrepont. Witness kept a livery stable in 1865, on Sixth street between B and Missouri avenue, and was a partner of Mr. Rainey: knew J. W. Booth, and knows John H. Surratt eleven or twelve years; was familiar with him; he addressed me as Doe, and I addressed him as John; Booth kept his horses at our stables, and the first horse brought there was a light built bay horse; Booth and Surratt came to the stables together, and afterwards, on January 25, 1865, Surratt came to hire a horse; previous to this time Booth and Surratt always came together; on this occasion Surratt came alone and ordered me to have Booth's horse ready at seven o'clock; Surratt, on January 25th, ordered the horse at three o'clock, and came for him at seven; it was then raining hard, and I asked him if he was going to the country on such a night as that? he said he was going to "T. B. to a party:" I asked him to go to the Clarendon to take a drink, and he said he had enough, and I thought he had, too; Booth had not yet come, and I asked Surratt to take a seat in the office; he did so, and said he and Booth were going to the country to meet a party to help them cross the river; that they were going to do some bloody work; that they were going to kill Lincoln, the old scoundrel, as he had ruined Maryland and the whole South, and he would kill him himself; Surratt showed his pistol, and said he represented two counties in Maryland; Booth came in at eight o'clock, and Surratt chided him for being so late and keeping him waiting; the witness said he was in Washington the day of the assassination: I was out that afternoon exercising a black horse, and rode to the navy-yard bridge: while going along H street that day I met John H. Surratt; he was riding along H street: I spoke to him, and said, "How are you, John?" and he nodded to me; he was dressed in a rusty-colored suit, and wore a sort of a jocky cap on his head.

Cross-examined by Mr. Bradley:—Surratt was dressed rather rough, and wore something around his neck like a victorine; I met him between the printing office and the railroad; it was about four o'clock when I met him. The witness was questioned as to his testimony at the military commission, and said he had not told them anything of what he said here to-day because he was not asked: witness knew that Surratt was implicated in the conspiracy, but did not deem it. necessary to mention the fact of having met him, because he knew Surratt and wanted to shield him if possible; I however told that Surratt came to my stable with Booth.

Q. Did you ever take a horse to break for me?

A. Yes, sir.

Q. Did you sell him?

A. Yes, sir.

Q. Did you ever give me any money for him?

A. No, sir.

Q. You sold him without any authority?

A. No, sir, I had your authority.

Q. Are you the same Dr. Cleaver who was convicted here of committing a rape upon a poor little girl, and in whose case a new trial has been granted?

Witness. I decline to answer that question.

Mr. Carrington said the question should not have been asked.

Mr. Bradley insisted that he had a right to ask the question. The witness could answer or not, as he pleased.

Witness was asked where he was within the last three weeks, and he declined to answer, as it would tend to degrade him.

Q. Have you seen and spoken to Sandford Conover, alias Charles A. Dunham.

A. Yes, sir.

Q. Did you tell Conover all about this?

A. I did, sir; I told him pretty much what I said here.

Q. How did you happen to tell Conover?

A. We were talking about the Surratt trial, and I told him about hiring horses to Surratt.

Q. Did Conover write down what you told him?

A. He did not as I saw.

Q. Where did you see Conover?

A. In this city, at a house on Fourth street; the house has a lot around it, and extends up to G street; have told other parties besides Conover; told a man named Lewis, who was in my employ; I would not have told all about it now if it had not been for Sanford Conover.

Mr. Bradley said that was enough, but Mr. Pierrepont insisted that the witness should complete a statement he was making.

Witness then said it was through Conover he was made a witness; Conover told what I told him, and a man came to the jail to see me; I was so mad at Conover I could have hit him over the head, and I did not talk to him for five or six days; I then talked to a man named Ashley, who came to see me about the case; Ashley was a short, stoutish man, and Conover told him about it; I told him all I tell here, but I failed to tell him many thingns I fail to tell now; saw Ashley at the jail in Conover's company.

By Mr. Pierrepont.—I understand that Mr. Ashley is a member of Congress: he came to the jail to see me.

By Mr. Bradley.—I have not received promises of reward from any one for the testimony I should give.

Mr. Brooks was sworn, and examined by Mr. Pierrepont.—Witness had charge of Mr. J. C. Howard's livery stable on G street, between Sixth and Seventh, in 1865; witness knew Booth, Atzerott, and Surratt; the latter put his horses at livery at the stable, and gave orders that Booth, but no one else but him, should get the horses; Booth, Surratt, and Atzerott came to the stables sometimes separately; Surratt gave orders that Booth, and none else, should have the horses.

Witness here produced a paper in Surratt's handwriting, and it was read to the jury. It was a note dated March 26, 1865, and was written by Surratt to witness, returning a team which he had hired, and requesting witness to let Booth have his (Surratt's) horses. The order was offered in evidence.

Witness resumed, and said he had seen Surratt ride out with Booth and Atzerott; he had received another note from Surratt, and also one from Mrs. Surratt.

Witness was asked if he had any conversation with Atzerott about Surratt, in April, 1865.

Mr. Bradley objected to the question, as the conversation related to a note which was not in court.

Mr. Pierrepont suggested that it would be best to postpone further investigation until the note was produced.

The court thereupon took a recess until 10 o'clock next day.

June 21.—The trial of John H. Surratt, was resumed this morning.

The interest in the case diminishes not, and the attendance on the part of ladies is increasing daily. Some of them merely gratify their curiosity by a look at the prisoner, and then depart, while others remain seated throughout the proceedings.

Surrat was brought into court at 10 o'clock, and the business of the day was commenced.

James W. Humphrey sworn, and examined by Mr. Carrington.—I keep a livery stable at No. 224 C street, between Fourth and Sixth streets; knew Wilkes Booth; he came to my stable, and asked for the propietor; I stepped up, and he wanted a saddle-horse to ride to the country; I told him I could accommodate him with a saddle-horse; I told Booth, as he was a stranger, he would have to leave security or give city reference; Surratt came up and said he knew Mr. Booth, and that he would take good care of the horse; Surratt also said he would see the horse paid for; have known Surratt a number of years; I then ordered the horse to be saddled, and when the boy brought him out Booth had gone across the street to the Pennsylvania House, and mounted the horse and rode away; I never saw Mr. Surratt after that; Booth frequently came to the stable afterwards, and generally got the same saddle-horse: this was about six weeks before the assassination: on the 14th of April, at 12 o'clock, Booth came and engaged a horse, and said he wanted the horse he had been in the habit of riding: I told him I could not give him that horse, but would give him a very good horse; I gave him a bay mare, and an English saddle and bridle, and Booth rode away: I have not seen either horse, saddle, bridle, or Booth since.

Miss Honora Fitzpatrick was sworn, and examined by Mr. Carrington.—I knew John W. Booth: I met him at Mrs. Surratt's. I first saw Surratt in 1865; met him there several times: I was boarding at Mrs. Surratt's: boarded there from October, 1864 until the time I was arrested: I was arrested on Monday following the assassination: I knew a man who came from Port Tobacco, who was said to be George Atzerott, met him at Mrs. Surratt's: met him in less than a year before the assassination. I saw him there more than once: I remember he stayed there one night: I don't remember what night it was, or how long before the assassination; I saw Lewis Payne at Mrs. Surratt's, but did not know him by that name; he was known as Mr. Wood; he called there alone one evening in March; that was the first time I saw him; I met him in the parlor: Mrs. Surratt, Mrs. Hallahan, her daughter, and Mr. Weichman were in the parlor; I never saw Payne there afterwards:

when I was arrested I recognized him at tee office where I was taken; I know John H. Surratt: the last time I saw Mr. Surratt was two weeks before the assassination. have seen John Surratt at the house during the visits of Payne and others, but I never heard them converse together; had been to Ford's Theatre with John Surratt, Mr. Wood, and Miss Dean before the assassination: we occupied a private box, and Booth came there and spoke to Mr. Surratt, and they both stepped out of the box and stood at the door; Wood or Payne afterwards joined them, but I could not hear their conversation; after the play we went home, and Wood went to Mrs. Surratt's in the carriage with us.

George F. Chapin was sworn and examined by Mr. Pierrepont.—I have lived at Stockbridge, Vermont, and am a farmer; have lived there since February, 1866; in April, 1865, was in Burlington most of the time; left Burlington on Friday evening, on my way to New Haven, Conn,: it was previous to the assassination; I heard of the assassination on my way to New Haven; I came back to Burlington on the train that left New Haven at 3. 12; this was on Monday after the assassination; after my return from New Haven I saw Mr. Charles Blinn at the depot in Burlington on Wednesday morning; he had an article that I wanted much to get.

Q.—What was that article?

A.—A handkerchief.

Witness examined a package and took out a handkerchief marked John H. Surratt; witness could not recognize this as the same handkerchief, because it was at that time very dirty.

Cross-examined by Mr. Bradley.—I gave the handkerchief to Mr. George Grinnet, who was represented as one of Baker's detectives; I was a detective at that time, but not one of Baker's: I received the handkerchief on Tuesday, April 12; got it from Mr. Blinn that day; saw the handkerchief for the first time previous Wednesday.

Benj. W. Vanderpoel sworn, and examined by Mr. Pierrepont.—I live in New York city, and have lived there all my life; at the commencement of the war I was in New York, an attorney in the office of Brown, Hall & Vanderpoel; I am now with Chauncy Schaffer, No. 243 Broadway; knew J. W. Booth; he used to visit the "Lone Star" Club, a club I belonged to; I was here at the time of the assassination; was here three days before it; I saw Booth on that day, and spoke to him: I saw him three times on that day.

The prisoner was asked to stand up.

Q. Did you see the prisoner on that day ?

A. I saw him at the place last mentioned : he was with John Wilkes Booth and two or three others: they were sitting around a table with glasses on it: I had been to the paymaster's, and coming down I heard music at the place referred to and went in, and a ballet dancer was performing: the table Booth was at was a round one, and he and his companions were talking: I saw them distinctly, as I was within a few feet of them : I cannot be mistaken about this.

Cross-examined by Mr. Bradley.—I did not speak to Booth when I saw him in the place : I saw Booth and his companions were engaged in conversation : I was only attracted there by the music ; I never saw Surratt before or since until now ; I took a good look at him this morning and recognized him as the same man I saw with Booth I am as confident that I saw Surratt as that I see you now.

Question by Mr. Merrick. Would you recollect the face of the woman who was dancing?

Answer. I did not pay much attention to her face; my attention was directed to her legs. [Laughter.]

The court took a recess at half past two until ten o'clock next day.

June 22.—The trial of John H. Surratt was resumed to-day. The defence asked that Benjamin W. Vanderpoel be recalled. The witness was not in court, and it was understood that the defence should have the privilege of recalling him at some future time.

W. II. Bell, colored, sworn, and examined by Mr. Pierrepont.—I am a servant of Secretary Seward, and was at the house on April 14, 1865 ; I remember the circumstances that occurred that day; the bell rang at quarter past ten o'clock, and I went to the door; a tall, heavy built man came and asked for Mr. Seward ; I refused to admit him, and he said he came from Dr. Verdi, and insisted, that he was compelled to see Mr. Seward; he insisted, and at last went up ; at the door of the room he saw Mr. Frederick Seward and said he had a prescription form Dr. Verdi; Fredcrick Seward went in and found his father asleep, and came out and said the man could not go in; the man insisted, and

some loud conversation ensued, when I reminded them to be more quiet; the man was very polite to me, and said he understood all ; the man then started apparently to go down stairs, and I was in front of him ; but after going down a few steps the man jumped back and attacked Mr. Frederick Seward, and hit him over the head with something ; I then ran down stairs and gave the alarm. and a soldier came up ; in the mean time, however, the man remounted his horse, and went off, and followed him as far as I street; witness afterwards saw the man at General Augur's headquarters, and recognized him as Lewis Payne, of the assassination conspirators.

No cross-examination.

Hon. Frederick W. Seward was sworn, and examined by Mr. Pierrepont.—I am Assistant Secretary of State, and was so in April, 1865 ; I reside at Madison place, on fifteenth street, and did reside there in April, 1865 ; General Augur's headquarters were just below my residence; on the night of April 14, 1865, I was in my room, which adjoins that of my father, in the third story; the house fronts on Lafayette Square ; my father's room was in the front part of the house, and my own room adjoins his.

The witness described the wounds his father had received by being thrown from a carriage, &c., and then resumed.

My father's right arm was broken ; he laid upon the bed with his arm toward the right side, and was in a recumbent position, but was supported by a framework ; my father was suffering from want of sleep, and it was an object to keep him as quiet as possible , in my father's room was my sister, who has since died, and a soldier named Robinson ; I was in my own room, and my wife was there also; my mother was in her room back of that of my father's: a little after ten o'clock on the night of the 14th of April, I heard some one come up stairs ; I stepped into the passage and I saw a stout, heavy built man, who said he was a messenger from Dr. Verdi, and that he had some medicine to deliver personally; I told him that we were trying to compose Mr. Seward to sleep, but he persisted and seemed to be determined to obey orders: after some further conversation I told him he could not see him ; and the man turned to go away, and I turned toward my room, when I heard a quick step behind me, and turning I saw the man come back with a navy revolver in his hands; it passed through my mind in a moment, and the pistol was an additional reason why the man should not see my father: the man then attacked me, and in the scuffle we fell into my father's room, and I remember nothing distinctly, but have a recollection of two persons picking up my father, who was bloody, and remember hearing some one say that he was not dead: I was then taken to my room, and knew nothing more until I recovered consciousness; I never saw the man afterwards.

No cross-examinaion.

Mrs. Frederick Seward sworn, and examined by M. Pierrepont.—She testified that when she entered the passageway on the night of April 14, she saw a man grapple with her husband; while she was looking, the door of the Secretary of State's room was burst open, and witness' husband and the man fell into the room: the next she saw was a man on the bed, upon Mr. Seward, and then two men fighting at the foot of the bed, apparently for the purpose of keeping some one from going around the bed; Miss Seward, my sister-in-law, asked me not to allow them to carry her father off: the Secretary of State was then lying on the floor, covered with. bedclothes; I then saw them lift the Secretary of State, and I attended to my husband, who was wounded about the head; it was some time before he spoke; I saw Colonel Seward come up stairs when Payne went out; he had a gash across his forehead.

Colonel Augustus Seward sworn, and examined by Mr. Pierrepont.—I was in bed the night of the assassination, and was awakened by the screams of my sister, and ran up stairs; saw two men scuffling, and at first supposed it was my father, who was delirious, and after seeing him, noticed I was mistaken I thought it was the nurse, and grappled with him, and was struck with what I suppose was a decanter from the table; the man was then pushed out, and as he passed the passage lamp I noticed that he was no one in the house who belonged there: I afterwards saw the man on the monitor, and recognized him as the man Payne, who was tried at the arsenal; I then got a pistol and went to the front door, and was told by William Bell that the man had gone off. No cross-examination.

The jurors asked if they would be permitted to attend church in a body.

Mr. Bradley said any church except the Catholic;

Mr. Pierrepont said they agreed the jury should go to any church.

Mr. Bradley said he was glad to hear that, for the prosecution had refused to allow Catholics on the jury.

The court directed however, that the jurors should be kept together, and if they went to church they must go in a body.

The court then took a recess until 10 o'clock Monday morning.

JUNE 24.—The trial of John H. Surratt was resumed this morning in the Criminal Court, Judge Fisher presiding.

John M. Lloyd was sworn, and examined by Mr. Carrington.— I live in the Seventh ward, in Washington I have lived here since October, 1865, previous to that I lived at Surrattville and kept a tavern there: I moved to Surrattville in 1864, and lived there until October, 1865: I occupied the house of Mrs. Mary E. Surratt. I have had a short acquaintance with the prisoner, and now recognise him: I rented the house from Mrs. Surratt; have sen Harold and Atzerott: saw them both at my house about six weeks before the assassination: Harold came to my house and stayed all night; the next morning Surratt and Atzererott drove up; half an hour afterwards they were all together, at my house; there were several persons at the house beside them; they came in and took a drink and played cards, after a while, Surratt called me in the parlor, and there I saw two guns and a rope lying on the sofa; there was also a monkey-wrench there: I never examined the articles, and cannot say that I could now identify them; the prisoner asked me to conceal the things; I at first refused, until he insisted that there would be no danger to me, and I then consented to take them; I told him there was no place to conceal such things, and he said he would show me a place, and I concealed the articles in an upper, room, under the joist; the prisoner said he only wanted me to keep the articles two or three days.

Mr. Carrington asked the witness if he saw Mrs. Surratt before the assassination.

Witness said he did not wish to go into an examination of Mrs. Surratt, as she was not here, and he would not answer unless compelled to do so by the Court.

The Court instructed the witness to answer.

The witness resumed, and said; On the Tuesday before the assassination I met Mrs. Surratt at Uniontown; she was in a buggy with a young man, whom I afterwards understood to be Weichman ; Mrs. Surratt told me to have the shooting-irons ready, and said that they would be called for soon ; I told Mrs. Surratt that the house was going to be searched, and I did not wish to have the things there. I was at Marlboro on April 14, 1865, and when I returned home at 6 o'clock I saw a number of persons there and among them was Mrs. Surratt; when I drove up Mrs. Surratt came to meet me, and handed me a package, and told me to have the guns ready and two bottles of whiskey, and to give them to whoever should call for them that night; Mrs. Surratt and Weichman left before dark ; the package handed me contained a field-glass; at 12 o'clock that night Harold came to my house, and a person was with him ; I do not know the size of the person referred to, as he was on horseback ; Harold remarked, when he came in, " For God's sake, Lloyd, make haste and get those things !" I then went up stairs and got one of the guns, a field-glass, and a cartridge box, which was all I could bring, and I did not go back.

Harold rode a bay horse and the other a gray horse : Harold took a drink and went out, and witness supposes the other man took a drink.

Question. Had you heard of the assassination of President Lincoln then ?

Mr. Bradley said the drift of this was to get out what Booth said.

Judge Fisher. It must first be shown that Booth was there. All that the other man said in the hearing of Harold was evidence.

The witness resumed, and said he was then asked if a doctor was near, and the other man talked about the assassination.

Question. When did you first hear of the assassination ?

Mr. Bradley objected, if it was in the course of that conversation.

The witness was disinclined to answer the question, and Judge Fisher said the witness could answer when he first heard of the assassination.

The witness said he first heard of it that night ; could not distinctly recollect, but he understood Booth to say that either he or they had killed the President. The witness thinks that Secretary Seward's name was also mentioned. The carbines referred to were covered when handed to the witness. The carbines were uncovered by Haorld, and the

witness noticed something peculiar about the locks, examined the field-glass, but could not fully recognize it as the one that was handed to him by Mrs. Surratt; he thought the glass he saw had large letters upon it. Witness was also shown the carbines, and thought the one was the same as the one Harold took the cover from; recognized it by the peculiarity of the lock ; the other carbine was taken away by the detectives; have not seen the cartridge-box since it was taken away by Harold.

Question by Mr. Pierrepont. On the night when these men were there, did you hear Harold use the name of Booth ?

A. No, sir.

Q. Did you use the name Wilkes ?

A. No, sir ; I don't know what Mrs. Surratt's business was down there on April 14 ; when Mrs. Surratt was there several other persons were there ; Mr. Jarboe and others were there, as was also Mrs. Offut; when I first saw Mrs. Surratt in the yard she was alone we were at Marlborough attending a trial, and after court was over drank a good deal, and went home much intoxicated.

I put no confidence in Harold telling me that the President was killed, because I thought he was drunk; the soldiers came early in the morning, and after I found what had happened I became frightened, and went to drinking ; do not recollect exactly what I told Clarvoe, the detective, but think I told him that the men, Harold and Booth, had not been there; I did not wish to be a witness in the case, and I might have said I knew nothing about it.

Colonel E. J. Conger was called and sworn, but his examination was deferred, and the court then adjourned until next day at ten o'clock.

JUNE 25.—The trial of John H. Surratt was resumed this morning in the Criminal Court, Judge Fisher presiding. The court-room was crowded, as usual, and the air was very oppressive. The court was opened at 10.20.

John M. Garrett was sworn, and examined by Mr. Wilson.—I reside in Caroline county, Virginia, and lived there in April, 1865, at the same place where I live now; I knew J. Wilkes Booth; I saw him at my father's house two days, I think, before he was killed there he was brought by two men, named Gett and Ruggles ; I saw Booth when he rode to the house ; he came in the afternoon, and was on horseback ; I can't describe the horse, as I don't remember what kind it was; I knew Harold; he came the day after Booth did: when Booth came he remained in the house; tho first night he was very lame, and said his leg was broken; Booth remained about the house during the day; he stayed there until after dinner, and then some cavalry came along, and he left the house for a short while; Booth went in the direction of the woods, and then returned when Booth came back from the woods he took supper at the house, and after supper he went to the barn with Harold, and stayed there until the cavalry came.

Colonel Everton J. Conger was then called and examined by Mr. Pierrepont. The witness is now a farmer in Richland county, Ohio, but was, in 1865, a soldier and lieutenant colonel of 2d District of Columbia Cavalry. Witness was asked to describe the capture of Booth, and said when he went to Garrett's house he was accompanied by Baker, Lieutenant Doherty, sixteen cavalrymen, a man named Rawlings, and a man named Jett; there was a sergeant named Boston Corbett; Jett went with us to show where Garrett lived: when witness and company got there they were informed that Booth and Harold were in the barn; witness posted the men around the barn.

Luther B. Baker sworn, and examined by Mr. Carrington.—Now reside in Lansing, Mich.; in 1865 was employed by General Baker as a detective: I had been quartermaster of the 1st District of Columbia Cavalry; I am one of the party who went in pursuit of Booth after the assassination; the date on which I left Washington in company with Colonel Conger and Lieutenant Doherty has now slipped my memory; I received orders to go to Belle Plains with this command to search for Booth and Harold; we went to Belle Plains, and Conger and I went in advance, under assumed names, and pretended we had been separated from a party crossing the Potomac—that we were being pursued by the Yankees: under assumed names we called on several persons and in tho morning breakfasted with a Doctor Ashton. I saw a man and his wife sitting at their door; I asked them if they had seen any citizens pass, one of whom was a lame man: they said they did, and I showed Booth's and Harold's picture, and they were recognized by the man, whose name was Rawlins, as the men who had passed: a colored boy named Lucas had

brought them to the ferry, and Harold offered Rawlins ten dollars if he would ferry them across, Booth saying that they had escaped from the Yankees; Rawlins said he could not ferry them then, as he had his nets to attend to; he went to attend to his nets, and meanwhile two Confederate soldiers, whose names were given as Jett and Bainbridge, come down, and Booth and Harold went off with them. I then sent for Colonel Conger, who came down, and we ferried across the river, taking Rawlins as a guide; we then proceeded to Bowling green, and we found Captain Jett there, and upon information received from Captain Jett, we proceeded to the Garratt House, Jett accompaning us; the Garrett House was surrounded; there were two gates, and I went in and held the gate open for the command to pass through: I came to a side door, and an old man put his head out, and wanted to know what the matter was; I told him to light a candle and open the door; he then came down, and I placed my hand on his shoulder, and, presenting my pistol, asked him where these men were; he seemed much frightened, and said the men had gone to the woods; Colonel Conger came up and threatened to hang the old man if he did not tell where the men were; a young man in Confederate uniform then came up and said; "Don't injure father, and I will show you where the men are," the cavalry then placed themselves around the barn, and I took young Garrett there, and told him he must go in and get the men to surrender; Garrett went in; I heard a low conversation: I could hear a man say, "You have betrayed me, and must get out of here;" Garrett then came out, and I dismounted the soldiers, and told the men inside if they did not come out I would fire the barn, and have a bonfire and a shooting match; Booth said "Captain, this is hard, we have been guilty of no crime!" and then made a proposition that I should range the men twenty yards off, and he would fight the whole party; told him we did not go there for that purpose, and that he must surrender: Booth then said a man inside wanted to surrender and come out: I told him to come out and bring his arms; Booth said "This man has committed no crime; the arms are mine, and I am going to keep them;" I then consented that Harold should come out, and he came out; Booth again made a proposition to fight the whole party, and said something about another stain on the banner: at

TRIAL OF JOHN H. SURRATT.

FORD'S THEATRE

BOOTH.   SURRATT.

THE FATAL HOUR DRAWS NIGH. THE CONSPIRATORS ABOUT TO EXECUTE THEIR
HELLISH DESIGNS.

that moment the fire sprang up, and I conld see every thing plainly inside, and Booth coming apparently from the centre of the barn; Booth then looked around some time, and then came toward the door where I was s anding : he dropped his crutch, and as he came towards the door I heard the crash of a pistol and Booth fell: I then ran in and grasped his arms to secure him, not knowing that he was mortally wounded ; Conger then came in and said Booth had shot himself ; I disputed this saying, as I was looking at him all the time, and said the man who shot him should be taken to Washington under arrest; Booth was then removed from the barn to the piazza of the house, and swooped away: a physician was sent for, and Booth was again revived, and said, "Tell mother I die for my country ; I did all for the best:" Booth then asked me to kill him, I told him it had not been our intention to kill him, and that the shot had been fired without orders ; some thing was then said about Captain Jett, and Booth looked up and asked if Jett had betrayed him; I told him not to mind Jett now ; Booth then asked to have his hands held up, and looking at them, muttered, " Useless, useless:" this is about all Booth said that I remember ; Colonel Conger then said he would go to Washington with Booth's effects, and I took from his person a knife, pocket compass, pin, his arms, and diary.

The business of the court here came to a dead-lock by the absence of witnesses.

The Court asked if the prosecution had any more witnesses ready ?

Mr. Bradley, pointing to the witness room. There are half a dozen waiting out there in the penitentiary, and have been there all the mo ning.

Mr. Merrick. Oh, no: not in the penitentiary yet, but they will be.

Mr. Carrington said he knew of no other way to keep witnesses here, except by attachment.

After waiting some time for witnesses, and none appearing, the court, at 2. 45, took a recess until 10 o'clock next day.

June 26.—The trial of John H. Surratt was resumed in the Criminal Court this morning, Judge Fisher presiding. The court was opened at 10 o'clock.

Mr. Carrington said that before calling the witness he desired to call the attention of the Court to a certain remark that had been made yesterday by the counsel, as reported in the morning papers. The remarks referred to are as follows;

" The Court asked if the prosecution had any more witnesses ready.

Mr. Bradley.— (pointing to the witness room (—There are half a dozen witnesses out there in the penitentiary, and have been there all the morning.

" Mr. Merrick. Oh, no, not in the penitentiary yet, but they will be."

Mr. Carrington said he had heard the remark of Mr. Bradley, but did not deem it necessary to call attention to it at the time, as he supposed it was made in a spirit of humor. He had not heard the remark of Mr Merrick, but he thought the remarks in-insulting to the witnesses and improper, and he felt it to be his duty to call the attention of the Court to the remarks. When th time comes for arguing the case to the jury every license will, of course, be allowed to the counsel, but during the examination of witnesses such remarks are not proper ; they reflect upon the character of the witnesses, and should not be tolerated; and he hoped the Court would not allow any such remarks in future.

Judge Fisher said he heard the remark of Mr. Bradley, and supposed it was made in a spirit of pleasantry.

Mr. Bradley acknowledged that he made the remarks attributed to him, and said he did it in a spirit of humor.

James J. Gifford, who was in 1862 the stage carpenter at Ford's Theatre, was sworn and examined by Mr. Wilson. The witness testified to the position of the box occupied by the President on the night of the assassination, its arrangement, the hole made in the wall, &c.; and a wooden bar having been exhibited, the witness recog nized it as the bar placed to secure the door of the box.

Colonel Henry W. Smith was sworn, and examined by Mr. Pierrepont.—Am an officer of the United States army, and stationed at Vicksburg, on duty with the Freedmen's Bureau: was in Washington at the time of the assassination, and remained here eighteen months afterwards; I commanded the party that arrested Mrs. Surratt; arrested her on Monday, April 18, and arres ed Payne at the same time ; I was ordered by Gen. Augur to arrest Mrs. Surratt and all I found in the house, and I proceeded with three men to 231 H street, and posted the men about it to prevent escape; I went to the house, and after going up the steps I looked in the window and saw four women sitting together, apparently in close conversation: I then rang the bell, and some one came to the window and whispered out, " Is that you Kirby?" I replied, " No, it is not Kirby: but it is all right; let me in;" I went in, and asked the lady who opened the door if she was Mrs. Surratt: she replied she was; I then told her I was ordered to arrest her and all in the house, and asked who the ladies in the parlor were, and she mentioned the names of Miss Anna Surratt, Miss Jenkins, and Miss Honora Fitzpatrick: I told the ladies they would go with me, and Miss Surratt then said something about being arrested, and for such a crime: Mrs. Surratt put her arms about her daughter's neck and whispered something to her, when Miss Surratt became quiet; I then told the ladies to get their wrappings, and after this was done Mrs. Surratt asked permission to kneel down and say her prayers, as she said she asked God's blessing on all she did; I told her there was no objection to that; in the meantime I heard some one come in, and I supposed I was going to get Kirby, but when the man came in I found it was Payne; he came in and had a pick upon his shoulder; he at first hesitated, and I cocked my pistol and ordered him to come in; I then questioned Payne, and he said he was a laboring man, and had been working about at different places; I asked him what brought him there at that hour of the night, and he said he came there to get instruction about digging a drain, which Mrs. Surratt had employed him to do that morning; I called Mrs. Surratt, and she denied all knowledge of the man, and said she had not employed him: I saw a colored woman in the house, named Susan Ann Jackson.

The ladies I have named were in the parlor when I entered: Miss Surratt was on the sofa, and Miss Jenkins on a chair, and Miss Fitzpatrick was near the sofa; Mrs. Surratt and I went in the parlor together, after she opened the door; when I told them I came to arrest them, Miss Surratt began to cry and Mrs. Surratt advanced and embraced her.

General U. S. Grant was sworn and examined by Mr. Pierrepont.—I was in command at Vicksburg in first part of 1863, and during that year.

Q. State when you first saw Jacob Thompson, and under what circumstances?

Mr. Bradley noted an exception.

The witness was allowed to proceed, and testified that while he was at Milliken's Bend, in the early part of 1863, one of our pickets brought in a sail-boat which was found coming up the river about opposite to where Admiral Porter's flag-ship was lying; witness sent to have the boat brought in; the boat had a white flag flying, and when the boat was brought in Jacob Thompson was brought upon the flag-ship.

Q. What did Thompson say?

Mr. Bradley objected, as Thompson was not mentioned in the indictment.

Judge Fisher asked if Thompson was indicted as one of the conspirators.

Mr. Pierrepont said he was not by name, but it was stated that the other persons unknown were engaged in the conspiracy.

Mr. Merrick asked if the gentleman proposed to prove that Thompson was in the conspiracy to kill the President.

Mr. Pierrepont said he proposed to show now who Jake Thompson was.

Judge Fisher said he understood that the counsel would show a connection between Thompson and the prisoner at the bar. If the connection be made the testimony will be relevant, and if the connection is not made it will not be relevant.

The Court therefore admitted the testimony, and General Grant continued, and said he saw Thompson on board of Admiral Porter's flagship, and he (Thompson) said he was an acting staff officer of one of the generals in Vicksburg; that he was an acting inspector general of the Confederate army; did not understand that he held a commission, but that he was an acting staff officer.

No cross-examination.

Charles Dawson was sworn, and examined by Mr. Wilson, and testified that he was a clerk at the National Hotel in 1865; when Booth left (April 14, 1865, he left a trunk and valise behind him, and they were placed in the baggage-room of the hotel: a few days before the arrest of Surratt witness was examining some baggage, and Booth's valise was partly open, and a card marked J. Harrison Surratt dropped out [card produced, but not offered in evidence]: during the progress of the conspiracy trial witness, in looking over the letter rack at the hotel, in letter B found a letter directed to "J. W. B." [letter identified]; the letter was offered in evidence; and an exception was taken by the defence. The letter is as follows, and is the same as was offered at the conspiracy trial;

SOUTH BRANCH BRIDGE, April 6, 1865.

FRIEND WILKES : I received yours of March 12. and reply as soon as practicable. I saw French, Brady, and others about the oil speculation. The subscriptions to the stock amount to $8,000 myself, which is about all I can stand. Now, when you sink your well, go deep enough. Don't fail. Every thing depends on you and your helpers. If you can get through on your trip, after you strike ile. strike through Thornton Gap and cross by Capon, Romey's, and down the branch, and I can help you safe from all hardships for a' year. I am clear of all surveillance, now that infernal Purdy is beat I hired that girl to charge him with an outrage, and eported him to old Kelley, which sent him in the shade; but he suspects too damn much now. Had he better be sentenced for good? I send this up by Tom, and if he don't got drunk you will get it the 9th. At all events, it can't be understood if lost. I can't half write. I have been drunk for two days. Don't write so much hifaluten next time. No more, only Jake will be at Greene's with the funds. Burn this. Truly yours,

"Lon."

Sue Guthrie sends much love.

Colonel Richard C. Morgan was sworn and examined. In April, 1865, was in the service of the War Department, and on the night of April 17 was sent to the Surratt house; went there after Colonel Smith had been sent there : I saw Mrs. Surratt, Miss Jenkins, and Miss Fitzpatrick there, and I saw a colored woman in the basement; the colored woman was tall and rather black; have a distinct memory of what occurred that night, as well as anything can be recollected that happened two years ago : I had directed that the persons in the house should be taken to the provost marshal's office, and there was some hesitation about getting ready, and I told them they must go: when they were prepared to go I heard a ring at the bell; supposing it was a man sent for the carriage, and as I opened the door a man came in with a pick over his shoulder, and dressed as a laboring man; the man came in, and as I turned Mrs. Surratt was getting from her knees: the ladies then passed out, and as they were going out Mrs. Surratt said, "I am so glad you officers came, as this man with a pick had come here to kill us :" after the ladies had passed out, 1 questioned Payne, and he said he came to dig a drain for Mrs. Surratt: I told him

that was an unseasonable hour to come, and asked him how he knew Mrs. Surratt; he said he met her on the street that morning and she engaged him to dig the drain; after further questioning Payne's answers appeared very unsatisfactory, and I put him under arrest and sent him to the provost marshal's office, I remained and searched the house until 3 o'clock a. m,: I found a bullet mould, some bullets, caps, cartes de visite, and portfolio and letters; we put all the articles we found in a trunk; I think the room these things were found in was Mrs. Surratt's room; it was the room back of the parlor; we found a pair of dirty boots in the room above we found also a little whistle, part of a spur, and a cash-book.

(Picture exhibited.)

It was a small framed picture of "Morning, Noon, and Night," and behind it was a photograph of Booth, in the back of it, and witness thought it was the same frame he had taken from Mrs. Surratt's mantle.

Mr. Merrick objected to this testimony.

Question by Mr. Pierrepont. Do you find anything in the back of the frame now?

Answer. Yes, sir, I find a card with "Morning, Noon, and Night" on it. The frame is not in the same condition now that it was when I found it; when I found it there was something else in it, which I handed to the provost marshal.

Mr. Pierrepont. (Handing a card to witness)—Is this the something you handed to the provost marshal?

A. It looks like it; it is a picture of J. Wilkes Booth, and it was Booth's picture I found there; don't know whether this is the same picture or not.

Col. John D. Pettit recalled.—A whistle was exhibited to witness, and he was asked if he had heard that whistle to-day?

Witness replied that he heard Mr. Carrington blow upon it to-day.

Mr. Carrington asked the witness if the sound of the whistle was a sound like that he heard in a lot back of his house on the night of the assassination, as testified to by him on a previous occasion.

Mr. Merrick said such an offer was a perfect farce.

Mr. Pierrepont said he could not see any farce about it. They proposed to show that witness heard a sound similar to that the whistle now made.

After some discussion witness was allowed to hear the whistle, and he testified that it was similar to the sound heard on the night of April 14, 1865, near Ford's Theatre. Mrs. Mary Benson (formerly Mrs. Mary Handspeth) was sworn, and examined by Mr. Carrington.—Witness now resides in Canada; was in New York in 1865, in November, and remembers the time from the fact of finding a letter about the assassination: General Butler had been in the city, but left that morning; General Winfield Scott was in the city, at the Hoffman House; I remember riding in the Third-avenue cars that day; my little daughter was with me; I remember two gentlemen riding in the car that day, and I heard their conversation at intervals; one of the men appeared to be educated, and the other was not; one of the men was very genteel looking; I was attracted to him by noticing that he was disguised, for as the car jolted I noticed that false whiskers were pushed forward, and the skin under them appeared whiter than the rest of his face; he had a scar on his right cheek; the other man was much more rough and coarse looking, and I noticed that the genteel-looking man who called the rough one Johnson, had a belt on his pistol; the genteel-looking man said he was going to Washington the day after, and the one called Johnson said he was going to Newbern, and he appeared to be very angry that he was not sent to do a certain thing; the man left before I did, and my little daughter picked up a letter and handed it to me, supposing it was mine, as I had some letters to post; I then went to a broker's office, and while getting out my purse I brought the letters out and found them unsealed, and they revealed a plot to assassinate; General Butler's name was mentioned in the letters, and having seen that he was in the city, I took the letters to the Hoffman House, and found that Gen. Butler had left the city; I then read the letters to General Scott, and at his directions I took them to General Dix. General Scott thought them very important letters [exhibited]; witness recognized them as the letters she had picked up on the car.

The letters were offered as evidence, and an exception was taken by the defence.

The letters were also used at the assassination trials, and are found on page forty of Pitman's report of that trial.

Cross-examined by Mr. Bradley.—I was living in Canada when I was summoned; no process was served, but the United States consul at Toronto asked me to come: it was agreed that if I came here to testify, my expences here and back were to be paid, and I was to receive $20 per day; my husband came with me, and his expences are paid.

By Mr. Pierrepont.—This agreement was made by Mr. Thurston, American consul: I would not come under any other terms.

Henry R. McDonough sworn, and examined by Mr. Pierrepont.—In 1864 I was cashier of Adams' Express Company in this city; John Surratt was employed by the company from December 30, 1865; to January 13, 1865: he was paid for two days service, and he never came back; I paid him for the two days, the 30th and 31st of December, and took his receipt; he was to be paid at the rate of $50 per month; the receipt is at the company's office in Baltimore; I do not positively recognize the prisoner.

Mr. Bradley.—It was him. We don't deny that.

The court, at 2.45, took a recess until ten o'clock next day.

JUNE 27.—The trial of John H. Surratt was resumed this morning, in the Criminal Court, Judge Fisher presiding.

There is no abatement in the interest in the case, and to-day the number of ladies in attendance was noticeably increased.

The prisoner was brought into court at ten o'clock precisely, and was escorted to his accustomed seat beside his counsel.

His brother, Isaac Surratt, who has not been noticed in the court-room for a day or two, was present again this morning, and for some time engaged in a very animated conversation with the prisoner.

The business of the trial was commenced at ten minutes past ten.

William R. Conger was sworn, and examined by Mr. Carrington.—Reside at St. Albans, Vermont; it is my native place, and have always lived there; the Tuesday and Wednesday after the assassination, I was keeping a saloon near the depot, at St. Albans; I think I saw the prisoner there, his eyes, nose, forehead and mouth look like the man I saw there; another man was with the prisoner; I paid special attention to the prisoner, as I suspected he had been engaged in the assassination conspiracy; the prisoner looks like the man I then saw; I crossed his path several times as he was going to the depot, and tried to have him arrested; and I went to seek an officer; and while going to the American House, I came across Albert Sawles, cashier of the National

Bank; I turned with Sawles, went to the depot, and pointed this gentleman out: we then started and went up town, and got in front of the American House, and we followed as far as the jail to find an officer, and could not find one: he turned back, and in front of the American I saw Albert Sawles' brother, Edward A Sawles, a lawyer; we did not arrest the man; the last I saw of the man was at the depot; I could get no officer; and I went through the cars and saw the man no more, and I do not know how he escaped,

Edwaad A. Sawles sworn and examined by Mr. Carrington.—I am a lawyer, residing at St. Albans Vermont; I know Mr. Conger: my attention was called to the fact that there was a person there who was supposed to have been connected with Mr. Lincoln's assassination, and that he was at the American Hotel at St. Albans, and it was supposed to be Booth; I went to the American Hotel with my brother, and we saw two persons who were pointed out to us; this was on Tuesday, April 17, 1865, in the forenoon; the men were in the bar-room, and one passed through; we heard there was a photograph of this supposed person, and we looked at the photograph, and when we came out these two men were going to the depot, and during this time we met Mr. Conger; we saw these two persons again in the depot, and while we were there a train was standing on the track, and my recollection is that it was about leaving for Montreal; we then left, and I returned to the National Bank with my brother; I did not see the persons afterwards.

Mr. S W. McClermont was sworn, and examined by Mr. Pierrepont.—I reside in Twelfth street, Washington, between E and F: I have lived in Washington from a child; in 1864 I lived on B Street, Island: in April, 1864, as near as I can recollect between the 12th and 15th of that month, I came from the Island, and was standing on the avenue, on the north side, at the corner of Tenth street, waiting for a car to go to the Navy Yard; it was in the forenoon; two men stood near me who seemed to be impatiently waiting for some one: in a few moments these two were joined by another, and I turned my head; why, I don't know; they spoke in an undertone to one another; the only name I heard was the name Jim, and then I heard the President's name mentioned, and one of the men spoke of coming from the Soldier's Home; then I heard the words "telescope rifle;" one of the others answered and said "His wife and child will be along;" another replied and said it "made no difference, if necessary they, too, can be got rid of;" at this I turned and one of them seeing I was looking, they ceased conversation and walked down the avenue. Harold and Atzeroth were the two men on the corner; the man who came down Tenth street was a young man, medium height, and I thought I had seen him before; I did not know where I had seen him, but I recollected afterwards I had seen him on the stage, and I recollected the third man as John Wilkes Booth.

Lewis J. Weichman sworn and examined by Mr. Pierrepont.—Reside in Philadelphia; I know the prisoner at the bar very well; I first met Surratt at St. Charles' College' Ellicott's Mill, Md., in September, 1829; in 1862, the latter part, I accepted a position as teacher in St. Matthew's Institute, on Nineteenth street, between G and H: I continued as teacher there for about a year and ten days; in the middle of January, 1863, I for the first time met Surratt since we left college. He visited me in 1863 and 1864, and he was treated with a great deal of kindness; Mrs. Surratt moved to the house here on November 1, 1864: I first visited the house by commencing to board there at that time; or rather I lodged there then, and I commenced to take meals there in December, 1864: I boarded there, and was there the night of the assassination; the first outside party I saw at the house connected with the conspiracy was Booth; in 1864 and 1865 I was invited by Surratt to take a walk, and we walked down Seventh street, and opposite Odd Fellows' Hall Surratt recognized Dr. Samuel Mudd, and he shook hands with him, and introduced the Doctor to me; Dr. Mudd introduced Booth to both of us: Booth invited us to his room at the National: at the room Booth requested us to be seated, rang the bell, and had the servant bring drinks and segars; I made some remarks about the appearance of the room, and Booth said it had been occupied by a member of Congress; the number of the room was 84: Booth took some documents down and remarked what nice reading he would have; Mudd then called Booth out, and afterwards Surratt was called out, and the three remained in the entry several minutes, and came back again; Mudd then came to me and excused himself for the privacy of the conversation, and said Booth wanted to purchase his farm, but would not give enough ; Booth afterwards told me something to the same effect; after a while Booth, Mudd and Surratt seated themselves around a table, and began a very private conversation; Booth took out an envelope and make marks, and Surtatt and Mudd were looking at him, from the motion of the pencil I concluded the marks were straight lines; after twenty minutes conversation they arose, and Mudd invited us to the Pennsylvania Hotel, on C street; at the Pennsylvania Hotel they had some conversation, and Surratt was shown letters, and appeared in much glee; Booth left at 10 30, and as Surratt and I were walking home, Surratt remarked that the accomplished gentleman I had been introduced to was J. Wilkes Booth, the actor; he told me Booth wanted to puchase Mudd's farm, and he was an agent, and some time afterwards, when I asked Mrs. Surratt about it she said the people of Charles county were tired of Booth, and wanted to push him off on John; in the summer of 1864, I met Harold at Piscataway Church, Charles county: I met Harold there for the second time, and Surratt was there; it was only a casual meeting; after this meeting with Booth, Surratt and I got home at 11 o'clock: in the latter part of 1864 Surratt was employed in Adam's Express Company; shortly after Surratt's introduction to Booth he wanted leave to go to the country, and could not get it, and he told me he took French leave; in January, 1865, he took leave and was away several days: when he returned I asked him where he had been, and his answer was to Port 'Tobacco. I met Atzeroth about four weeks after Surratt's introduction to Booth, and about a week or ten days after Surratt returned from the country ; I met Atzeroth at Mrs. Surratt's and was introduced to him by John Surratt; some called him Atzerow, and others Atzeroth, and the ladies called him Port Tobacco; I met Atzeroth after four o'clock p. m. after I came from work: Surratt presented me, and nothing unusual was said ; Atzeroth stayed there half an hour, and he and Surratt conversed together, and Mrs. Surratt conversed with them; I was seated in the parlor one evening, and heard the door bell ring, and I went to the door; at the door I met a man, tall, of very black hair and ruddy countenance, and he asked

me if Mr. Surratt was at home, and I said no; he then inquired for Mrs. Surratt; he gave his name as Wood, and I went to the parlor and told Mrs. Surratt: she told me to admit him, and I brought him to the parlor and introduced him as Mr. Wood ; Mrs. Surratt said the gentleman would like to have supper, and as the dining-room was disarranged, Mrs. Surratt asked me to give him his supper in my room, and I did so; there was no sign of recognition between Mrs. Surratt and Wood; I asked him where he was from, and he said Baltimore, and he said he was in a china store—the store of Dr Parr; on March 13 I again saw the man ; he came to the door and I let him in ; his first visit did not make much impression on me, and I did not recognize him, and he said his name was Payne: I took him to the parlor, and during the conversation he was addressed as Mr. Wood, and I then recognized him; on this occasion he was not a clerk in a china store but a Baptist minister; his luggage consisted of two linen coats and two shirts: the next day he came back and walked into my room; I was writing at a table and Surratt was lying on the bed: Payne said he wanted to converse privately with Surratt, and I left the room: the next day when I came home, on March 15, I found a mustache lying on my table; I then went up to an attic room, back, and saw Surratt and Payne seated on a bed conversing, and surrounded by new spurs, two revolvers and two bowie-knives; when I went to dinner I told Mrs. Surratt I had seen John and Payne fencing with these things, and I said, "Mrs. Surratt, I don't like this:" I told her I had seen this on the bed; she told me I need not think anything of it, as I knew John was in the habit of riding in the country, and he had to have these things for protection; that night John showed me a ticket for a private box, and said he was going to the theatre, and I wrested the ticket from him and said I was going to the theatre ; he wrested the ticket from me and, said he had private reasons for not wanting me to go: Surratt took with him a little girl named Dean, about eleven years old, and he asked Miss Fitzpatrick to go, and she consented; the theatre party was Payne and Surratt, Miss Dean and Miss Fitzpatrick: before they left for the theatre Surratt borrowed a blue military cloak from me, and said he wanted Payne to wear it: this was on March 15, four weeks before the assassination; they went to Ford's theatre: at 11 or 12 o'clock Surratt and Payne came to my room, and Payne picked up a pack of cards, and they went out and stayed out all night; I afterwards met Surratt with Mr. Brophy, and Surratt said he had spent the night of March 15, at Gautier's, and that he would introduce us but it was a private club ; seen Surratt again on the 16th; they returned at 7 o'clock in the morning.

On the 3d of March I had been down the street with Surratt in the evening, and there was a good deal of music; Surratt left me, and when I went back to Mrs. Surratt's I saw Booth and Surratt there, and conversing in the parlor; this was after seven o'clock; I proposed we should walk to the Capitol, and Surratt, Booth and I went there, and on our return Surratt and I left Booth at the corner of Sixth street and Pennsylvania avenue; Surratt and I then went home; I met Harold at Mrs. Surratt's one day in March, after four o'clock; Harold was in my room, talking with Atzeroth and John Surratt: he came there on horseback; I saw Harold only once at Mrs. Surratt's house ; on the 20th I met Surratt at the post office, and he asked for a letter addressed to himself under the name of James Sturdy: I saw the letter; it came from New York, and was signed " Wood;" on getting this letter Surratt said nothing particular; he only showed me the letter: he said the letter was from Wood, who had been at Mrs. Surratt's house; he did not tell me where Wood was; do not remember seeing any of the parties on the 21st: on the 23d of March Mrs. Hollahan came to the office where I was employed.

Mr. Bradley objected to giving any conversation with Mrs. Hollahan.

The witness resumed, and said Mrs Hollahan handed him a telegram from New York.

Mr. Bradley objected, unless the telegram was produced.

Telegram exhibited, and witness recognized it as one he received.

The telegram was dated New York, March 23, 1865, and was directed to "Wichman," and read—

"Tell John to telegraph number and street at once.

J. Booth."

The witness resumed :—Two things about the telegram struck me as singular; my name was spelled wrong, and I knew of no one to telegraph to me; I took the telegram home, and showed it to John Surratt, and

said that it must be for him, and asked him what number and street was wanted, and he replied, " Don't be so d—l inquisitive ;" that afternoon Surratt and I took a walk, and at the corner of Tenth and F streets, we met a Miss Anna Ward ; we then went to the Herndon House, and John Surratt asked for Mrs. Murray, and said he wanted to speak to her privately; Mrs. Murray did not seem to understand, and Surratt asked if a room had not been engaged by Miss Ward for a man who was expected the next Monday, and who was délicate, and wanted his meals sent to his room : Mrs. Murray then seemed to recollect that the room was engaged: the man's name was not mentioned by either of us; I think that Surratt stated, upon our return home, that the rich man was to come from New York.

A paper was exhibited, and witness recognized it as Booth's handwriting.

Mr. Pierrepont proposed to offer the paper in evidence, as the original of the telegram above referred to.

Mr. Bradley said it must first be shown what knowledge the witness had of Booth's handwriting.

The witness said he had seen Booth write, and knew his writing by the way he made his B's.

By Mr. Bradley—Booth had given witness his autograph: had seen him write his name.

The paper was admitted in the evidence, and the witness resumed in chief. On March 25 I saw John Surratt, his mother, and Mrs. Slater, in a carriage drawn by two white horses, which Mrs. Surratt subsequently said had been hired from Brooke's stables; Mrs. Surratt returned it on the next evening, and said John had gone to Richmond with Mrs. Slater, to get a clerkship; saw the horse again the following Saturday, driven by a Dr. Wyril, and I was asked to tell at the stables that the horses would be returned the next day: I objected, and Mrs. Surratt said, " Oh Brooke thinks Atzerott, Harold and Surratt are a party of gamblers, and I want him to think so ;" on Sunday, March the 26, as I was going to church, Mrs. Surratt asked me to go to the National Hotel, and tell Booth she wanted to see him that afternoon: at the hotel I met Atzerott, and was introduced by Booth to John B. McCullough, the actor; I delivered my message, and Booth came that afternoon and had an interview with Mrs. Surratt at the head of the back stairs; I went to church that day with Mrs. Surratt, and on this occasion she did not stop at any place; on Sunday she went to St. Aloysius' Church, and on week days to St. Patrick's Church; after the 27th of March. Anna Surratt, Miss Jenkins, Miss Fitzpatrick, Mrs. Surratt and I went to St. Patrick's Church, and on returning, Mrs. Surratt stopped at the Herndon House, and said she was going to see Payne; she went in and staid twenty minutes, and came out; the others of the party had walked around the square and we met Mrs. Surratt as she came from the Herndon House, and we went home together: a day or two afterwards I met Atzerott, and he said he was going to see Payne, and I asked if it was Payne who boarded at the Herndon House, and he said yes; I told Mrs. Surratt afterwards what Atzerott had said, and she appeared angry that he should have told me. That afternoon Mrs. Surratt said her brother wanted to return to the country, and she requested me to ask Atzerott to lend Mr. Jenkins, her brother, one of his horses: I asked Atzerott, and he said before he could loan the horse he must see Payne; I asked what Payne had to do with it; I remarked, "You say one is Booth's and one is yours, and John Surratt says they are his:" the reply was Payne had a heap to do with it; we then walked to the Herndon House, and Atzerott went in and in twenty minutes came out and said Payne would not consent to loan the horses; I went and told Mrs. Surratt of the interview, and she seemed much annoyed that Atzerott should have refused, saying she had loaned him the last five dollars she had in her purse; Mr. Jenkins walked home the next day. On the evening of April 10, Mrs. Surratt asked me to drive her to the country; on the 11th I went with her; on the following morning she asked me to go to the National Hotel and tell Booth she sent me for his buggy and horse; I found Booth in his room and delivered my message; he said he had sold his horse and buggy, but handed me $10 to hire a horse; in speaking of the horses I said I thought they were Surratt's, and he said they were his own; I hired a horse and buggy at Howard's stables, and we left the house at nine o'clock. I went to the buggy, and Mrs. Surratt came down in a few moments, and was about to get into the buggy when she said, "Wait, Mr. Weichman, I must get those things of Booth; she returned to the house, and came back with a package in her hand, tied up in brown paper; said package was about five

or six inches round: Mrs. Surratt laid it on the bottom of the buggy, saying it was glass, and was afraid of its getting wet; we then started, and the buggy was halted once on the road at a place where there were some pickets of soldiers: Mrs. Surratt halted the buggy, and wanted to know how long the pickets would remain there, and she was informed they would be withdrawn at eight p. m.; Mrs. Surratt said, " I am glad to know it," and we drove off; nothing further occurred on the way to Surrattville.

Mr. Pierrepont said he must ask the court to stop here. He was not through with the witness, but he did not fell very well.

The court then took a recess until 10 o'clock next day.

Weichman's appearance upon the stand created quite a sensation. and when he first appeared he seemed to be much agitated. As soon as he appeared upon the stand the prisoner fixed his eyes upon him, and without a change of countenance, all through the long examination. All the testimony was given slowly and with the utmost deliberation.

June 28.—The trial of John H. Surratt continued to be the topic of conversation, and the court-room continues to be the centre of interest here, and applications for admission are increasing daily. Fearful of not getting an eligible position, crowds of ladies and gentleman hang about the court-house long before the hour opening, Among the spectators to-day were several members of Congress, and many of our most prominent citizens.

The business of the court commenced at 10. 15.

Lewis J. Weichman was recalled for the continuance of his examination in chief by Mr. Pierrepont.

The witness resumed and testified as follows:

Mrs. Surratt's manner all the way down, to Surrattville was lively and cheerful; we arrived at Surrattsville, and I removed the package from the buggy and gave it to Mrs. Surratt, and she went into Mr. Lloyd's parlor. I left Surrattville to return home at 6 30; on the way home Mrs. Surratt said she was anxious to be at home at nine o'clock; that she was to meet a gentleman there; I asked if it was Booth, and she made no reply: I said something about Booth's not acting, and she replied, " Booth is done acting, and is going to New York very soon, never to return:" and she asked me if I did not know that Booth was crazy on one subject: I said I did not, and she did not state the subject to me; on returning I saw the pickets returning to Washington; about two miles from Washington is a high hill and the city was illuminated, and I made some remark about the return of peace, and she replied, "I am afraid all this rejoicing will be turned to mourning, and all this gladness to sorrow," I turned to her and asked what she meant, and she said, "After sunshine there is always a storm:" she said, also, "The people are becoming too licentious, and God will punish them;" just as we came to Pennsylvania avenue, at the capitol, we saw a torchlight procession, and the horse shied at the light, and we turned up Second street, and arrived at home at nine o'clock, and Mrs. Surratt, after awhile, asked me which way the torchlight procession was going; I replied I thought they were going to serenade the President, and she said she would like to know, as she was interested in it; as I recall her manner now, she appeared nervous, and I asked what was the matter; she said she did not feel well; she had beads in her hands, and was walking up and down, and she once asked me to pray for her intentions; I asked her what her intentions were, and said I never prayed for one's intentions unless I knew what they were; Annie Surratt and others were laughing and talking, and Mrs. Surratt said, "Oh, you are making too much noise," and in a playful manner drove us from the room; Miss Surratt, Miss Fitzpatrick, Miss Jenkins, and I left the room together, and left Mrs. Surratt alone in the parlor; I went to my room in a few minutes afterwards: Miss Surratt and Miss Jenkins occupied a room above me, and I bade them good night at my door; Miss Fitzpatrick occupied Mrs. Surratt's room; I was unwell that night, and was out in the yard during the night; about two o'clock I got back to bed, and was just falling asleep when the bell rang vicently; I went down stairs and rapped on the door inside, and asked what was wanted: I was told Government officers were there, who wanted to find John H. Surratt and Wilkes Booth; I told them neither of those men were there; they demanded admittance anyhow, and I went in and informed Mrs. Surratt, who said, "Let them in, for God's sake;" I expected the house would be searched; I then let them in; there were half a dozen, and among them I remember Clarvoe and McDevitt of this city;

the house was then searched, and they searched my room, and I asked them for God's sake to tell me what has happened, and why this search was made: one of them turned and asked if I did not know what had happened that night; I replied I did not: the officers appeared to be astonished that I did not know what had transpired: then Mr. Clarvoe said; "I will tell you," and he pulled out a piece of cravat with blood on it, and he said; "Do you see that blood? It is the President's blood; Wilkes Booth has murdered Abraham Lincoln, and John H. Surratt has assassinated the Secretary of State;" I then went down stairs with Clarvoe and McDevitt, and Mrs. Surratt came out of her room, and I said; "What do you think? President Lincoln has been assassinated, and Booth did it;" she raised her hands and said; "My God! you don't tell me so;" at this time Miss Surratt Miss Jenkins and Miss Fitzpatrick were not in the parlor, but they afterwards appeared: after talking some time Annie Surratt wept and said, "Oh ma, this will bring suspicion on our house:" we were speaking of Booth having been there an hour before the murder: Mrs. Surratt said, "Annie come what will, I think Booth was only an instrument in the hand of Providence to punish this proud and licentious people: I returned to my room and did not see Mrs. Surratt again till the morning of the fifteenth at breakfast; I told Mrs. Surratt that I had suspected something, and that I was going to the Government, and would state the names of all I had seen in Booth's company, and bring the guilty parties to justice.

Question. Did you go to the Government and give information?

Answer. Yes, sir.

Mr. Bradley objected and noted an exception.

Witness resumed.—Mr. Hollohan was in the house, and he went with me and told all he knew. I was at Mrs. Surratt's house on March 10, and Payne, Booth, and Suratt came in my room at 6 p. m.; Surratt came in first, and had his pants tucked in his boots and was much excited, and had a four-barrelled pistol; Surratt raised his arm, and said in an excited way, "My hopes are gone, my prospects are blighted; I want something to do; can't you get me a clerkship?" he was much excited, and I told him not to be foolish; Payne came it next, dressed in gray clothes, and wearing pistols, Booth came in third, and was dressed in black, and had a riding whip in his hand; Booth walked about, and at first did not notice me; Payne, Booth and Surratt then went to Payne's room, in the attic, and in about half an hour the three left; Booth was at Mrs. Surratt's very frequentey: Mrs. Surratt liked Booth, and called him her pet; she said on one occasion, that pet stayed in her parlor from 10 o'clock p. m. until 1 a. m.; Booth was as intimate at Mrs. Surratt's as I was. [Telegram exibited.] I know the handwriting.

By Mr. Bradley. What means have you of knowing the handwriting?

Witness. I have seen Booth write, and have had his autograph, and have received a telegram, and I know Booth's handwriting. The witness was allowed to testify to the handwriting, and said it was Booth's.

Mr. Bradley noted an exception.

Telegram is as follows:

WASHINGTON MARCH 13
To Mr. McLaughlin, Exeter street, Baltimore;
Don't you fear to neglect your business. You had better come at once.   J. Booth.

Another telegram was exhibited, directed to the same party, and dated March 27, 1865, as follows:

Get word to Sam; come on with or without him Wednesday morning. We sell that day, sure; don't fail.
J. Wilkes Booth.

Witness recognized this also as in Booth's handwriting.

Mr. Pierrepont said he had some letters which he had omitted to show the witness, and he desired to offer them. [Letters exhibited.]

Witness recognized one as in Surratt's handwriting; it is dated Surrattsville, November 12, 1864. Another letter was shown, and was declared to be in Surratt's handwriting, and is dated September 21. 1864; both letters are directed to me.

The following are the letters;

SURRATTSVILLE, Nov. 12, 1864.
DEAR AL: Sorry I could not get up. Will be up Sunday. Hope you are getting along well. How are times and all the pretty girls? My most pious regards to the latter. As for the former, I care not a continental d—n. Have you been to the fair? If so, what have we now I'm interested in—the ,, bedstead?'' How's Kennedy? Tight as usual, I suppose. Opened his office, I hear. Fifty to one tis a failure. Am very happy I do not belong to the "firm.'' Been very busy

all the week taking care of and securing the crops. Next Tuesday and the jig is up. Good-bye Surrattsville. Good-bye God forsaken country. Old Abe, the good old soul, may the devil take pity on him.
JOHN H. SURRATT,
To Lewis J. Weichman, Esq., Washington City, D, C.

SURRATTSVILLE, MD
SURRATTSVILLE, Sept. 21, 1864,
Lewis J. Weichman, Washington, D. C.;
Dear Friend; John Surratt is neither dead nor drafted, though he ran the gauntlet of both. I am just able to walk but a little; yet very weak. I have had the chills and fever pretty severely. In hopes I have entirely escaped. I shall be in Washington soon as possible. I intend to stay up now a few days, in order to recuperate; possibly we may move up sooner than we anticipate, on account of certain events having turned up. I am quite sorry Miss Estelle has gone to Philadelphia. There is no attraction there now for me. Miss Fanny and I were getting on a fair road to a flirtation when she huddled up baggage and left for Washington. She says she is glad Mrs. Surratt intends moving to town. All right! we will see. Write soon, and tell me all the news. Nothing would give me greater satisfaction than to write a long letter. I am very glad to state that I escaped the draft. I sincerely hope you may do the same. Family are well, and send respects to you.   Yours, as ever,
J· HARRISON SURRATT.

At three o'clock p. m. the court adjourned until ten o'clock next day.

JUNE 29.—The trial of John H. Surratt continued to attract immense crowds to the Criminal Court-room. Ladies congregate about the doors an hour, and sometimes an hour and a half before the time for the opening of the court, and many of them endure the close, oppressive air of the courtroom all day long. Members of Congress arriving in the city seem to make the courtroom the first point of interest to visit.

Lewis J. Weichman was recalled, and Mr. Bradley continued the croos-examination. The witness was asked if he had not prepared a written statement, and then revised it from the published book?*

* Trial of the Assassins and Conspirators Published by Barclay &Co 602 Arch St and sent free of postage on receipt of 25 cents.

Mr. Pierrepont objected to the question as irrelevant.

Judge Fisher ruled that the question was proper.

The witness said he did write out a written statement, but he did not compare it with the book; he did not prepare the statement and read it before the grand jury in this case; I prepared a statement and gave it to Mr. Wilson, Assistant District Attorney, and did not have a copy of it in my pocket when before the grand jury.

JULY 1.—The Criminal Court Room was again crowded this morning with spectators.

By the agreement of the counsel the cross-examination of Lewis J. Weichman was temporarily suspended in order to admit of the examination of Mr. Charles C. Dunn. The witness testified that in 1864 he employed John H. Surratt in Adams' Express office, the witness being at the time agent of the company in this city. He was employed in the military freight depot, and entered upon his duties on December 30; on January 13 Surratt asked leave of absence, and the witness expressed his surprise that such an application should be made in so short a time after he had been employed; Surratt said he had business in the country, and wanted to go there with his mother, and the witness still refused; the next day Mrs. Surratt came, and the witness refused her also, and Surratt left and never came back to the office to resume his duties, and did not even return for his pay. No cross-examination.

Lewis J. Weichman was then recalled and was cross-examined by Mr. Bradley. I do not know that Mrs. Surratt remained at the table and that Anna Surratt answered the door on the night of April 14; on the morning after the assassination I met Hallohan in the street and we then went home to breakfast; and I said I believed that Atzeroth had assassinated the President; at the breakfast table I said I would disclose all I knew: I remember a remark that was made at the table, that "the death of Abraham Lincoln was nothing more than the death of a nigger in the army."

Q. Who said that? A. Anna Surratt.
Q. Did you tell that at the assassination trial? A. I did not.
Q. Why did you not? A. Because I had too much sympathy for the poor girl.
Q. Why did you tell it now, then? A. Because you drew it out of me, and because

I have been hunted down and persecuted fo the last two years on account of these people.

Mr. Bradley—1 did not ask anything to induce you to make a volunteer statement.

The witness resumed, and in answer to a question said I don't remember telling either Carlin or Brophy that I did not wish to return from Canada, and would not have done so if the detective had not compelled me; that is simply an absurdity, and you will be satisfied that it is before you have done with this trial.

Mr. Bradley—Well, suppose you let the counsel attend to that, and give the facts.

The witness resumed I might have told Howell that my sympathies were with the South, because I often talked Secesh with such fellows for buncombe; I was in Carroll prison with Mr. Hollahan and others; I was there thirty days, but I think Hollahan was released before I was.

At twelve o'clock the court took a recess for half an hour.

Upon re-assembling, Lewis J. Weichman was recalled, and his cross-examination was continued by Mr. Bradley: since court took a recess I saw Mr. Carlin, and shook hands with him, and said, "Hello, old fellow, I see you are to be a witness against me:" he replied, " He could not help it, that it was his duty;" don't remember telling Mr. Carlin that my conscience troubled me for the testimony given, and that I was going to confession to unburden my conscience; do not remember Carlin telling me I had better go to a magistrate and make a statement, nor do I remember telling him that I would do so if I did not fear a prosecution for perjury; do not remember telling Mr. Carlin that the testimony was written out for me, and that I was compelled to swear to it; do not remember telling Carlin that I could have given an explanation of Mrs. Surratts' visit had I been allowed to do so; I say upon my solemn oath that I never said any of these things, and will put my word against the whole world on that point: the questions are perfectly surprising to me.

Re-direct examination by Mr. Pierrepont. —I was confined in Carroll prison as a government witness ; I was not confined there for any crime. (Paper exhibited.) I recognize it as a copy of the order appointing a special officer: the original is in Mr. Mc-Devitt's possession.

Mr. Pierrepont proposed to read the paper, and Mr. Bradley objected.

The objection was overruled, and Mr. Bradley noted an exception.

The paper is as follows:—

HEADQUARTERS, DEPARTMENT OF WASHINGTON, Office Provost Marshal-General, Defenses North Potomac, Washington, D. C., April 16, 1865.—Special Orders, No. 68.—(Extract)—Special officers James A. McDevitt, George Hollohan and Lewis J. Weichman are hereby ordered to proceed to New York city on important government business, and after executing their private orders, to return to this city and report at these headquarters. The Quartermaster's Department will furnish the necessary transportation.

By command of Major-General Augur.

(Signed) J. INGRAHAM,

Colonel and Provost Marshal-General, Department of North of Potomac.

Witness resumed.—It was on the morning of April 15, 1865, at breakfast, that Miss Anna Surratt said the death of Lincoln was no more that the death of a nigger, &c.

Mr. Pierrepont asked witness to state something more about his confession to Carlin, and about his going before a magistrate, &c.

Witness said he never spoke to Carlin or Brophy about confession; I never said anything to them about confession.

Mr. Pierrepont—That is all, then.

Witness—Are you done with me, Mr. Bradley?

Mr. Bradley—I do not know that I am. For the present I am, but I may have something further to say to you. The witness then retired from the stand.

Dr. Lewis Archibald McMillan was called and sworn.—I am a surgeon, and am out of service now; two years ago I was in the service of the Montreal Ocean Steamship Company, and from April to October, 1865, was surgeon of the steamer PERUVIAN; I know the prisoner at the bar; he crossed the ocean with me to Londonderry; I first saw the prisoner on the mail steamer Montreal, running between Montreal and Quebec, on the 15th of September, 1865; about a week or ten days previous, a man named La Pierre, a priest, who at the time lived in Montreal, came to me and said somebody was coming, and on the 15th of September, as I was going to Quebec on the steamer Montreal, I there met this Mr. La Pierre again, and he said he would introduce me to his friend;

he took me to a state-room, of which La Pierre had the keys; the state-room was locked and he unlocked it, and in the room I found the prisoner at the bar; Mr. La Pierre introduced the prisoner under the name of Mr. McCarty; I never suspected who the person was, and I passed the evening and night with him; the prisoner's hair was then short and of a dark brown color; I did not perceive then that it was dyed, but I afterwards found it out; the conversation that evening was general; La Pierre went to Quebec with us; when we got to Quebec we had breakfast on the steamer at seven or eight o'clock, and between nine and ten the passengers were transferred to the steamer Peruvian; upon reaching the Peruvian, La Pierre said to me, in Surratt's presence, that he wished me to let Surratt occupy my room till the steamer left; I did so, and he occupied my room till the steamer left; the steamer left in half an hour, and La Pierre went ashore; that day I remember that either after lunch or dinner the prisoner came to me, and, pointing to one of the passengers, asked me if I knew who the gentleman was, and I said I did not know; Surratt said he thought the man was an American detective, and was after him; I told him I thought nothing of the kind, and I asked him what he had done that he should be afraid of an American detective; he said he had done a good deal, and that if I knew all he had done it would make my eyes stare; I said he need not be afraid of an American detective, because he was on a British ship and in British waters; he said he did not care if he was, for that if he attempted to arrest him this would settle him, and he exhibited a pistol; we sailed about 10 o'clock a.m.; after we got on board the steamer I perceived that Surratt's hair and mustache was dyed; he wore a pair of spectacles; he said he did not wear the spectacles because he was short-sighted, but because they aided in disguising him; I had conversation with the prisoner every day until we arrived at Londonderry; I remember Surratt's telling me that he had been in the habit of going to Richmond with despatches during the war, and bringing despatches back to Washington and Montreal; he stated he at one time was told in Montreal that he would meet a lady in New York r that he met a woman in New York and came to Washington and started to Richmond with four or five others; tha tafte:

much trouble they crossed the Potomac, and getting south of Fredericksburg they saw some men approaching, and found out they were escaped soldiers, and were most starved to death, and that the women said "let us shoot the d—d Yankee soldiers," and they shot them and then went on; he told me the name of the woman, but I cannot now recollect it: I can't remember the name, and would not like to say it; it sounded like Slater; the soldiers referred to were unarmed.

Mr. Bradley said he could not see where this evidence was tending.

Judge Fisher, said he could not see to what it tended now.

Mr. Pierrepont said they would connect it with the conspiracy-

Witness resumed, and said Surratt told him he had received money from Benjamin, the Confederate Secretary of state; the amounts he named were $70,000 and $30,000; he said this was in Richmond, a few days previous to its fall; he said one day that several of them were crossing the Potomac in a boat, when they were pursued by a gun-boat and were ordered to surrender, or they would be fired upon; a small boat was sent to them, and they fired into the small boat as soon as they came alongside. Witness was asked to repeat this evidence, and retorted by telling Mr. Merrick that he (Mr. Merrick) could understand if he kept his ears open: he (McMillan) was not to be insulted, as all the witnesses had already been insulted, and he thought to insult the witnesses, was the act of a coward and a sneak.

Mr. Merrick asked if that was proper language for the witness to use.

The Court said it was not, but counsel must not worry and annoy the witnesses.

Witness said that Mr. Merrick had said the other day that all the witnesses ought to be in the penitentiary, and he wanted it understood that he was as good as Mr. Merrick.

Witness then resumed, and said Surratt stated that he had frequently travelled to Richmond under the assumed name of Harison and Sherman: upon reaching the coast of Ireland, Surratt called witness behind the wheelhouse and remarked that he saw foreign land at last, and putting his hand upon the pistol in his pocket, he said he hoped to live to see the day when he could return and serve Andrew Johnson as Abraham Lincoln

had been served; he said, also, that if an English officer atempted to arrest him, he would shoot him; I told him if he did that he would meet with very little mercy in England; he replied that he knew that, but that he would do it nevertheless, for he would sooner be hung by an English jury than a Yankee one, and if he went to the United States again he knew he would swing

Mr. Bradley asked that the latter statement be repeated by the reporter.

The witness was about to reply, when it was stated that he was not asked.

The witness said he could tell all that was necessary, and, continuing his remarks said that Mr. Merrick was not at all dangerous; witness was not afraid of him.

At 2.20 p. m. the court took a recess until 10 o'clock next day.

WASHINGTON, July 2.—The trial of John H. Surratt was resumed this morning in the Criminal Court, Judge Fisher presiding The court-room was again crowded with spectators.

Mr. Bradley said that before the examination was proceeded with he desired to call the attention of the Court to an incident that occurred just prior to the adjournment of the court yesterday, and he would ask that the reporter's notes be read, in order that the Court might see what led to the attack, and that its attention might be directed to the facts.

Mr. Clephane, the official reporter, then read an extract from his notes of yesterday, including the passage between the witness and Mr. Merrick.

Judge Fisher said I have never seen a case in which there was so much warmth and so much bitterness of feeling, and I never saw witnesses cross-examined in such a way as they had been in this case, and it was not to be wondered at that they sometimes felt insulted, and especially at such remarks as had been made by the counsel, that all in the witness-room should be in the penitentiary. Some most respectable witnesses, as Gen. Grant, Mr. Frederick Seward, and others, had been placed upon the stand, and the remark might be understood to apply equally to all, and the Court could not help it if witnesses helped themselves.

Dr. McMillan then resumed his testimony, and testified that Surratt told him that he was in Montreal on the first day of the week of the assassination; that he was summoned to Washington by Booth, by letter; Surratt also told me that a day or two after the assassination he was at St. Albans, and, the train being late, he strolled through the town, and went to a hotel for breakfast: while sitting at the public table he saw a great deal of excitement among the people at the same table, and asked his neighbor what all the excitement was about, and his neighbor said, "Don't you know that President Lincoln has been assassinated?" the prisoner said, "The story is too good to be true;" the man then showed him a paper, and the prisoner then saw his own name mentioned, and that was the last of his breakfast: that morning he left the table, and at the moment a man came in and said Surratt's handkerchief had been found: the prisoner then felt for his handkerchief, and found he had lost it, and then made himself scarce, went to Canada, and stopped at the house of Mr. Porterfield, Confederate agent, and stayed there until the detectives' search after him admonished him to leave; Surratt described to me how he got away from Mr. Porterfield; two carriages were brought to the house, and Surratt was placed in the one and a man dressed like him was placed in another, and they were driven in different directions; Surratt said he was driven to the foot of the Island of Montreal, where he crossed the St. Lawrence river, and was piloted by a boy to a small town called Saint Laboise; he said he stayed there some two weeks in the house of a priest named Charles Bouche; he told me that one day the priest being absent he was lying on a sofa in the priest's bed-room, and between the bed-room and sitting-room there was a place for a stove, and under the stove was a trap-door, and one of the female servants being desirous of seeing who the priest was concealing, put her head above the trap-door and Surratt frightened her off; the rumor then got out that the priest was keeping a woman in his room, and the priest then told Surratt he could conceal him no longer, and Surratt went to Montreal and was concealed by Priest La Pierre for four months in a dark room, which he never left, except late at night to take a stroll; on ship board the prisoner's appearance and conduct were gentlemanly, but he was very nervous, especially when any one would come behind him; on the evening before we landed at Londonderry, between 11 and 12 o'clock, I was called out of a brother officer's room, and passed the prisoner standing on what is

called the after-square: he was all dressed ready to go ashore; he had previously asked my advice about landing, and I would give him no advice, and he said he would go on to Liverpool; I was therefore surprised to see an apparent intention of landing at Londonderry: after some conversation I told the prisoner he had been telling me a good deal, and I expressed doubts of his travelling under his correct name, and asked him to give me his right name; he looked around, and then whispered in my ear, "My name is Surratt;" he went ashore twenty-five minutes afterwards: before going ashore the prisoner asked for a drink, and I woke the barkeeper, and we all three took a drink; it is the custom in England and on board ship for the barkeeper to help a customer to the drink asked for, and not to place a decanter before him; but in this instance the barkeeper put the bottle up, and Surratt poured out and drank half a tumbler of raw brandy; I then treated and the barkeeper treated; Surratt at all times took the same quantity; the prisoner then landed; the ship went on to Liverpool; I next saw the prisoner on the Wednesday following at my own boarding-house, in Birkenhead, opposite Liverpool: when he called upon me he asked me to show him the place he had been recommended to go to; I did so, and then called a cab, and that was the last I saw of him that night; I remember Surratt telling me one day that he, Booth, and others had planned the abduction of President Lincoln; he said they found they could not carry on the plan of abduction, and had to abandon it.

Henry Benjamin St. Marie was sworn and examined by Mr. Pierrepont.—In 1866, in April, I was in the Papal States, at Velotra; it was about forty miles from Rome; I was a soldier of the Papal army, and in the ninth company; these were called Papal Zouaves [the dress worn by Surratt was exhibited]: that is the dress worn by the Zouaves; I saw the prisoner there and I knew him; I think the time I referred to was the 14th or 16th of April: about the 18th or 19th of June, 1866, I saw the prisoner again; he came to my quarters with two other Zouaves, named Libart and Lebau, and we four took a walk; we took the road to Naples; we had some conversation at that time, and I was occasionally speaking to my companions in French and to Surratt in English; I asked the prisoner how he got from Washington, and he told me he left the night of the assas-

SURRATT HOUSE, WASHINGTON.

TAVERN AT SURRATTVILLE.

ATTACK OF COUNSEL UPON JUDGE FISHER.

sination or the next morning. and he said he was so disguised that no one could recognize him as an American, and that he was disguised as an Englishman, with a scarf over his shoulders; I then went to Malta, and did not see Surratt, but I afterwards saw him on the Swatara.

No cross-examination.

Judge Fisher said he had already exceeded the limits prescribed by his physician, and the court, therefore, at 2 10 adjourned until ten o'clock next day.

JULY 3.—The trial of John H. Surratt was resumed this morning in the Criminal Court.

Mr. Merrick asked if there would be a session of the court to-morrow, July 4.

Mr. Pierrepont said he doubted whether it would be legal to hold court. In some States it was not recognized as a legal day.

Judge Fisher said the matter had been under advisement, and the room had already been promised to the "Oldest Inhabitant Association," and there would be no session.

Charles H. M. Wood, colored, sworn, and examined by Mr. Pierrepont.—I am a barber by business, and have been in that business here since December, 1862: I knew Booth before the assassination : I have cut his hair and shaved him, and knew him well [the prisoner was asked to stand up] : I have seen the prisoner before ; on the morning of the assassination I saw him at Booker & Stewart's barber-shop ; I shaved and trimmed the prisoner's hair: Surratt came to the shop with Booth, McLaughlin, and another: the three named talked about coming from Baltimore: I also trimmed Booth's hair that morning ; I was waiting on Booth, and Surratt was in the rear of me, and a small, thickset man, whose name I do not know, was sitting near the glass; when I was done waiting on Booth he got out of the chair and went to the back part of the shop, where McLaughlin was, and the latter was standing at a glass disguising himself with false hair ; Surratt had by this time taken the chair vacated by Booth, and told me to clean him up nicely; Surratt looked like a man who had been travelling a short distance.

Frank J. M. Heaton sworn.—Reside at No. 462 Eleventh street, in this city ; on the day of the assassination when the President's carriage came saw the party get out and go in the theatre; was standing in front of the theatre at the time : saw no face at the time that attracted my attention: when the car-riage came up half a dozen persons from the restaurants came up: on last Thursday week witness came to court and saw the prisoner, and recognized him as one he saw at the time coming up to the President's carriage.

Theodore Benjamin Rhodes sworn.—Witness lives on Capitol Hill. in this city : was here the day Mr. Lincoln was assassinated ; knows Ford's Theatre; on that day was in the theatre; while there saw one of the box. doors open a little, and being desirous to see the stage from that point. went down there : as witness approached, whoever was there walked away, and witness stopped there some time and went out, and the party behind, who had been in the box previously came up and spoke to witness, and said he was connected with the theatre; he had a piece of wood in his hand about eight feet long and two inches wide, and remarked that the President would be there that night, and he was going to fix the box so the President could not be disturbed : he then placed the stick, which was of oak or pine, against the door and a niche in the wall, and adjusted it, asking if witness thought it would hold.

The prisoner was requested to stand up, and witness stated that he should judge that was the man ; had no doubt about it.

The court took a recess until half past ten o'clock next day.

JULY 5.—The trial of John H. Surratt was resumed.

Mr. Pierrepont proposed to put in evidence the almanac for the year 1865. for the purpose of showing when the moon rose on the night of April 14, and the condition of the moon at that time at Washington.

Mr. Merrick objected.

Mr. Pierrepont said he did not suppose there was any serious objection to the almanac, on account of the maker of the almanac.

Judge Fisher suggested that the American Almanac would be the most correct one to use, and, after further discussion, a messenger was despatched to the State Department for an American Almanac.

Thomas Lincoln sworn.—Is a son of the late President; was with his father at City Point, in March, 1865 ; was on a steamboat with him during the time he was there; while there a man came to the steamer and said he wanted to see the President; he asked to see the President; said he came from Springfield, and wanted to see the President on particular business ; he tried twice to see the President and was not permitted [the prisoner made to stand up]; witness stated that the party who attempted to see the President on the boat looked very much like prisoner.

The court here adjourned until next day.

JULY 6.—The trial of Surratt was resumed in the Criminal Court, Judge Fisher presiding.

Mr. J. H. Bradley, Jr., opened for the defence, and said that the time had at last arrived in this case when the prisoner could say something in support of his own innocence, and when not only his guiltlessness may be shown, but the pure fame of his departed mother may be vindicated. The difficulty of at first summoning a jury was adverted to, and after complimentary remarks to the jury, Mr. Bradley said the attorney for the defence came to the trial of this case in full confidence of the innocence of the prisoner. They had come to this conclusion, not from sympathy, but after a full and candid investigation of all the circumstances surrounding the case. All that the prisoner asked was a fair and full trial, and he trusted the verdict of the jury would set at rest all the misunderstood circumstances of the case.

Every prisoner was presumed to be innocent until proven guilty, and yet, in this case, the Assistant District Attorney, in his opening remarks, held him a monster of iniquity. Mr. Bradley then traced the tenor of Mr. Wilson's argument, and argued that he had not proven what he, with an eloquent flourish, said he would prove. The accusation made against the prisoner had not been sustained, and he [Mr. Bradley] argued that all such arguments on the part of a prosecuting officer were out of place. He reminded the jury that in its moral aspect the crime was no more heinous in the sight of the judge of all mankind than that of the most obscure citizen. He depicted the horror of feeling that attended the assassination of President Lincoln, and he then referred to the fact of a conspiracy to murder, and that the prosecution endeavored to show that Surratt was the head and front of the conspiracy. There was no doubt but that Booth was in the conspiracy; there was no doubt that Payne was one of the conspirators, but there was a doubt as to guilt of Harold and Atzerott. As to Mrs. Surratt, it would be shown that at least a grave error had been committed in that case, and they would prove the entire innocence of the prisoner. The conspiracy had not been traced back to 1863, as was promised it would be. Booth

was the head and front of the conspiracy, and it was in evidence that the prisoner never made his acquaintance until 1865.

The circumstances of the introduction of Surratt and Booth were rehearsed. The character of the two men were described, and it was argued that Booth was just the man to corrupt one like Surratt. To prove the intimacy of Surratt and Booth Weichman, and John M. Lloyd were the two witnesses most depended upon by the defence. The defence would contradict Lloyd in many important particulars. Who was John M. Lloyd? A man who was a self-proclaimed low, grovelling drunkard; who was so drunk on April 14 that he did not know whether he fell down before Mrs. Surratt or not.

Mr. Bradley then detailed some of Lloyd's testimony, and said Mrs. Offut would be put upon the stand, and would contradict his statment from a sober standpoint. She will show who was present on April 14, and said that was said and done, and she will show what transpired as Mrs. Surratt drove away. It will be shown, also, that Lloyd on the morning of the assassination denied all that he has testified to on the stand, and has called God to witness the truth of his denial.

The next witness was Lewis J. Weichman, a clerk in the War Department, and a quondam student of divinity—a man who was treated as a son by this murdered woman—a man whose dastard heart made him quake for the position in which he was placed, and he became the principal witness upon the other trial. This man Weichman testifies that he drove Mrs. Surratt to the country, and that on the way they met Lloyd, and that Lloyd and Mrs. Surratt whispered to each other; but this is falsified by the testimony of Lloyd himself. It will be proven that it was not one of the conspirators who called at Mrs. Surratt's on the night of April 14.

It will be proven, also, that Mrs. Surratt did not answer the door on that night; that she never said the murder of Mr. Lincoln was a punishment upon this people for their pride and licentiousness: that the conversation detailed by Weichman as having taken place at the breakfast-table on April 15 had no place except in the brain of the witness. What transpired at the station-house will be shown, and it will be proven that Weichman was at all times under arrest. The statement and confessions of this witness will also be shown, and it will be proven that he was intimate with the conspirators. It will be shown also that the information he obtained by virtue of his office at the War Department, and which could be of benefit to the rebels, was communicated to blockade-runners. The man's character will be fully shown. These two witnesses, Lloyd and Weichman, are the principal ones to prove the conspiracy, and then they attempt to prove that Surratt was here on that night. It is necessary to prove his presence here, or all charges of guilt fall to the ground. The first witness to prove this is Sergeant Joseph M. Dye, the dreamer. Now, assuming that Dye did see these men, whom he described, we will show to the jury who the men he described were. We will produce the man who looked in the carriage, and the man who called the time, " ten minutes past ten, " in an audible tone of voice. We will further prove the record of Dye's indictment as a counterfeiter, and will show that he never had the conversation with Mrs. Surratt, as sworn to.

Who else do they produce? David C. Reed, a gambler for twenty years. If allowed, we will contradict him out of his own mouth, and we will prove his indictment for a criminal offence, and will prove him unworthy of belief. As to Cooper's testimony, it is so indistinct that it is unnecessary to attempt to contradict him. Another is John Lee, and him we will contradict by showing that he stated that he never saw and never knew John Surratt.

It will be shown, also, that Lee is not entitled to any credit on his oath. Another witness is Wm. E. Cleaver, just fresh from the jail, admitted to bail since the jury was sworn, but originally committed for a crime of murder committed in the vilest manner upon a little girl. This man, after being manipulated by that most infamous of all criminals, Sanford Conover, alias Dunham, comes here and swears he saw Surratt here on April 14. A worthy successor to Cleaver on the witness stand was Benjamin W. Vanderpool, who says he is a member of the New York bar.

It will be shown that this witness asserted that he never saw John Surratt; that he was summoned here, and did not come voluntarily ; that he was not a partner of Mr. Chauncey Schafer in New York, but was allowed to keep his desk there: that he would not have seen an afternoon performance at Metropolitan Hall because there were no afternoon performances there, and it will be shown that he was utterly infamous. It will be shown that Mr. Schafer sent duplicate telegrams to the prosecution and the defence, setting forth Vanderpool's infamy, and that this knowledge was not given to the jury. As to the testimony of Wood, the barber, it will be shown that he is mistaken.

Mr. Bradley reviewed at length the testimony of other witnesses brought forward, to prove an ALIBI, and said he would prove them false or mistaken in all particulars.

The defence would prove that John Surratt was in Canada in 1865, and went thence to Europe, and after two years he is found in the Papal service. It is claimed that he received $200,000 from the Confederate government, and yet he is so poor that he is compelled to seek service as a private soldier; at the end of two years he is lodged in the jail here as one of the assassination conspirators, and he is shut out from the world, and his tale is known to no one except his counsel. His tale is plain and simple, and will be developed. He will be traced from Richmond in March, 1865, to Montreal in April. It is conceded that he paid his bill at the hotel there on April 12 ; and we will show that he was not near Washington, except when brought back here in the Swatara. We will show where Surratt was on April 14 and April 15, and will show that he was not within four hundred miles of Washington.

It will be shown that he went to a certain town and registered his name John Harrison, and that he remained there to attend a mission he was entrusted with, and was there on April 14. It will be shown that the register of that hotel has mysteriously disappeared. He will be followed back to Montreal, where he arrived on April 18. Facts and circumstances will be shown to conclusively demonstrate that Surratt could not have got to the places named for the purpose of covering up his tracks. It will be shown that while Surratt was in Montreal, after the assassination, he was not allowed to read a newspaper in his place of concealment, and he was not aware of his mother's peril until the eve of her execution, and he then wanted to hasten to Washington to give himself up, but was not permitted to do so.

It will be shown that he first heard that he was implicated in the assassination at

Albany, and he then turned back to Montreal. He did not flee for fear, but because he knew, as well as we all know, that Justice dropped her scales when she entered that building at the foot of Four-and-a-half street. As to the handkerchief, of which so much has been said, it will be shown that it was not dropped by Surratt, but by an officer of the Government, who was in pursuit, and who carried the handkerchief with him for a purpose. It will be shown that the Government knew that the officer dropped the handkerchief, but did not choose to divulge it.

The defence would also show the agreement between the conspirators and signed by them, and upon which neither the name of Mrs. Surratt nor of John Surratt appears. This agreement will be produced as it came direct from the chief conspirator, and contains the genuine signatures, in which they pledge themselves to commit this act of assassination, and upon that neither the name of John Surratt or of Mrs. Surratt appears, and after these things are shown, the jury cannot be asked to say that the prisoner is guilty of the charge preferred against him.

At the close of Mr. Bradley's remarks the court, at 12,30, took a recess until 10 o'clock next day.

On Monday the defense began the examination of their witnesses. Several witnesses testified in relation to the calling of the time in front of the theatre on the night of the assassination, and to the probabilities of Surratt's presence on the same day in the box of the theatre in which the President was assassinated. The object of this evidence was to explain away the testimony of Sergeant Dye, who swore to having seen Surratt and Booth in front of the theatre on the night of the assassination, and to Surratt as the man who called the time; and also the testimony of Mr. Rhodes, who swore to having visited the theatre at the time the box was being repaired for the reception of the President, and to having seen Surratt then and there fixing the bar with which the door was fastened that night when Booth entered and committed the deed. The defense evidently failed in their object. The cross examination to-day was conducted by Judge Pierrepont, and most ably he did it. He destroyed several of the strong points of the counsel for the defense.

The session of the Court was occupied yesterday with evidence showing the state of the moon on the night of the 14th of April, 1862, and testimony impeaching the characters of witnesses for the prosecution. A witness who lives in the house adjoining No. 541 H st. testified that he did not hear any conversation proceeding from No 241, as testified to by Dye, but could have heard it had there been conversation. A number of witnesses were called to impeach the character of John Lee, one of the witnesses, who testified to the presence of Surratt in Washington on the day of the assassination. The witnesses give Lee a bad reputation for truth.

Mr. Merrick proposed to offer in evidence the record of the trial and conviction of Cleaver.

Mr. Carrington objected to the admissability of the evidence. A new trial had been granted in the case. For what purpose could it be proper to put in evidence the record of a trial where a man was convicted but not sentenced, and where a new trial had been granted?

Mr. Merrick said he should offer the record as to the conviction of Cleaver, and then the prosecution could rebut that in any way they chose.

Mr. Pierrepont—You can't offer a part of the record.

The discussion was here waived, and Mr. Merrick stated that he should have to ask the indulgence of the Court to adjourn at this point, as his colleague (Mr. Bradley, sr. was suffering from severe indisposition, and it was desirous that the defense should not be deprived of its right arm at this time.

Mr. Carrington stated that it was not the purpose of the prosecution to press the trial, if counsel on the other side was sick.

The Court concurred in the propriety of suspending for to-day, as Mr. Bradley appeared to be suffering from indisposition; and, therefore, at 2 p. m. ordered a recess until next day at 10 o'clock.

Further testimony was offered on Wednesday to invalidate the evidence of Lee. Testimony was also given impeaching the testimony of Tibbitts and Cleaver. The record of Cleaver's conviction in the Criminal Court on a charge of rape and manslaughter was offered by the defence. Mr. Merrick stated that it was a record of conviction and sentence, Cleaver was sentenced to five years in the Albany Penitentiary. He held that the record was admissable as affecting both his credibility and competency as a witness.

Judge Fisher said the Court would take cognizance of its own record, and not a portion of it, whether it was complete in one book or not—it made no difference. He could not ignore the fact that he had helped to reverse his own ruling in the case, Judge Wylie and himself being on one side and Judge Olin on the other. Since the reversal of his ruling and the granting of a new trial, Cleaver had been bailed out, and the case now stands as though he had never been tried at all, because NON CONSTAT. At the subsequent trial he might be enabled to prove his entire innocence. Therefore he could not see what there was in the record to offer. Besides, the crime for which Cleaver had been tried was manslaughter—a crime not affecting the truth or falsity of a man. The law presumes every man innocent until convicted ; therefore, the record could not be admitted.

Additional evidence was given Thursday impeaching the character of Cleaver. Tallmadge J. Lambert, a clerk in the Paymaster-General's office, was called to describe the house in which he lived in 1865. It is on H. st., between 4th and 5th-sts., a square and three-quarters distant from the house occupied by Mrs. Surratt.

Mrs. Frederika R. Lambert then testified : Between eleven and twelve o'clock that night I heard a voice indistinctly from the street calling out—" The President is shot ;" I went into my parlor and I opened the window and two soldiers were passing by ; I asked what was the matter, and the soldiers said that the President was shot and that Wilkes Booth shot him ; I asked the soldiers if they saw it and they said they did not but were about the theatre at the time ; one of the soldiers stepped forward when I spoke to them and said they were going to Camp Barry.

The proceedings of the Surratt case on Friday were interesting. Counsel for defence endeavored to have admitted as evidence the register of the Webster Hotel, in Canandaigua, New-York, on which appears the name of "John Harrison," Surratt's assumed name, as registered on the evening of the 15th of April, 1865. The prosecution, however, objected, and held that said name could have been written there by the prisoner himself at any time during the five months that he spent in America prior to his departure for Europe, or by one of his friends within the last two years. Judge Pierrepont charged that the evidence was manufactured for the ocasion, a common practice, to which notorious crimi-

nals had recourse, and said that the prosecution would consent to the admission of the register only when a man would be produced who saw Surratt write his name in the Webster Hotel on that evening, and not until then. This brought Merrick to his feet, who replied in an earnest and excited manner, and spoke as though the issue of the whole case depended on this single point. In fact, it so looks, and if the Court rules that the register is not admissible, then an alibi for the defense is utterly destroyed, inasmuch as it was impossible for Surratt to have been in Elmira or Canandaigua on the night of the 15th of April, and at Burlington on the night of the 17th of April. The trains did not run in New-York State on Sunday, the 16th, and supposing that he left either Elmira or Canandaigua on the morning of Monday, the 17th, he could not by any means have arrived the same night at Burlington, where he lost his handkerchief. The defense expected to prove that he left the United States by way of Rochester and Niagara Falls, and it is of course manifest that when the Canandaigua register is ruled out the whole theory of the defence falls to the ground. The witness Holohan swore that he had lost the handkerchief with Surratt's name on it at Burlington on the morning of the 20th of April, but Mr. Charles Blinn testifies that he found it on the morning of the 18th, and in this he is corroborated by Mr. Chapin, who deposes that he saw the same handkerchief at noon on the 19th of April. Consequently, Holohan, who did not reach Burlington before the night of the 19th, and who left that place on the morning of the 20th, could not have lost it. All this proof, however, is as nothing against Surratt's own confession on the steamer Peruvian, to Dr. McMillan, that he had lost that very handkerchief, and was in consequence compelled to leave St. Albans as fast as he could. The animus of Holohan and his wife, Miss Fitzpatrick, and Miss Jenkins, former boarders at Mrs. Surratt's, toward Weichman, is unmistakable. They all swear as to Weichman's intimacy with Atzerott and Booth : but, as mere intimacy is not conspiracy, all this amounts to nothing. Miss Fitzpatrick and Mrs. Holohan were intimate with Mrs. Surratt, but there is no reason for saying that because they were intimate they knew of the murder.

On Monday Judge Fisher gave his opinion that the register could not be admitted in evidence, after which two witnesses were examined to prove that Surratt could not have come from Washington to Elmira after the assassination so as to be at the latter place at times specified by witnesses.

E. G. Lee, a Brigadier-General in the Confederate Army, was put on the stand, when the following offer was submitted in writing:

"On the further trial of this cause the defendant offered to give in evidence tending to show; First; That on the 6th of April, 1865, he arrived in Montreal, Canada; was the bearer of a dispatch from Mr. Benjamin, the Secretary of State of the Confederate States, to the witness. . E. G. Lee, which dispatch related to and directed the disposition of the funds in the hands of Jacob Thomson, named in the testimony of the prosecution, and to show that no part of the same was to be paid, nor was any paid to the prisoner at the bar or to any one charged in the indictment in this case as concerned in the conspiracy therein alleged, and in point of fact what disposition was to be made of said funds. Second; And the Government having also given evidence tending to show that the prisoner was in Elmira after the 12th and before the 18th of April, 1865, and was there co-operating with the alleged assassins of the President; and the prisoner having given evidence tending to show that he was in point of fact in Elmira on the 13th, 14th, and 15th of April, 1805, he now offers further to prove that on the 12th of April, 1865, then being in Montreal, he was specially employed by the witness, E. G. Lee, then holding the commission of Brigadier-General in the army of the Confederate States, and absent on sick-leave in said Montreal to visit Elmira, with a vew to ascertain the position and condition of the Confederate prisoners confined at or near said town of Elmira, and to make sketches of the stations of the guards and the approaches to said prison; and, also, the numbers of the army and troops there; that, in point of fact, the prisoner left Montreal on the afternoon of the said 12th of April to go to Elmira, and was absent untill the 17th day of April, on which day, or the next succeeding day, he returned to Montreal, and made his report, and brought back with him what purported to be rude sketches of the said prison and its approaches, and the number of the forces, and that he paid the prisoner for his expenses and for his services. Third: That the prisoner at the bar having left

Washington, as given in evidence by the prosecution, on the 25th of March, 1865, reached Richmond, Va., on the 29th of said month, and on the 31st of March was charged by Mr. Benjamin, Secretary of State, as aforesaid, with a dispatch for the said witness E. G. Lee, at Montreal, where he arrived as hereinbefore stated on the 6th of April, where he remained until the 12th of April: all of which evidence and each several part is offered tending to show the whereabouts of the prisoner, and how in point of fact he was occupied from the 25th of March to the 17th of April; and also to show that he did not receive money from Jacob Thompson, which it is pretended by the prosecution he did receive.

Mr. Pierrepont stated that there were several points in the proposition to which he did not object.

The Court said the proper way would be to place the witness on the stand and put questions to him, which could be considered and decided on as they were asked.

The witness was then placed on the stand and questioned as to the points mentioned in the above paper, which were ruled out by the Court.

A number of witnesses were examined yesterday, among them an actor named John Mathews. He testified that he saw Booth on the day of the assassination; conversed with him near five minutes; he was leaning over from the horse to speak: he shook hands nervously, and appeared to be excited; he placed a sealed paper in witness's hands; witness placed it in his pocket: witness saw it afterwards in witness's room, after the shot was fired, witness read it, and then burned it; it was in Booth's handwriting.

Question.—What were the contents of that letter, and by whom was it signed?

Mr. Pierrepont—I object to that, and don't desire to discuss such a proposition.

Mr. Bradley said it was a serious matter, and asked the Court to indulge the counsel to discuss it the remainder of the evening. It was expected to show that the contents of the letter was an agreement between four conspirators, neither of whom are on trial. He didn't know whether the matter had ever reached the ears of the Court. This witness had been examined before the Judiciary Committe, and that was how that the defense had found the matter out.

The Court said he had studiously avoide

hearing and reading anything concerning this matter, promising that he might possibly have to try some case connected with the conspiracy. He did not think counsel would hold so meanly of him as to approach him with anything of the kind before hand.

Mr. Bradley stated that he did not think it would be wrong for the Court to see or read the contents of the letter, and form an opinion as to its admissability, but he thought it was a grave matter, as showing who were the original plotters who had entered into an agreement, and signed it together, and directly touching the innocence of the prisoner.

Without further discussion, at 2:42 o'clock p. m. the Court adjourned.

On Wednesday the defense made an argument in favor of admitting, as evidence, a copy of the paper purported to have been written by Booth, and signed by him, Payne, Harold, Atzerott, wherein they made an agreement to kill President Lincoln. Judge Fisher however, ruled it out. Matthews, the actor, finished his evidence. The defense look upon him as one of their strongest witnesses. This Matthews was examined by the War Department officers previous to the military trial of the conspirators, At that examination he knew so little about the matter that he was not summoned to testify at the trial. Matthews was cross-examined very closely on Wednesday, and put himself in rather an uncomfortable position before he got through, as counsel prosecution made it apparent to everybody that he remembers a great deal more now than he did immediately after the assassination.

A number of witnesses were examined on Thursday who gave testimony to impeach the character of Dr. McMillan and St. Marie for veracity. A priest who had been Weichman's confessor was introduced on the stand to show that Weichman had admitted inside the confessional that while in the War Department he had given information to the rebels. Weichman said, in his testimony, he never gave such information. The evidence was not admitted. Another priest was placed upon the stand to show that Mrs. Surratt avowed her innocence to him on the day of execution, but the testimony was not admitted.

In the trial of Surratt on Friday, Mr. Bradley, sr., said that one or two witnesses, instead of coming themselves, had sent certified copies of time-tables, showing

that in April, 1863, a train on the New-York Central Railroad left Albany at 7 a. m. and reached Syracuse at 1:20 p. m. The train left Syracuse at 1:30, and arrived at Canandaigua at 4:52.

Mr. Pierrepont agreed that the time-table should be admitted in evidence, but he would not agree that the trains actually run at the time specified, in the absence of further proof.

Mr. Merrick said that before going further in the case he desired to call the attention of the Court to an authority with reference to reopening the question of the admission of the Webster House register at Canandaigua. He then referred to a decision in 12th Howards, U. S. Supreme Court. The case was one in which a letter written by a defendant was admitted in evidence to show where the defendant was on a day stated.

Judge Fisher did not deem the case analagous. Letters were never admitted unless they bore a post-mark, and the fact of mailing the letter was evidence of the presence of the party at the place of mailing. The evidence of Surratt's signature upon the Webster House register, it will be remembered, was ruled out, because there was no proof that it was actually written upon the day indicated upon the face of the register.

Dr. Bissell was examined on Saturday, to prove that Surratt was in Elmira on the day of the assassination. The witness was subjected to a very severe and extended cross-examination.

Father Boucher, a priest from Canada, with whom Surratt lived after the assassination, before he went to Europe, was on the witness stand on Monday. His testimony went to impeach the character of Dr. McMillan for truth. The defense offered to prove by this witness that Surratt wished to come to Washington when he heard of his mother's condition, but was restrained. The evidence of Father Boucher closed the case for the defense, and the prosecution then offered testimony in rebuttal. The rebutting testimony referred mostly to the running of trains in April, 1835, between Williamsport and Elmira.

Yesterday the prosecution offered testimony to sustain the character of the witnesses Tippetts and Dr. McMillan, and also introduced evidence impeaching the character of the Rebel Chaplain Cameron and Hollohan.

JULY 24.—The trial of John H. Surratt was resumed this morning.

Francis C. Speight sworn, and examined by Mr. Pierrepont.—I live in New York, and am Captain of the Twenty-ninth Precinct Metropolitan Police; I know a Dr Bissell, but I don't know whether his name is Augustus or not - he keeps a drug store on the corner of Twenty-third street and Seventh avenue; Bissell also had a restaurant on Broadway; he was there several months; I have heard Bissell's reputation for veracity spoken of very frequently, and as a mysterious and bad man: Bissell's character for truth is bad.

By Mr. Bradley.—I have heard Mr. Campbell, a jeweler, at No. 339 Fourth avenue, speak of Bissell's character; I heard a policeman, named Gleason, speak of him: I have known Bissell about two or three years; Bissell has told me he kept a drug store; I was told by Mr. Eaton that Mr. Bissell purchased the restaurant; I have seen Bissell about there, and he appeared to control the restaurant · I have read Bissell's evidence; I have read all the evidence, and the moment I read Bissell's testimony I was satisfied I knew the man; I wrote to Mr. Pierrepont on Sunday, and on Tuesday I was subpœnaed; I have frequently heard Bissell's character spoken of within the last year or two: I do not know where Bissell came from to New York; Bissell's general reputation for truth and veracity is bad; I cannot recollect who spoke of it, except the two men named; I do not know exactly many of Bissell's associates, but many say he associates with Chris. Hogan; when I saw Bissell to know him he was lame and on crutches.

Patrick D. Kilduff sworn, and examined by Mr. Pierrepont.—I live at No. 948 Broadway, New York; I have lived there since 1858: have known Dr. Bissell two years this month, and have had business transactions with him: I know of his purchase of a restaurant; Bissell has a bad reputation for truth.

By Mr. Bradley.—Bissell is not a man of honor; if it is to his interest to be so, he is a liar: his reputation is bad; I have heard Mr. McMahon, Mr. Eaton and others speak of him; I know half a dozen who know Bissell, and they would not believe him.

Major A. C. Richards, Superintendent of Police, recalled and examined by Mr. Pierrepont.—Weichman was not arrested to my knowledge on the day after April 14 : if he had been arrested I should have known it; there is no record of Weichman's arrest on the 15th of April.

By Mr. Bradley.—There is no record of arrest on the 16th; I had a conversation with Weichman on April 15; I found Weichman in my office and McDevitt introduced him to me: McDevitt and I had a conversation as to the propriety of putting Weichman under arrest, and it was decided not to let him know that he was under arrest, but at the same time it was understood that he would not be allowed to escape us; we wanted to use him and intended to keep our eyes upon him; I do not know that McDevitt told him he was under arrest; on Saturday or Monday Weichman wanted to go away, but we persuaded him to remain, but we used no force or positive command.

Michael Mitchell, sworn and examined by Mr. Pierrepont. — Resides at Waterloo, and knows Dr. McMillan and testifies to his good character for veracity.

Thomas Brawsard, sworn and examined by Mr. Pierrepont.—Resides at Waterloo, and am a notary public; know Dr. McMillan; has a good reputation as a man of truth; I never knew a man of better repute. No cross-examination.

Edmund Freithett, sworn and examined by Mr. Pierrepont.—Reside at Montreal; have known St. Marie many years; know his associates: his reputation was good for truth and veracity.

Alexis Burnet, sworn and examined by Mr. Pierrepont.—I reside in Montreal, and am a lawyer; I know a Mr. Nagle, a lawyer; I knew St. Marie, also; from 1853 to the time he left Montreal I knew St. Marie all the time, and his character was very good for truth and veracity; I know Mr. Nagle, and I know his reputation for truth to be good; have heard something against him, but it came from enemies; I had a conversation with Nagle about this trial, and he said he received about $500 in gold.

Charles Kimball recalled and examined by Mr. Carrington.—Live in Seventh Ward, Washington, and have lived here all my life. I am a constable, and know William E. Cleaver, and know persons who know him: I never heard Cleaver's reputation questioned for truth.

No cross-examination.

Henry Goss, sworn and examined by Mr. Carrington.—I have lived in Washington all my life, and have known William E. Cleaver for ten years : never heard anything against Cleaver in regard to truth.

By Mr. Bradley —I live at the corner of Eighth and D streets, Island ; I knew Cleaver some years : knew Cleaver before he was inspector of horses ; I never heard anything in connection with Cleaver's passing horses or as to truth and veracity:

Robert Pywell, sworn and examined by Mr. Carrington:—Live in D street, Washington, and have lived there since 1843 ; I keep a livery stable ; I know Wm. E. Cleaver; have known him fifteen or sixteen years ; I know his reputation for truth and veracity ; I never heard it questioned.

By Mr. Bradley.—Cleaver is an Englishman and so am I ; I am his bail in the indictment against him.

Q. Is there any understanding that Cleaver is to be benefitted in the case against him by working in this case.

Mr. Carrington objected. He was not afraid of the answer, but he thought the question improper. Objection sustained and exception sustained.

George W. Shearer sworn, and examined by Mr. Carrington.—I reside in Georgetown, D. C., and was born and raised there ; I keep a restaurant ; I knew John Lee: have known him three years : I knew him as a detective, and, as a justice of the peace ; I never heard anything bad of him ; never heard his character questioned prior to this trial.

Charles H. Merrill sworn, and examined by Mr. Carrington.—I live on H street, No. 378, in this city : know William Cleaver, and have known him twelve years ; know his reputation for truth and veracity, and never heard any thing against him until this trial.

George F. Waldo sworn, and examined by Mr. Pierrepont.—I reside at Waverley, N. Y., and have lived there twenty years ; have known Dr. Bissell part of eight years ; knew him in Waverley ; he came there as a physician in 1828, and he stayed there about two years ; then he went away, and has not been there since : at Waverley Dr. Bissell's reputation for truth was very bad.

By Mr. Bradley.—When I speak of general reputation I mean what people said of him ; Bissell was reputed to be a common liar ; I believe he could tell the truth under some circumstances, but he had but little regard for truth ; I would not believe him ordinarily ; if Bissell were to tell me my horse was in a ditch I would hesitate somewhat before believing him ; I am a druggist ; Bissell dealt with me ; I never quarreled with him : Waverley is on the New York and Erie Railroad, two hundred and fifty miles from New York.

The prosecution having sworn all the witnesses in attendance, it was agreed that witnesses should be called for the defence.

Daniel Bratton sworn, and examined by Mr. Bradley.—Reside at Elkton Md : have resided there twenty-seven or twenty-eight years : knew Stephen F. Cameron, and had opportunities to learn the estimation in which he was held ; never heard his reputation for truth questioned until this trial ; would not hesitate to believe him under oath.

R. G Recse sworn, and examined by Mr. Bradley.—Resided in Elkton twenty years, know Stephen F. Cameron, and was intimate with him : never heard his character for truth doubted ; would believe him under oath : he was an eccentric man.

James B Groome sworn, and examined by Mr. Merrick.—I reside in Elkton ; knew Mr. Cameron ; his general reputation for truth and veracity was good.

By Mr. Pierrepont.—Have heard Mr. Cameron discussed unfavorably, but never heard his truth or veracity questioned ; he was a very versatile genius.

At 3 25 p. m. the court took a recess until ten o'clock to morrow.

July 25.—The trial of John H. Surratt was resumed this morning in the Criminal Court, Judge Fisher presiding.

The rebutting testimony for the prosecution was resumed.

Charles F. Wetmore sworn, and examined by Mr. Pierrepont.—I reside at 18 Clinton place, New York city ; I know Dr. Bissell ; I am the person referred to as conducting a suit for him against the Erie Railway Company: Bissell never attended me as a physician ; I do not think Dr. Bissell was in Elmira April 14, hunting up witnesses for his suit ; when I saw Bissell's testimony in this case I thought he was mistaken ; my reason for thinking so was that yesterday, after being subpœnaed, I went to the office of Mr. Eaton, who was opposed to me in the suit, and he handed me some letters dated 11th, 12th, and 13th of April, 1865, and the letters confirmed me that Bissell was then in my office; I have heard the character of Dr. Bissell very much canvassed ; his general reputation for truth and veracity was bad.

By Mr. Bradley.—In the settlement of the suit Dr. Bissell was satisfied ; I settled it on the 5th of June, and gave him the money on the 6th; the amount I paid him was $5,100, and the company paid me my fees; Bissell's general character for truth is bad.

Dr. Wm. Elmer sworn, and examined by Mr. Pierrepont.—I reside in New York, and know Dr. Bissell; I know what people say of him; his reputation for truth is bad.

Francis Archambault sworn, and examined by Mr. Pierrepont.—I reside in Montreal: have lived there eight or nine years; am a lawyer; know Mr. Nagle, who testified against Dr. McMillian; I had a private conversation with Mr. Nagle; I do not wish to tell it, but if compelled I will do so; Mr. Nagle told me he was coming here as a witness; and he said he was bringing other witnesses; and I understand he first got a draft for $1,000 or $2,000, and that not being sufficient, he got more; I know St. Marie, and studied law in the same office with him; his character was always good.

No cross-examination.

Morell Marean sworn, and examined by Mr. Pierrepont.—I am a telegraph operator; in 1865 I was in the office of the American Company here; on the 13th, 14th, and 15th of April there was telegraph communication between Elmira and Washington.

John George sworn, and examined by Mr. Pierrepont.—On April 15, 1865, I was through baggage-master between Washington and New York; we left Washington at 7.30 a. m.; were detained at the Relay House, and reached Baltimore at 4.20 p. m., and left Baltimore at 6.40 p. m.; it made the train twelve hours late in reaching New York.

Mr. Bradley said he could not understand what this would rebut, and unless it was in rebuttal he would move to strike it out.

Mr. Pierrepont said it would show that Surratt could have reached Lake Champlain at the time stated.

Mr. Bradley said that was original proof.

Mr. Pierrepont said it would tend to show Surratt was not in Elmira on the 14th of April, if Dr. Bissell did say so.

Mr. Bradley said if Dr. Bissell was the most unmitigated liar on earth, this testimony was not rebuttal. It could not show that Surratt was not in Elmira on April 14.

Mr. Pierrepont said he never heard that it was to be assumed that an 'ALIBI would be attempted to be proven; but when an ALIBI is attempted, it is proper to know that he was not at the place set up. There is a legal

right to prove anything that goes to contradict the ALIBI set up.

The prosecution were now about to put together all the links of the iron chain. He [Mr. Pierrepont] would, before the case closed, demonstrate that Surratt was in Washington, and that he was not in Elmira; and if he did not fully demonstrate that fact he would never try another case in this or any other court.

As to the telegrams, they were to show that the prisoner could have communicated by telegraph with Washington, and in support of the assertion that he was at one time and another in Elmira, making efforts to release the rebel prisoners, which was a part of the damning scheme to spread anarchy and confusion all over the country.

Bradley recapitulated some of the testimony given, and said how far the prosecution had succeeded in fixing Surratt here on April 14 was a question for the jury. They then attempt to show that he fled on the 15th, that he was in Burlington on the night of the 17th, and in Montreal on the 18th. In reply to that, the defence had offered evidence to show that it was not so, and that he was not in Washington on the 14th, but that he was in Elmira.

But gentlemen on the prosecution say that on April 13 Surratt was in Elmira, and if he was there then, they were bound to show that he was here on the 14th, on the evening of that day. It must be fully shown that the prisoner was here, or that he was within reasonable distance, and if that is not shown they have no case. The defence has given evidence to show that the prisoner could not have got here, and they cannot now offer evidence in rebuttal, for it was part of their argued case that the prisoner's presence here should be proven. If they failed to do it in chief they cannot prove the fact now. Whatever is confirmation of the original case cannot be given as evidence in reply.

Mr. Pierrepont rose to reply.

Mr. Merrick said he believed the defence had the close of this argument.

Mr. Pierrepont said he did not propose to make a speech. They had expected to prove that Surratt was in New York on April 15. They were going to prove that by a woman who had not arrived, but was expected by the next train. But a challenge had been thrown out by the defence to close the case The prosecution accepted the challenge.

Mr. Bradley, Sr.—We agree, sir; and are

now willing to submit the case without argument. The case is closed.

Mr. Merrick. We will now agree to submit the case without argument.

Mr. Carrington said that in a case of so much importance he could not consent to that course.

Judge Fisher asked what became of the point about which there had been so much argument.

Mr. Merrick said that it went over with all the rest of the case.

Judge Fisher said it was a point of some importance, and intimated that he was not now prepared to decide it.

Mr. Merrick asked what rule prevailed as to the speeches, and whether each side was entitled to two speeches.

Judge Fisher replied that such had been the practice.

Mr. Merrick then asked whether if the defence decline to argue the question to the jury, the speech of one of the gentleman on the other side would not close the case.

Mr. Carrington said that as this was a case of great importance, and had occupied some time, the counsel had divided the duty.

After some further discussion Mr. Merrick said that the agreement would be withdrawn unless the case was considered entirely closed.

Their proposition had been to submit the case without further argument, and let it go to the jury at once.

Mr. Pierrepont said he had not so understood it. He understood the evidence only was closed.

It then appeared that counsel had misunderstood the agreement, and the case was reopened and the examination of witnesses was resumed.

Judge Fisher said he would decide upon the point argued to-morrow morning.

At 3.30 o'clock p. m. the court took a recess until 10 o'clock the next day.

JULY 26.—The trial of John H Surratt was resumed this morning in the Criminal Court, Judge Fisher presiding.

Judge Fisher delivered an opinion upon the question argued yesterday, relative to the admissibility of certain testimony, as follows;
Before we took a recess yesterday, witnesses were examined by the counsel in reply to the testimony offered by the defence, that the telegraph line between Washington and Elmira, N. Y., was in good working order, and that communications were passed to and fro between these two points on the 12th,

13th, 14th, and 15th of April, 1865, and witnesses were also examined who testified as to the running of trains between Washington and New York on the 15th and 16th of April. After the evidence had been given by the witnesses the counsel for the defence moved that it be stricken out, upon the ground that it was not responsive to the testimony offered by the defence to establish an alibi on the part of the prisoner.

In support of their motion, the counsel for the prisoner contend that the rule by which evidence offered in reply is to be admitted or rejected is, that no evidence which might have been adduced originally in support of confirmation laid in the indictment can be received by the Court as evidence in reply, and that the only evidence which can be given in reply is that which goes to cut down the case on the part of the defence, without being in any way confirmatory of the case on the part of the prosecution.

In my opinion any evidence may be given in reply which tends to disprove the matter set up in defence, and which it was not necessary to have proved in making out the original case.

In the case which we are now trying it was not necessary to prove that the prisoner at the bar was ever in New York city, or elsewhere than in Washington. It was necessary to prove that he came here from Elmira on the 13th or 14th. It was sufficient for the original case to prove that he was here participating in the deed of murder, and unnecessary to trace his history further, either in the past or future. When it is attempted to show that he was at Elmira, or some other place in the State of New York, at such a time as would have made it impossible for him to be present here at the time of the murder, common sense would certainly dictate to men of but ordinary intelligence and reflection that to prove him on the cars coming in this direction at such a time as would place him here on the night of the murder, is directly responsive to the matter set up in the defence.

I shall therefore not strike out the evidence given as to the running of the trains between here and New York, as delivered yesterday, unless the counsel for the prosecution shall have failed in some way to connect the prisoner with one of these trains. The testimony respecting the telegraphic communication between Elmira and Washington, whereby it was possible for the conspirators to communicate with the prisoner, stands upon the same footing, and will be stricken out if the prosecution shall fail to connect the prisoner with the conspiracy by that instrumentality.

Mr. Bradley noted an exception to the opinion and ruling of the Court.

Franklin Frazer sworn, and examined by Mr. Pierrepont.—I reside in Montrose, Pennsylvania, and am an attorney at law; have been prosecuting attorney there: Montrose, is my native place; I have but little personal acquaintance with Dr. Bissell, but I know his reputation about Montrose for truth and veracity from 1856 until 1862; that reputation was bad, and Bissell was not considered worthy of belief.

No cross-examination.

Dr. J. W. Cobb sworn, and examined by Mr. Pierrepont.—I am a physician of Montrose, Pa.; while Dr. Bissell lived there his reputation was bad for truth.

A. D. Butterfield sworn, and examined by Mr. Pierrepont.—I reside at Montrose; Dr. Bissell's reputation for truth, while he lived at Montrose, was bad.

Dr. C. M. Noble sworn, and examined by Mr. Bradley.—Am a practicing physician of Waverly, N. Y.; have resided there fourteen years, I first knew Dr. Bissell seven years ago; knew what reputation Bissell had, and his character for truth and veracity was good; from his general reputation I would not hesitate to believe him under oath.

At 3 p. m. the court took a recess until 10 next day.

JULY 27.—The trial of John H. Surratt was resumed this morning in the Criminal Court, Judge Fisher presiding,

The crowd of spectators within the bar, has of late, been so great as to seriously inconvenience the movements of the officers of the Court in the performance of their duties. The presence of so large a crowd too, has prevented to some extent a free flow of air through the room, and this has been a source of great annoyance. Judge Fisher accordingly this morning decided to limit the number of spectators within the bar, and has directed most of the old tickets to be withdrawn, and will on Monday issue a different style of ticket. After the opening of the court, Judge Fisher made an announcement of the above fact, and also announced that during the arguments he wanted no signs of approbation or disapprobation at anything that might be said. The marshal would have his force properly placed, and would remove from the court-room any one giving any sign of approbation or disapprobation.

Mr. Merrick asked the Court to rule upon the question submitted by him relative to the speeches, and whether, if the defense declined to speak, one speech by the prosecution would not close the case.

Mr. Pierrepont said this was no ordinary case and he intimated that no restriction should be placed upon counsel in addressing the jury.

Judge Fisher said this was one of the most voluminous cases, and even if the defence did not wish to address the jury, he thought he could not restrict the prosecution to but one speech,

Mr. Carrington contended that this case was one of too much magnitude to be permitted to be thrown upon the court and jury without argument; proposed to divide the labor; the defence should be advised of that division in justice to the prisoner. He would suggest, therefore, that the prosecution officers make their speeches first, and let the defence reply, and then one or both of the counsel for the prosecution could reply. He did not know what arrangement had been made, but he believed the prosecuting attorney had always closed the case, except in one instance, in the Gardner case.

Mr. Carrington said he had given way to other counsel in the Van Dervenkin case, and he received a severe excoriation for it from Mr. Carlisle.

Mr. Bradley said he deserved the excoriation and would always deserve it if he resigned his rights as prosecuting attorney to his associate counsel.

Mr. Pierrepont contended that the defence had no right to close in any case. It was a matter for the direction of the court. He had been asked to close the case by the District Atorney, and he had agreed to do so, and would now speak unless the Court said he could not do so in the event of the defence declining to speak.

Judge Fisher said it was best to proceed in the usual way, and he directed the prosecution to proceed with the argument to the jury.

Mr. Carrington, District Attorney, opened the argument, and said he was not surprised that the counsel for the prisoner had offered to submit the case, because their only hope was that, in the jury groping through this mass of testimony, they might find some reasonable doubt of the guilt of the prisoner, which doubt would all be dispelled by an analysis of the case, He explained to the jury that it was not customary for the District Attorney to yield the close of the argument to his associate counsel, but he referred to precedents to show that it had sometimes been done, and he had therefor yielded the place of honor to Mr. Pierrepont, who had been employed by the Goverment to assist in this case.

In arguing this case he would endeavor to treat the prisoner in a spirit of fairness, but he would speak of this murderer, traitor, and assassin as he deserves, and would also refer in proper terms to the rebel spy who came to defend him on the witness stand. He could not look upon this murderer and assassin, as a representative man of the South, and if it was attempted to make him appear such a representative, he hoped the jury would spurn it, for Southern men did not desire assassination; he spoke to a jury of Southern men, but what Southern man would shield the murderer or the assassin? What honorable Confederate officer or soldier has taken that stand to shield this assassin from the consequences of his crime.

A spy thrust from Morgan's band of guerillas or robbers alone comes here to shield this man by testifying in his favor. An honest jury of Confederate soldiers would, after hearing this evidence, hang this wretch as high as old John Brown or Haman. Upon this point all honorable men can agree, the murderer or assassin of any man is a criminal who deserves the anathema and indignation of every man who has a heart to love or a soul to feel for the honor of his country. Who are the men who sympathize with the prisoner and his horrid crime? The original secessionists, who filled the land with widows and orphans, and the men who stirred up strife, but whose cowardly hearts prevented them from boldly avowing their sentiments, and he hoped the jury would wipe this damning stain from the escutcheon of the country.

This is a solemn scene. The jury have before them a dying man who has forfeited his life by his crimes. You, gentlemen of the jury, have sworn to decide this case according to the law and the evidence. with an appeal to your conscience and your God. It is a matter of congratulation that a jury has been selected acceptable to both parties—a jury with whom any man could entrust his life—and this case is to be decided according to the law and the evidence, and this law is to be taken as laid down by the honorable judge, and you are to look to him exclusively for the law. From the judge the law must be taken, and the juror who departs from the law as laid down by the judge commits the Heaven-daring crime of perjury.

The province of the jury is to ascertain whether the law and evidence justify a verdict of the guilt of the prisoner. He [Mr. Carrington] would undertake to show that every fact essential to the guilt of the prisoner has been established, and every link in the chain has been forged by honest links, to bind the prisoner at the bar to the body of this atrocious murder. Every privilege has been accorded to the prisoner. He has a jury selected mutually, and he has been zealously defended by counsel of ability.

Where is the woman and where are the men who perpetrated this great crime? I do not ask who fired the pistol, but where are the men who concocted this crime? The satan of this conspiracy has gone to hell, there to atone.in eternal fires his infernal crime; but the beelzebub of this infernal conspiracy still lives, and in John H Surratt you see him. False to his country, while professing allegiance to its laws; false to his Government, not like one of the misguided men, shouldering a musket and going gallantly into the fight; false to the mother who bore him, and deserting her in her hour of peril and trial; false to every principle of patriotism and honor, he sought security in flight, on the plains of Italy and on the sands of Egypt; but the avenger of blood pursued, and John H. Surratt is now here to answer for his crimes.

The conspiracy might have been an infant at first, but it assumed the proportions of a giant. It was one great artificial person, animated by the same spirit and moving toward the same end, and the act of one member was the act of all; and by the law of nations and the law of God, every man connected with it is guilty of this great crime which shook the great heart of Christendom.

Mr. Carrington then said he would show that the legal consequences of the facts which he assumed to be proven in this case is the guilt of the prisoner at the bar, and second to satisfy the jury that the facts he assumes in his argument are proven beyond a reasonable and rational doubt, and if he succeeds in maintaining these propositions he would be entitled to a verdict of conviction. For the Court he would submit the following proposition of law.

First. If the jury believe from the whole evidence that Abraham Lincoln received a wound from a pistol fired by John Wilkes Booth in the city of Washington, on or about the time named in the indictment, which resulted in his death in pursuance of a conspiracy to murder or assassinate said Lincoln, of which conspiracy the prisoner was a member, and that the prisoner was at the place and performed the part assigned him toward the execution of the common design, they should find him guilty as indicated, no matter what distance may have separated the conspirators, or how far apart they may have been apart at the time the wound was inflicted as foresaid.

Second. If the jury believe that the object of said conspiracy was to abduct the said Lincoln, the President of the United States, with general resolution on the part of the conspirators to resist all who might oppose them in the execution of the common design, and that while engaged in said unlawful conspiracy, one of the conspirators, without the knowledge, and contrary to the wishes of the other conspirators and the original plan and purpose of said conspiracy, killed the President as foresaid, the jury should find the prisoner guilty as indicated.

Third. If the jury believed from the evidence that, at the time President Lincoln was killed as foresaid, the prisoner was either actively or constructively present, encouraging, aiding, abetting, and maintaining the principal murderer they should find him guilty as indicated, although he was neither an ear nor an eye witness to the transaction, leaving it open for the Court to explain constructive presence, for we contend that he was constructively present no matter how far off, he was at the place, and performing the part assigned him where and in the manner the conspirators supposed he would be most effective.

Fourth. If the jury believe, from the evidence, that President Lincoln was killed as aforesaid, in pursuance of said conspiracy, of which the prisoner was a member, he being either actually or constructively present at the time, it is a legal presumption that such presence was with a view to render aid, and it lies in the prisoner to rebut such presumption, by showing that he was there for a purpose unconnected with the conspiracy.

Fifth. That the defence of alibi being an affirmative defence, the burden of proof rests upon the defendant to establish it to the satisfaction of the jury by a preponderance of evidence.

The facts to be submitted to the jury would be as follows:

1. Does it appear from the evidence that the assault charged in the indictment was made in the manner and about the time therein stated and within the jurisdiction of the honorable court?

2. Does it appear from the evidence that the wound which deceased received, as charged in the indictment, caused his death?

3. Does it appear from the evidence that the assault and death were the result of a conspiracy of which the prisoner at the bar was a member?

4. What was the original character, plan and purpose of the conspiracy?

5. If it be true that the prisoner was a member of this conspiracy, what part did he perform in the general plan?

6. Where was the prisoner in point of fact at the time the assault charged in the indictment was made? Was he in aforesaid commonwealth, or was he in the city of Washington, D. C. ?

7. Has not the prisoner at the bar confessed his guilt expressly and by implication?

The court at 1.12 took a recess for half an hour.

Upon reassembling, Mr. Carrington proceeded to consider the several proposition of the case.

In regard to the first proposition, it could be maintained that upon principal and authority, if the prisoner was a member of the conspiracy, he was an accessory either before or after the fact. Assuming that he is guilty, he must either be an accessory, a conspirator, or the principal. The first point to be noticed was whether the prisoner was an accessory before the fact. Counsel then defined an accessory before the fact, laid down in Wharton's Law Dictionary. In Bishop's Criminal Law the character of a criminal is well defined. An accessory before the fact is one who contributes his will toward the execution of a criminal design, but he does no principal act.

If in addition to contributing his will, he does some overt act at the time the crime is

PORTRAIT OF MRS. SURRATT.

PORTRAIT OF DR. MUDD.

LEWIS C. PAYNE.   DAVID C. HAROLD.

THE SCENE OF THE GREAT TRAGEDY.

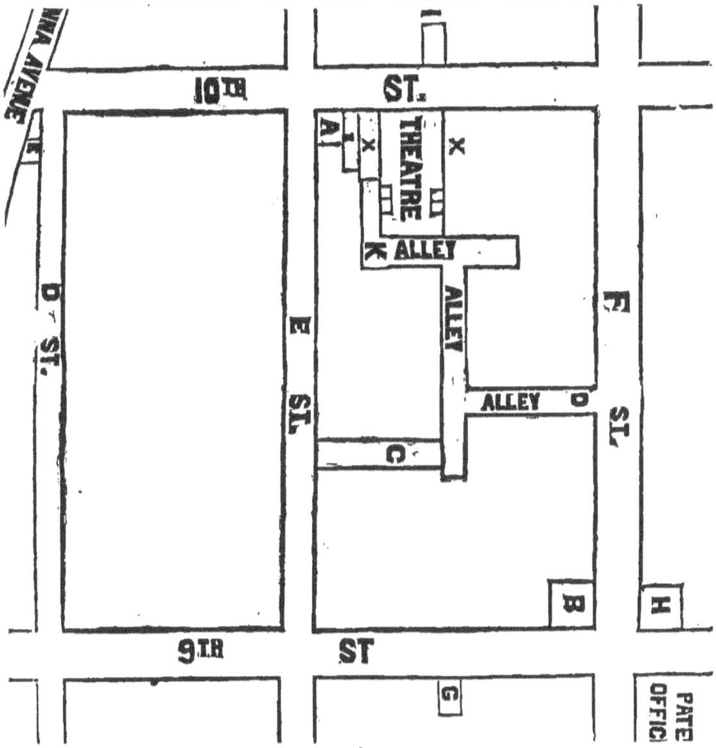

A—Public School.   B—Herndon House, (Hotel).   X—Restaurants.   G—Newspaper Office.
C—The only vacant lot communicating with alley.   H—Model House.
D—The only alley outlet to F street.   I—House taken to after the act.
E—Bank (formerly Savings Bank).   K—The alley by which the murderer escaped.

committed, he ceases to be an accessory before the fact, and becomes a principal in the second degree. An accessory after the fact is one who does nothing before the crime is committed, and if present at the act he ceases to be an accessory.

If a man engages in a conspiracy he is a conspirator, and amenable to trial for a misdemeanor : and if he continues in the conspiracy until an act is committed he becomes a felon, and ceases to be merely a conspirator,

Where a number of persons conspire to commit an act of murder, the act of one conspirator is the act of all, and in this connection we are led to the inquiry of what the law implies by constructive presence. When a murder is committed as a design of conspiracy, every conspirator is supposed to be engaged in it, no matter how far distant he may have been when the felony was committed.

Suppose, in the judgement of the conspirators, he could render more aid 1,000 miles away than he could here, would he not in contemplation of law be responsible for the act of any one of the conspirators ? Conspirators know best how to dispose of their own forces, and each was assigned a position in which he could best serve the interests of the conspirators ; and under this theory, the act of Booth in shooting the President, was the act of all the conspirators.

In confirmation of these views, Mr. Carrington referred to 1 Bishop on Criminal Law, third edition, section 601, and argued from that decision, that if the prisoner could render any aid, however minute, though it might be from New York or New Orleans, he was a principal in the second degree. He also cited from page 67 of Wharton's Criminal Law, later edition, page 127, to show that where a number of persons engage in a conspiracy against the public peace, and murder ensues by the act of one, all are equally guilty, though the others were neither ear nor eye witnesses ; and if that principle was true, he contended that the distance separating the conspirators was entirely immaterial.

If being one mile from the place of crime does not exonerate a conspirator, one hundred miles or one thousand miles does not in the least alter the principle. If that be sound law it applies to this case. A conspiracy was formed to strike at the nation's life by striking out its head. It was a conspiracy, the natural consequence of which was murder, riot, and blood-shed, and any con-

spirator, no matter where he might be, is equally guilty with the man who struck the fatal blow or fired the fatal shot.

The probable consequences of such a conspiracy was murder, and consequently all engaged in it were equally guilty. A conspiracy was formed to strike at the nation's heart, by striking down the nation's head, and the law of the land protects the nation against such conspiracy, and views all the conspirators alike. Upon this point the old common law of England was the same as it is now, and in support of this he would refer to volume first of Hale's Pleas of the Crown, page 427, which enunciated the principle that it was not necessary for a conspirator t be an ear and eye witness of the act to mak him amenable to the law for the commission of the actual crime.

In a decision of the Supreme Court of the United States in 1 Peters' Supreme Court Reports, page 363, in which report a reference is made to 1 Wheaton, page 648, it is decided that whatever an agent does or says in performance of his duty is considered the act of the principal, and it may be proven in criminal as well as civil cases. If the agent is employed for a lawful purpose, and he commits an unlawful act, the principal is not responsible ; but if an agent is employed to do an unlawful act, and in the performance of that unlawful act he commits a murder, then the principal is responsible.

In a conspiracy each co-conspirator is an agent of the other, and in this case, while Booth fired the fatal shot, the prisoner at the bar was brought on from Montreal to perform his allotted part. In 12 Wheaton the law is clearly laid down of the culpability of the principal for the act of his agent, committed while in pursuance of an unlawful act directed by the principal. It must be shown that the agent has the authority ; but this being admitted the principal is liable, and it may even happen that the agent may be innocent while the principal or procurer is guilty, as in the case of an idiot or an infant employed to administer poison.

This principal was maintained, Mr. Carrington contended, in Chief Justice Marshall's decision in the Burr trial, as reported in 4 Cranch. The doctrine there is that when war is actually levied, and a conspiracy is formed, a man is guilty if it is proved, first, that he was leagued in the conspiracy, or second, that he committed some overt act

He knew this would be objected to, on the ground that it applied to treason.

Yesterday, Mr. Merrick asked if the prisoner was to be indicted for the crime of treason. He [Mr. Carrington] would answer, no! He was indicted for murder; but in this murder there was an element of treason.

He contended that it was a treasonable conspiracy, and that the prisoner was in it, giving aid to the enemies of the country for money, and compassing the death of the President. While endeavoring to commit treason, he commits the crime of murder: while engaged in the lesser crime, he commits the higher crime, and it is proper to offer evidence of the lesser crime. The man who strikes at the head of the commander-in-Chief of the army of the United States is a traitor, and deserves a traitor's doom, and if the prisoner was indicted for treason he would, without doubt, be convicted. As a matter of law, if this was a conspiracy to murder the President, then all engaged in that conspiracy were constructively present when the act was committed.

In support of the second proposition of law, Mr. Carrington referred to 1 Russell, page 28, to show that a man cannot apportion his own wrong, and he contended that it applied equally to a body of conspirators as to an individual. Suppose there is a dangerous riot, and a number of persons assemble to resist a law for the purpose of doing a personal violence to some individual, and while engaged in that unlawful act one of the rioters commits a murder, all will be held responsible for the act of the one.

Where a number of men engage in a war against each other, and men combine to go to the house of the President and adduct him, the natural consequence of that act was murder, violence, and bloodshed, and as human life was taken, every man engaged in the conspiracy was guilty, although it was no first principle of the scheme to murder.

Can it be claimed in this case that because the original plan was to abduct, and not to murder, therefore the conspirators were not all guilty because one of their number committed the murder? Can they claim that they only intended to abduct the President, but that they missed their aim and only killed an old man sitting in a theatre by the side of his wife? He regretted the other day to hear Mr. Bradley say that the murder of Mr. Lincoln was no more :- the sight

of God than the murder of a common vagabond.

He hoped his friend did not desire to re-echo the sentiments of Anna Surratt, that "it was no more to shoot Mr. Lincoln than it was to shoot a negro." He [Mr. Carrington] had some respect for many of the rebel dead, for he believed many of them fought under a delusion, and they would turn with horror in their graves if this man were claimed as the representative of a lost cause. The prisoner seemed to think it was nothing to kill Abraham Lincoln, and he boasted of his exploits to Englishmen and French Canadians, and threatened to serve Andrew Johnson just so, thus seeming to glory in his very shame.

He [Mr. Carrington] could, to some extent, appreciate how men, born and reared in the South, could be deluded and give their support to a cause in opposition to the Government, but he could not understand how a man living in Washington could profess allegiance to his country and yet raise his hand to strike it down by engaging in this horrible conspiracy.

The third point of law was so clear that he did not deem it necessary to refer to any authorities upon the subject. As to the fourth point it was in reference to the burden of proof, and was settled in 9 Pickering, page 406, and in Roscoe's Criminal Evidence, page 213. From this decision, assuming that the prisoner was a member of this conspiracy, and that he was in Washington, and if this be assured there was no doubt of the preponderance of proof; and to show an alibi is upon the defence, and they must show conclusively that he was here for some purpose other than to aid and abet the assassination. It must be shown that he was endeavoring to prevent the consummation of the act with which the conspiracy is formed.

Being connected with that conspiracy, the presumption is that Surratt was here in furtherance of the scheme of the conspirators, and it must be shown by positive and affirmative proof that he had repented and retired from the conspiracy. There must be evidence that this man had repented and had confessed, for there is no true repentance except in confession. He never confessed, except when he crossed the ocean. Supposeing he was secure, he bosted, not confessed, that he was engaged in the murder of the President.

Mr. Carrington here concluded his remarks upon the legal points, and the court took a recess untill ten o'clock on Monday morning, when he will conclude his speech. The counsel for the defence will follow, and Mr. Pierrepont will close the argument, which argument will probably consume all of next week.

JULY 29.—The trial of John H. Surratt was resumed.

Among the auditors, were several ladies who have been regular attendants since the beginning of the trial. Mrs. Ann S. Stephens, the authoress, occupied her accustomed seat within the bar.

Mr. Carrington resumed the floor and continued his address to the jury, and discussed the questions of fact submitted on Saturday. In regard to the first fact, whether the act charged was committed about the time therein stated, and within the jurisdiction of this court, he had but little to say, for the evidence upon that point was clear and explicit.

As to Booth, he enters the President's box, which had been carefully prepared for his ingress beforehand, and pours the contents of his pistol into the brain of the representative of this nation. The President bows his head and dies as he lived, with no expression of malice to any one. When did such a crime as this ever before occur? Is it necessary to call up this scene, which never can be forgotten by American citizens?

The scene was graphically described by our own citizen, Colonel Stewart: and if he had held Booth in an herculean grasp the assassin's blood would never have stained the soil of Virginia. The testimony of Dr. Barnes could not but satisfy the jury that the President's death ensued as the result of the shooting by Booth, and this settles the second proposition, that the wound the deceased received caused his death.

The third proposition is: Does it appear that the assault and death were the result of a conspiracy, of which the prisoner at the bar was a member? and that is the great question, for if it appears that the death was the result of a conspiracy, no matter for what other purposes that the conspiracy was formed, then was it murder, and God grant the day will never come when an American or English judge will ever decide that such an act is not murder.

Mr. Carrington cited from 3d Greenleaf, section 89, to show what a conspiracy was,

and contended that the prisoner conspired to commit an unlawful act, and that act was committed by some one of the conspirators; then he was guilty, and guilty of murder. Where would our safety be if the law were otherwise? Now apply that law to the facts in this case.

The first scene of that conspiracy is laid on Pennsylvania avenue, in April, 1864. Three men are engaged in conversation, and the subject is the murder of Abraham Lincoln, President of the United States. One suggests as the instrument of death the telescopic rifle; another, whose heart is touched with pity, says, "No, we might kill his wife and child." "But yes," says the first, "we will kill all, if necessary: we'll murder all, if necessary to the execution of our bloody purpose." Is this doubted? It does not depend upon imported testimony, but on the testimony of Mrs. McClernand, a lady born and bred in your own city, whose character no attempt has been made to impeach. What do you see? In April, 1864, malice, hissing and hot, and murder contemplated against the President of the United States.

Who were that party? John W. Booth, the friend and associate of the prisoner, and the especial pet of Mrs. Mary E. Surratt; Atzerott, to whom the ladies at No. 541 gave the name of "Port Tobacco," and Harold, who drank whiskey given him by Mrs Surratt to nerve his arm for his bloody deed.

The second scene of this bloody act occurs in a Third avenue car of New York, where a lady overheard a conversation relative to the murder of the President. The conspirators attract her attention. They are disguised, but by one of the mysterious providences of God, they drop certain letters, which are secured by the lady and taken to General Scott, who conceiving them to be of importance, sends them to the authorities.

Mr. Pierrpont here read the letter found by Mrs. Hudspeth.

Mr. Carrington resuming, said; The jury had heard the testimony of Mrs. Hudspeth. He cared not who the persons overheard were, for it showed that, by solemn vows, there was a pledge to murder Abraham Lincoln with the pistol, the dagger, and the cup. Do you remember that at this very time, Harold was the clerk in a drug store, and the command was very plain; "If the the pistol and the dagger will not do its work, then use the cup."

That letter from St. Louis, signed by some one's wife, may we not infer was from the wife of Louis Payne, the friend of Surratt? But Payne was deaf to this appeal, and bent upon his murderous purpose. He goes on until this murder is consummated, and the land is filled with tears and mourning. Let us leave the city of New York and return to Washington, the metropolis of this great Christian nation, and I visit there 241 H street, the third scene in this bloody tragedy. Visit that place, and the first figure we see is that of Payne, the Moloch of this infernal conspiracy. Next we have Atzerott, the Belial of this infernal conspiracy. He was the pet of the ladies at 541 ; they gave him the sobriquet of " Port Tobacco." They petted him. Who next? There was Howell, the blockade runner. I would call him Mammon, for he had no other ambition than whiskey and money.

Who next? There sits old Satan—Booth, and next to him Beelzebub—Surratt. For he would show that Surratt was second in power in command to Booth. Who next do you see? Oh, that it were not so, that an American woman could be found in such company, giving her support and countenance to this conspiracy. There sat Mrs. Surratt. There was no infernal deity she could properly personate, for hell has no fury like the hatred of a depraved and wicked woman. Has the English language words to express the depravity of this woman, who in cold blood, requests the prisoner at the bar to shoot down Union soldiers escaping from rebel prisons? A brave man's heart melts with pity when he sees his bitterest foe at his feet ; but here is a man and a woman murdering in cold blood men in distress, who appeal to their clemency.

But what is the next scene in the bloody tragedy? Do you doubt the testimony of Mrs. Honora Fitzpatrick? If not you cannot doubt the truth of the fourth scene in this tragedy. This lady goes to the theatre with the prisoner. Booth enters and calls the prisoner aside, and they have a private conversation. What was it? No ear heard it but that ear that has the gentlest sound ; but can it be doubted that the subject of this conversation was the murder of Mr. Lincoln? What is the next scene? On April 14, 1865, we find the conspirators at Ford's Theatre. Booth enters the theatre and fired the fatal shot. A whistle sounds. A whistle making a singular sound is found

at the house of Mrs. Surratt. At that signal, Payne invades the sacred precincts of the family circle, and, raising his murderous arm, he makes an assult upon the faithful nurse. He enters the sick chamber, and strikes with the fury of a demon, at the almost lifeless corpse of a feeble and emaciated old man. By a miraculous interposition of Providence life is spared. Payne escapes and where does he go? To the arms of Mary E. Surratt, the mother of the prisoner at the bar. He goes there reeking with the blood of an American citizen. He goes to the general rendezvous, whence all had issued on their murderous undertaking. Does not all this prove a conspiracy? It has not been necessary to refer to the testimony of Lewis J. Weichman, for without it the conspiracy is proven complete. But he [Mr. Carrington] now came to Weichman's testimony. Why should it be discarded?

Ignorant men are governed by prejudice, but not so an intelligent jury. No witness testimony can be discarded unless his character is proven bad, or a different state of facts is proven by other witnesses. From what had already fallen from Mr. Merrick, it would be attempted to be shown that Weichman was one of the accomplices. He spurned the imputation. It has been said that it was fortunate a Union clerk was boarding at the house of Mrs. Surratt. A Union clerk among those infernal spirits!—for was ever such a congress assembled this side of hell? Weichman was, among the faithless, faithful. If Weichman had been an accomplice, Surratt would have made him a confident, and would have conversed in his presence. If Weichman was a liar. how easy would it have been to have sworn, I saw the prisoner here on April 14, 1865. He did not see him, because the prisoner did not permit him to see him, and he told the truth and the whole truth.

But suppose Weichman was an accomplice. If he turned and repented that was his conciliation. During this conspiracy Weichman met the officer face to face, He told them all he knew. He pursued the prisoner, and, like a true American citizen, he comes here and testifies against him. It must be remembered, too, that Weichman remonstrated with Mrs. Surratt, and she replied that John was with this party, and Booth was crazy upon one subject. But has Weichman been contradicted in any one material point? He defied the defence to point to one prominent fact where Weichman has been contradicted by any creditable witness in behalf of the prisoner.

He was somewhat amused at Weichman's cross-examination, and he asked if Weichman did not bear himself manfully ? Mr. Bradley found himself foiled for once in endeavoring to discredit this witness. He came through the fiery furnace well tried, and confirmed by all the witnesses.

The first testified to by Weichman is corroborated, and that is that 541 H street was the rendezvous of these conspirators.

Secondly, he testifies to the intimate relation of the prisoner and the other conspirators, and no one contradicts him in that.

Weichman also testifies to the myster ious meetings and conversations, ciphers and geographical projects, after he forms the acquaintance of John W. Booth, upon the introduction by the prisoner at the bar. In this he is uncontradicted.

In relation to the conversation at the theatre he is confirmed by Miss Honora Fitzpatrick. (Weichman's testimony in relation to Payne and Surratt practicing with bowie knives was here read). This Mr. Carrington said, was also uncontradicted. Again ; when Weichman receives a mysterious telegram from Booth, and asks Surratt what it means, he is told not to be so inquisitive, and is given no satisfaction. Couple this with the fact of Surratt's immediate visit to the Herndon House, and it shows that Surratt and Booth were endeavoring to secure a hiding place for Louis Payne. Booth telegraphs to his tool, Surratt, to prepare a room where they may conceal one of their instruments. He is concealed, and whenever he leaves his room he goes to the house of Mrs. Surratt, or else to his bloody work at Mr. Seward's. Again Weichman testifies to Mrs. Surratt going to the Herndon House, and to Mrs. Surratt's refusal to say who she went to see there. But Atzerott says it is Payne, and he is then censured for giving information. I sit not all plain ? Booth orders the preparation of the room ; Surratt secures the room, and his mother nurses him as a game cock would be nursed for the final blow. Can you not see them altogether, gentlemen, like a bunch of herrings ? Pardou me for using such a commonplace expression. Upon this point Weichman is confirmed by Miss Fitzpatrick, who testifies to Mrs. Surratt's visit to the Herndon House.

On April 2 Weichman saw Booth at Mrs. Surratt's house. He testifies to those war maps, and he is not contradicted. On April 14 Weichman drives Mrs. Surratt to Surrattsville. Is he contradicted in that ? He is entrusted with a small package, and is told to be careful of it. This is delivered to John M. Lloyd, and it turned out to be a field-glass, and after the dead body of Booth is brought from Virginia to Washington this very field-glass, which Weichman carries to Surrattsville, is traced to Booth's possession. In the next place Weichman testifies to the departure of the prisoner and Mrs. Surratt for the confederacy, where Surratt expected to receive a clerkship. In this Weichman is confirmed by their own witness, Mr. David C. Barry, who shows that the prisoner had communication with the rebel authorities. It is true there are some little immaterial discrepancies about the buggy and certain dates, but he would ask if any one was not liable to be contradicted as to dates, or some immaterial facts about a transaction. As to the fact to which Weichman testifies, that Mrs. Surratt, in a state of excitement, asked him to pray for her intentions, does he lie on that subject ? If Weichman testifies to that, he either did it truly or falsely ; for it was a matter that he could not forget. It was natural that Mrs. Surratt should have made that request under the circumstances. Although Mrs. Surratt was bent on murder, she felt the necessity of divine assistance ; and it is not strange, for a man or a woman sometimes looks to God when about to commit a crime, especially when it is done in a spirit of fanaticism, and that is the most charitable construction that can be placed upon this act.

Who contradicts this statement of Weichman's ? Miss Honora Fitzpatric is brought here for that purpose, but she simply testifies negatively, and says she did not hear it. She does not say the remark was not made, but only says she did not hear it. Weichman says he did hear it, and affirmative testimony must be taken in preference to negative testimony. Weichman says he heard footsteps on the stairs, and in this he is not contradicted, except again by negative proof, for Miss Fitzpatrick says she did not hear the footsteps. Has Weichman lied as to Mrs. Surratt's saying that Booth was an instrument to punish this wicked and licentious nation ? He did not care whether this was true or false. It was not necessary to prove the murder and conspiracy. But his testimony, from the record and the fact of this conspiracy and murder, would still be amply proven. In relation to the trip to Canada, Weichman is confirmed in every part; but he did not deem it necessary to elaborate on all these items of testimony.

Mr. Carrington, in continuation, had certain items of testimony read, and said: It appears, first, that Booth has communication with one McLaughlin. Then it is shown that Surratt tried to get leave from his place of employment at Adam's Express Company. He makes strenuous efforts to get leave, and it is not granted, and Surratt takes French leave? Why? Because the man who commanded the conspiracy leaves a card, and tells him not to mind his business. Then, hand-in-hand, he goes through this bloody business with Booth, until the scheme is consummated. Does not all this recapitulation of evidence show that there was conspiracy, and that Surratt was a part of that conspiracy, and that Booth, Payne, Atzerott, and Harold were part of that conspiracy?

It having then been shown that Surratt was a part of this conspiracy, the next point was what part did he perform in that general plan and conspiracy? Mr. Carrington said, in referring to this matter, he would not use his power to insult or hurt the feeling of the prisoner by unnecessary allusions, but it was his business to denounce crime, and he would say that any man who would cruelly shoot down a man by the side of his wife was a coward. All cruel men were cowards, and if McMillan's testimony was true, the man who would shoot down unarmed soldiers was a coward, and he could find no other name wherewith to designate what his opinion was of the prisoner.

At this point, one o'clock, the court took a recess for half an hour.

Upon reassembling Mr. Carington resumed and said, before discussing the proposition of facts referred to before the recess, he would refer to a fact alluded to by the counsel for the defence. Mrs. Surratt had been designated by counsel a murdered woman and a butchered woman, and he thought this was doing the greatest injustice to the men who had tried Mrs. Surratt. Suppose, after the verdict in this case, if it should be guilty, would it not excite a feeling of indignation for you to be denominated murderers? Or would it not equally excite your indignation if in the event of a verdict of acquittal

if he should call the jury a set of perjured individuals? Yet Mr. Merrick has, by implication, if not directly, charged these honorable men, who tried the conspirators, to be murderers! Acting under the orders of the President of the United States they tried Mrs. Surratt, and found her guilty of murder.

Mr. Bradley said there was no evidence to that point in this case.

Mr. Carrington said it was strictly responsive to the arguments of the defence, who had said Mrs. Surratt was a murdered and a butchered woman; and he had a right to repel any such insinuations, which he denied, and would show that Mrs. Surratt was neither a murdered nor a butchered woman.

Mr. Bradley said the fact was now open, and it could be discussed.

Mr. Carrington asked why he was interrupted then?

Mr. Bradley said he wanted to understand if the point was open, in order that the defence might not be stopped.

Mr. Carrington said the first allusion had come from the defence. They had cast the first stone, and it was his duty to repel the insinuation. He regretted that an American tribunal ever found it necessary to declare a woman guilty of murder. But when Herodias murdered John the Baptist she deserved hanging, when Lucretia Borgia shed blood she deserved hanging, and when Mary E. Surratt compassed the murder of President Lincoln, and permitted her house to become the headquarters of the conspirators, public safety demanded that she should be condemned when found guilty. Who composed that military commission? They were men not more honorable than these jurors, but they were equally honorable. They were officers of the United States Goverment, and were supposed to be honorable men. Yet they were denounced as murderers and butchers, who took the life of an innocent woman.

But whether Mrs. Surratt was innocent or not has nothing to do with this case. It is to be considered whether the prisoner at the bar is guilty, and not whether Mrs. Surratt was. He did not know for what purpose this subject was introduced, but he wanted the jury to consider well before they believed the members of the military Commission were murderers and butchers.

Mr. Carrington then proceeded to trace the connection of Mrs. Surratt with the conspiracy. He regretted to do this, but it had been forced upon him by the defence. First, her house was the rendezvous of the conspirators; and can this fact be reconciled with innocence? Is it reconcilable with innocence that any house could be the rendezvous of Booth, Atzerott, and Harold? Second, who furnished the arms with which the bloody deed was done? The person who furnishes arms, the woman who puts an arm into the hands of husband, lover, or brother, and urges him on to murder, is equally guilty with the person who actually commits the act.

If John M. Lloyd is to be believed did not Mrs. Surratt place the arms there? He was her servant, he lived in her house, he drank her liquor. Why it is even in evidence that Harold, and Surratt drank and played cards there. Lloyd was the tenant and confidential agent of Mrs. Surratt, and did not wish to testify against her, but he did say that he concealed the arms in a place designated by the prisoner. The mother knew of this because she afterwards asked where those shooting irons were.

On the night of April 14, Booth and Harold, in their flight, reached the Surratt House. Booth had broken his leg and they needed refreshment, and knew where to get it. They drank out of the very bottle which Mrs. Surratt had left in the custody of Lloyd, saying it would soon be called for. But Booth needed something else than whiskey and arms. He needs a field-glass, and that is ready to his hand, placed in proper place by Mrs. Surratt. Booth is slain, and in his grasp is found the very gun left for him by Mrs. Surratt.

But that is not all, although it is enough. Mrs. Surratt goes home, and the officers find their way to No. 541, and while there a man apparently a workman, comes in, and he proves to be Louis Payne. That would at least prove Mrs. Surratt an accessory after the fact. It was proven that she visited Payne at the Herndon House, and yet upon this night she denied all knowledge of the man, and it is a well settled principal that a deliberate lie is an evidence of guilt. Putting all these facts together, it is apparent that Mrs. Surratt was in the conspiracy, and, if in it at all, in the most minute particular she was guilty.

No reference has here been made to Weichman's testimony, for there is ample evidence without it to convict Mrs. Surratt. Womans' weapon is her tongue, and with her tongue did Mrs. Surratt urge these young men on to their deed of blood.

Mr. Carrington then left the subject of Mrs.

Surratt and referred to his point as to what was the original plan and purpose of this conspiracy. It was immaterial what its character was; if it led to murder, all the conspirators were equally guilty.

Mr. Merrick interrupting, asked Mrs Carrington if he was to be understood as saying that if entering into a conspiracy to abduct, and some members of the conspiracy changed the plan to murder, whether all of them would be equally guilty?

Mr. Carrington replied that if the plan was to abduct, and murder was committed in pursuance of that plan, then all the conspirators would be guilty.

Mr. Carrington said he would now proceed to notice some of the other points submitted. He did not deem it absolutely necessary to prove the prisoner's presence here on the 14th. But, out of abundant caution, they have fixed the prisoner here by thirteen witnesses; but let us see if we did not trace him here. On April 12, 1865, he was at Montreal, and he left at 3,30 for the New York train. McMillian testifies that Surratt left Montreal, and that, too, in obedience to a summons from Booth, who said it was necessary to change the plan of operation. According to the testimony of St. Marie, Surratt left Washington on April 15. According to the testimony of Maurice Drohan Surratt is seen at the ferry at Williamsport on April 13. He remembered Mr. Bradley's conduct on that occasion, when he said he did not wish to ask the witness a question. Has Drohan been contradicted? Has he not been confirmed by Westfall, who says a man inquired anxiously when the trains would run. He [Mr. Carrington] knew the Irish character. They would fight and drink whisky, but would not lie, and Mr. Bradley did not dare to cross examine the witness. One witness starts him from Montreal, another sees him him on the way, a host of witnesses testify that the trains were running, and St. Marie says he acknowledged he left on the morning of the 15th. Can it be doubted that Surratt was here? He is seen here by thirteen witnesses, among whom are Reed. Susan Jackson, Vanderpool Grills, Lee, Cleaver, Dye and Cooper. All, see him here at different hours, and not one witness has on this point contradicted the other. The first witness on the list was David C. Reed, who Mr. Bradley, Jr., said was a notorious gambler.

Mr. Bradley—Well, isn't he?

Mr. Carrington said the jury must decide

this case upon the evidence, and the defence had not attacked the character of Reed. They had attacked all the other witnesses, and did not care to attack Reed. The fact that his character was not attacked warranted the assertion that the defence did not dare to make the attack.

Mr. Bradley said they could have done so very successfully.

Mr. Carrington said it was nevertheless a fact that it had not been done, and he had a right to say that they did not dare to attack him. It was observed that Mr. Reed took the stand with emotion. He had known this boy, and he had known his father before him, and he swore positively that he saw him on the 14th.

Mr. Merrick said he had not sworn to a positive recognition.

There being some question as to the testimony, it was read by Mr. Pierrepont, and Mr. Carrington contended it was a positive descriptive recognition of the prisoner.

According to Reed's testimony, then, the prisoner was on Pennsylvania avenue, booted and spurred, and prepared for action. The next witness is Susan Jackson, who identifies the prisoner positively. She says she not only saw him, but heard his mother say, "That is my son." It is for the jury to say whether she has sworn falsely. Her character has not been successfully attacked, but on the contrary many have sworn to her good character for truth and veracity.

It is true that Eliza Hawkins attempts to contradict Susan Jackson, but she is in turn contradicted by Samuel Jackson. The third witness is Mr. Vanderpoel. Judging from the cross-examination, and judging from the remarks of counsel, he supposed something startling was to follow. Mr. Bradley had said that he [Mr. Carrington] allowed the witness to go on and tell a falsehood without stopping him.

Mr. Bradley said the witness did state a falsehood, and he was not corrected by Mr. Carrington.

Mr. Carrington replied that Vanderpoel had never been summoned. He was asked if he had been summoned. He said he had not. If he had been asked if he had received a telegram from Washington, he would have answered differently. But Vanderpoel has not been contradicted. They first attempted it by showing that the tables in the concert saloon referred to by him were square, and not round, but in point of fact the tables in the Winter Garden and in Teutonic Hall were round, and the testimony is conclusive that the prisoner was not only in Washington, but also in the concert saloon with Booth, stimulating himself for the act of the evening. Another witness was clearer, and as to him Mr. Carrington would say fairly that he would not convict any man on the uncorroborated testimony of Wm. E. Cleaver; but even if a bad man knew a fact, it was the duty of the prosecuting officer to put that man in the stand; but he had no objection to striking all of that from the record, as the case was made without it.

Mr. Carrington reflected severely upon the witnesses brought to discredit Cleaver's character, and said one was Bill Horner, a modern Æsculapius, who had invented a medicine and was killing the people here; another was Harry Middleton, who had coined money out of the tears and widows of orphans by dealing out liquid poison for years. John C. Cook was another one. He would not say anything more about Cook than he was a horse-dealer, and one of the last characters in the world who should be brought to show a man's reputation for truth.

The next witness, said Mr. Carrington, was Mr. Wood, the colored barber, a man of good character, who identified Surratt as having been in Booker's barber shop on the morning of April 14. (Wood's testimony was here read.) Wood could not be mistaken. It is certain he saw John Wilkes Booth, for he had the scar on his neck. No man could grease the head, (pointing to Surratt) and no one could see that face and forget it. No man could say that he had perjured himself.

Rhodes is the next witness, and he stands before the jury an honest man and uncontradicted.

The next witness is St. Marie. A number of witnesses are brought here to discredit him: but others yet have testified to his good character. It was true that he had been guilty of an indiscretion in connection with the Educational Board, but it was also in evidence that he had made restitution, and what honest jury would discredit a man for a youthful indiscretion of which he had repented?

He had no object in coming here to swear Surratt's life away. They had been fellow Zouaves, said Mr. Carrington, in the army of his Holiness the Pope. The next witness was Sergeant Dye, who saw Surratt in front of the theatre on the night of the assassination.

At this point (3 20) Mr. Carrington gave way, and the court took a recess untill next day at ten o'clock,

JULY 30.—The trial of John H. Surratt was resumed,

Mr. Carrington renewed his remarks, and said he hoped the jury would bear with patience until he had concluded his argument. Yesterday afternoon he was considering the assaults upon the witnesses for the prosecution, and he was defending their characters. The witness upon whose testimony he was commenting was Sergeant Dye. Who was Sergeant Dye ? He was a soldier, who had risen from the ranks to be a non-commissioned officer. Credit was due to any one who attains rank and position, but the private soldier who by merit fights his way up to be a first sergeant comes before a jury with the presumption in his favor. No witness was produced to question the character of Dye, and he stands before you an unimpeached and unimpeachable witness.

Who denies that Dye is a man of nerve, of courage; or who denies that he was a man of truth? Show me a courageous man and you see a truthful one. Liar and coward are synonymous terms. Valor and veracity are also synonymous terms. It is true, imputations were thrown out by counsel against the character of this witness; but the jury must remember that they must consider only the evidence, and not the statements of counsel. What right had the counsel to utter this libel against a brave and honorable man? But Dye had said he had seen the pale face of the prisoner in his dreams, and this was sneered at by counsel. But is it not a fact that circumstances that impress themselves upon the mind in the waking hours are called up again in dreams? Dye well illustrated his meaning when he said he had so often dreamed of a woman who became his wife. No man ever loved who did not dream of the woman he loved, and no lover of his country failed to dream of that country when it was in danger.

Was it strange, then, that a man who had attested his devotion to his country upon the field of battle, should be impressed with such a scene as that which Dye witnessed on the night of the assassination? The very fact that Dye dreamed of this scene shows that his heart and mind were in the matter, and that he remembered it, and

that he was telling the whole truth in relation to it.

The witness Grillo says he believes he saw the prisoner. He did not swear positively, but all the thunder of the artillery of the defence was hurled against his devoted head. Who is John Lee? You have heard the testimony of men who knew him in Philadelphia and in Washington. He came here from Philadelphia, and became first a detective and then a justice of the peace—a most responsible position, and one in which he could not fail to make enemies if he did his duty faithfully, because no public officer ever clearly did his duty without making enemies.

The next and last witness is Mr. Coleman, who also thinks he saw the prisoner; and this completes the list. Eight witnesses swear positively to seeing Surratt, and five others think they did. Each see him at a different place. Have all these witnesses lied? It is possible, but not probable. Are all these witnesses mistaken? It too, is possible, but not probable.

Now, we have proved, first, the existence of the conspiracy; second, the object of the conspiracy, which was to murder, and that was the original plan persisted in. It was murder at first, murder in the interim, and murder in the last. It was argued, out of abundant caution, that even if it were not to murder, if the conspiracy resulted in murder, the prisoner was guilty. John Surratt had a family and a home in the capital of the nation. He was timid and needed assistance. Booth had nerve, desperado as he was. Surratt furnished a rendezvous, and Booth appeared there to indoctrinate his ideas. Surratt furnished whiskey, and Booth and Harold drank it. Surratt furnished a rope Booth did not need it. One of the Surratt's furnished a field-glass, and Booth used it in his fight. Booth died by the hand of justice - not regularly by an interposition of Providence. As he lay weltering in his blood a weapon is taken, which was furnished by Surratt. The man who commits a crime and goes to hell, deserves his fate : But how much more the man who urges on the crime?

Booth has been called Satan and Surratt the Beelzebub of this infernal conspiracy. He would beg the prisoner's pardon, for perhaps Surratt was the Satan and Booth the Beelzebub. The difference between the two is that one died game, and the other was hunted down and pursued. Booth died game like a true fanatic. Booth's last prayer was the mention of his mother's name. Surratt deserted his mother in her hour of peril and danger. Surratt's sin was avarice, for he was a spy, which Booth never was. Booth died saying he died for his country, and that he had done what he believed to be right. Surratt fled, and boasted of his bloody exploit, and threatened to serve Andrew Johnson as Abraham Lincoln had been served. If, then, the prisoner has been shown to be one of the chief conspirators, should not this jury wipe this blot from the country? But has not the prisoner confessed his guilt? He has done so, both expressly and by implication; and out of his own mouth he is condemned. God grant that the day may never come when such a crime as this, self-confessed, shall go unrebuked in an American court.

Who is the witness to this point? Dr. McMillan, a French Canadian by birth, but with Scotch blood coursing through his veins, and an honorable man withal. Who discredits Dr. McMillan? They bring on Nagle to discredit him, and he [Mr. Carrington] would pay his respects to Mr. Nagle, although Mr. Bradly, Jr., seemed to intimate that it would be dangerous to do so. He wanted no personal difficulty, but would do his duty, although Mr. Bradley seemed to make it a personal matter.

Mr. Bradley, Jr., said he had never said so.

Mr. Carrington said he had so understood it in some remarks made by Mr. Bradley, Jr.

Mr. Bradley, Jr., to Mr. Carrington. You are only creating a·bubble to blow yourself up on.

Mr. Carrington resuming, said he was glad Mr. Bradley disclaimed making it a personal matter. Mr. Nagle was a lawyer, and it was admitted that he had been employed and had been feed in this case. He had no objections to that, but he did object to a lawyer receiving a fee in a case and then being placed upon the witness stand to blast a man's character, and all such testimony should be received with many grains of allowance. But enough of this. Dr. Mc Millan has proven an excellent character, and he says he gave his testimony from a sense of duty: and will any jury discard a man's testimony because he desires to expose a terrible crime and a gross villainy? He believed Dr. McMillan told the truth and he would credit all of his testimony, and believed that the jury would do the same.

[Dr. McMillan's testimony was here read.]

Mr. Carrington resuming, said the jury would perceive that there were several confessions in this testimony. In one Surratt distinctly confesses that he had done a deed that deserved capital punishment. What clearer admission could there be of his guilt, and of the commission of some act from the consequences of which he was then fleeing? What clearer confession could an American jury desire? Does he not again confess his guilt when he says he received a letter from Booth announcing a change in their plan? By responding to that letter he confesses that the original plan was his, and according to the testimony the original plan was murder. Upon this point of confession St Marie also testifies, and if these witnesses are believed, there is an end of this case, for these confessions all prove his presence, his co-operation, his flight, his own conviction that he had done an act worthy of death, and an honest American jury must so decide, But this is not all. There is such a thing as an implied confession, and upon this point Mr. Carrington read an extract from that great man and jurist, Daniel Webster, and afterwards paraphrased it to apply to the pending case. Surratt fled, for in flight was his only security; and to disguise himself, he stained his hair and wore glasses. Upon the vessel he trembles, because conscience pursues him. Dr. McMillan notices his tremor and asks him about it, and he says he fears an American detective is aboard, and acknowledges he has cause for fear. A few days ago the American people congratulated the Emperor of Russia on his escape from a violent death, and yet here he had been for three days endeavoring to convince an American jury that they should avenge the death of Abraham Lincoln, whose blood cries aloud for vengeance. With such confessions staring them in the face, it was an insult to the intelligence of the jury almost to pursue this matter further. Mr. Carrington here read, as part of his speech, the thirteenth chapter of Romans, to show that the Bible itself commands that the officers of the law should avenge the blood of innocence. The Bible condemned the lawless, and it was a spirit of lawlessness that led to this infamous murder.

Mr. Carrington said he would now briefly review the testimony for the defence, and would then submit a few general remarks to the jury, after which he would leave the case with the jury, so far as he is concerned.

A movement was here made by one or two of the jurors which Mr. Carrington observing said that they need not be alarmed, as he did not propose to discuss the propositions seriatim; he thought he had already met them. He then reviewed some of the points made by the defence, and said he would now refer particularly to the route travelled by Surratt. If the jury would cast their eyes over the map they would find that the direct route between Washington and Montreal was by New York, Albany, and Burlington; and he thought the idea that Surratt could have gone to Canandaigua was utterly unreasonable. If he had gone to Canandaigua he would have taken the lakes to Toronto, and not a circuitous route to Montreal. It is probable, therefore that he took the most direct route, If he was in Canandaigua on the 15th, he could not have been in Burlington on the 17th of April; but all the witnesses show that he took the direct route to Montreal. and was there secreted by Father Boucher. Another point is, whether Surratt was in Elmira on April 14. Even if he were, as he [Mr. Carrington] interpreted the law, it was immaterial, the other facts being proven, and as a question of fact he was not in Elmira on April 14.

This is a mixed question of law and fact, and must be decided by both Court and jury. An alibi is affirmative proof, and relying upon an alibi. the defence must prove it. He has been traced to Washington and Montreal, and this affirmative defence of an alibi must be proven by a preponderance of proof. In support of this proposition Mr. Carrington read from Chief Justice Shaw's decision in the trial of Webster for the murder of Parkman. In that important trial, said Mr. Carrington, the doctrine was enunciated, that an alibi must be proven beyond a reasonable doubt, and by a preponderance of evidence. That, too, has been the doctrine enunciated in this court in the cases of the United States vs. Foley, and the United States vs. Mary Harris. In the former case the doctrine was enunciated by Judge Merrick, a brother of one of the counsel for the defence who even decided that where insanity was set up, it must be proven beyond a reasonable doubt.

Mr. Merrick said the decision was wrong whether his brother decided it or not.

Mr. Carrington said it was the decision, and this court would stand by its own decisions, and invoked a decision from the court that the burden of proof was upon the prisoner. Five witnesses were brought here to prove Surratt's presence in Elmira on April 14, and thirteen witnesses swear to his presence here. This gives a preponderance to the evidence of the prisoner's presence here' and the jury cannot escape the conclusion, in considering the evidence, that he was here. Cass says he saw Surratt in Elmira. Reed says he saw him here. Both are honest men, and it is for the jury to say who is mistaken. He would put Carroll, the witness for the defence, against Wood the witness for the prosecution, and the jury must decide who was mistaken. Cass never knew Surratt before. Reed knew him from boyhood, and knew his father before him. Carroll saw Surratt when he was disguised, while Wood knew Booth, saw Surratt with him, and rubbed and greased his head. Who had the best opportunity for knowing? It is for the jury to decide, and if the law is correct that the jury must decide by the preponderance of proof, then they must decide by the majority of the evidence. As to Dr. Bissell he would place in opposition to him Lawyer Vanderpoel. There was a Roland for an Oliver, and it was for the jury to decide who told the truth.

There now are three against three, and the prosecution has yet ten behind to show Surratt's presence here on April 14, thus giving the preponderance of proof to the prosecution, and showing that an alibi had not been proven, as the law required.

Mr. Carrington said he had now touched upon the evidence for the defence, and he would be brief in what few observations he would yet make.

He then referred to the fact that, in connection with this trial. imputations had been thrown out against the loyalty of this city and District, and proceeded to defend it from the charge, and alluded to the fact that Mr. Lincoln was inaugurated under the protection of District of Columbia soldiers, and that they were the first to invade Virginia. He contended that the citizens of Washington had ever been loyal, and then pronounced a panegyric upon the power of this country, and asked what this country was worth, if its rulers were subjected to assassination with impunity? What is the Union worth, if your sons fight for its preservation, and you fail, by the execution of its laws, to restrain and punish its enemies? He charged the jury to maintain the majesty of the law, and wipe this damning stain from the escutcheon of the country. We must be cruel to be just, for justice to the guilty is mercy to the innocent. It was their duty, then, to assign to the prisoner at the bar that punishment he so righteously deserves. He is a murderer, and deserves a murderer's doom.

Mr. Carrington here concluded his remarks, and Mr. Pierrepont said he would call the attention of the court to some additional legal points upon the question of alibi, and show that the burden of proof was on the defence. He cited from Wills on circumstantial evidence, as found in the law library, page 51, side paging 115. He also cited from page 53, side paging 130. Also, from page 71, side paging 168. He also cited upon this subject from Allison's practice in the criminal courts of Scotland, pages 624, 626, and 627. Mr. Pierrepont said the other legal points had been so fully considered that he would not now waste the time of the court, but would simply state the points without reading. In this, as in all other long cases, there was at last but a limited number of points. He then read the points upon which he claimed this whole case at last rested. The real question in their case is, whether the prisoner was engaged in aiding and abetting the conspiracy which resulted in the killing of Abraham Lincoln, President of the United States. If he was so engaged he is guilty under this indictment. If he was not engaged in the conspiracy which led to the killing, then he is not guilty. The conspiracy being established, it is well settled law—

FIRST. That each confederate in the conspiracy is liable for the acts of every conspirator, and the declaration of each may be given in evidence against every other; and though the conspiracy may have been formed years before the prisoner ever heard of it, yet, having subsequently joined in the conspiracy, he is in all respects guilty as an original conspirator.

SECOND. That when several persons are finally confederated in a conspiracy they are like one body, and the act of each hand, and the utterance of each tongue, and the conception and purpose of each heart touching the common plan is the act of each and all; and every one of the several persons forming the confederate body is responsible for the acts, sayings, and doings of each and of all the others.

THIRD. That a conspiracy to kidnap, abduct, or murder the President of the United States in the time of rebellion or other great national peril, is a crime of such heinousness as to admit of no accessories, but such as to render all the conspirators, their supporters, aiders and abettors, principals in the crime; that such is the common law of England, and is the law of this country.

FOURTH. That such conspiracy, either to abduct or to kill the President, and thus to overthrow the Government and promote anarchy in the nation, is a crime of such a nature as to render every supporter of the conspiracy a principal in the crime, and liable for all the consequences of a murder perpetrated by a coconspirator while carrying out the common design, though no such murder may have been originally intended, and though the accused conspirator had never personally participated therein.

FIFTH. That a killing by a coconspirator, in pursuance of a common plan to abduct, makes each conspirator guilty of the killing, though no such crime was contemplated by the other conspirators.

SIXTH. That the personal presence of the prisoner in Washington is not necessary to his guilt in this case. He could perform his part in the conspiracy as well at Elmira as at Washington, and be equally quiet at one place as at the other. That if he left Montreal, in obedience to the order of his coconspirator Booth, to aid in the unlawful conspiracy, it matters not whether he arrived in time to bear his allotted part or not. Being on his way to take his part, any accident which may have delayed him does not change his guilt.

SEVENTH. That in legal contemplation, each conspirator is present where the crime is committed towards which the confederate had conspired, or which was committed as a consequence of the confederated plan, though in fact the conspirator on the trial may have been absent when the acting conspirators did the deed.

EIGHT. That a conspirator performing his part in a conspiracy to abduct or kill the President in the capital, though not personally present, may be lawfully convicted and punished for the crime whenever brought within the jurisdiction of this district.

NINTH. That a conspiracy is proved by facts and circumstances which convinced the mind, precisely as any other crime or agreement is proved in a court of Justice.

It is the first time, said Mr. Pierrepont, that an opportunity was ever afforded to test the fourth point, for the fact seems to be lost sight of that this whole conspiracy was for the purpose of overthrowing the Government, but neither the court or jury could escape from that view of the case, and if this was considered only as an ordinary murder, the country would hold both court and jury responsible.

It was a monstrous doctrine to communicate, that if an abduction merely was contemplated, and a murder ensued, that therefore the conspirators to abduct were not guilty of murder. Mr. Pierrepont here stated a hypothetical case, and contended that if the prisoner remained at another place, and yet aided and abetted the conspiracy, he was equally guilty with the principal. It does not matter where the man is so that he commits the crime, and he is liable the moment he comes into the jurisdiction where the crime was committed.

In support of the points submitted Mr. Pierrepont cited from 1 Comstock, page 175, to show that actual presence was not necessary: and also referred to 1 Russell on Crimes, pages 32 and 39; to 4 Wendell, page 256—case of The people vs. Matthew; 1 Russell, page 27, and page 29 and 30; to 2 Starkie, page 237: 12 Wheaton, page 360; 2 Peters' page 368; 3 Connecticut Report, page 8: 10 Pickering, page 498; Bishop's Criminal Law, vol. 1, page 81; and Archibald, page 7.

Mr. Pierrepont said he would only add that these authorities cited contain the principles for which the prosecution contend.

At this point Mr. Carrington announced the death of E. C Morgan, Esq., a member of the bar, after which the court took a recess until 10 o'clock next day.

JULY 31,—The trial of John H. Surratt was resumed.

The attendance upon the part of spectators was much greater than it has been for some days past.

Mr. Merrick proceeded to address the jury for the defence, and said the feeling with wich he approached the discussion of the case was indescribable, as the magnitude of the case was beyond any he had ever known, and its surroundings were painful beyond description. The prisoner is in the hands of the jury, and his future destiny is committed to them; but there is something in this trial beyond the ordinary arraignment of the prisoner. He finds arrayed against his client the best talent, and some high officers of the Government aiding a legal combination surrounded by spies and detectives, aided by the Treasury of this Government, and all arrayed against one man to urge him on to the judgment.

In discussing this case he would go into some of the motives that actuated the prosecution in this case, and he would show there had been a conspiracy here to commit a murder under the form of law. Why is it all these appliances and this vast machinery are in the case? Why all the wonderful array of counsel here and elsewhere? They nominally represent the Government, but all the trial convinces that there are two sets, one representing the Government in its assumed offended majesty, and the other the officers of the United States, seeking for their own purpose the shedding of innocent blood. In a case of this kind, all evidence that would bring light should be given to the jury, but in this case all the technicalities of law have been used to exclude that testimony, I would not question the decision of the Court on points presented, but would say that no opinion changed my view that the testimony should have been left in.

Instead of representing the United States upon law, every feeling and sentiment to excite prejudice have been persistently urged. The District Attorney in one breath congratulates the jury upon the return of peace, and in the next tears open old gaping wounds made by the war. Why did he speak of the murder of Union soldiers? Why call the prisoner, beforehand, a traitor and a murderer? Why ask the jury to decide the case according to the human prejudice engendered by the war? Peace has come, but all its consequences never will come if the United States, before a jury, continues to tear open the wounds made by the war. There will never be peace as long as fratricidal strife is again stirred up.

Mr. Carrington is mistaken in talking of God as a God of vengeance and a God of wrath; assuredly mistaken, as he is in saying that peace has returned. God is a God of love, and not of wrath. But I would seek to excite no prejudice. The jury are under oath to do their duty, and they must discard all prejudice and stand forth as men with unclouded minds. What is John H. Surratt charged with? In the wide discussion of the counsel the jury have almost lost sight of the cause, and it is necessary to recur. The first count of the indictment charges Surratt with the murder of Abraham Lincoln. The second count charges him with assassinating Mr. Lincoln, in connection with Booth.

The third count unites the prisoner with Booth, Harold, Payne, and Mrs. Surratt, in the killing of Mr. Lincoln. Bear in mind one feature in the indictment, "The fourth count specifies that the persons named and other persons unknown did make an assault upon Mr. Lincoln. The jury must find whether what is laid in the indictment is true. It is charged that the parties then and there made an assault. It puts them all in Washington, and the jury must find if they all were here. The charge in the third and fourth counts is that these parties murdered Lincoln then and there. Are not you then trying Surratt for the murder of Mr. Lincoln? there is nothing else in the indictment, and the verdict must be guilty or not guilty as indicted. The question is did Surratt kill Mr. Lincoln? The prosecution want to try Surratt for being a spy and conspirator, a member of the Southern Confederacy, anything and everything except the crime laid in the indictment. To conspire is one thing—to do the act is another. It is a crime to conspire, and it is another crime to commit the act for which the conspiracy was formed.

When Mr. Wilson made his opening address he spoke of the indictment as a simple indictment for murder, and it was not until they found their original view thwarted that they commenced to try the prisoner for conspiracy. They brought witnesses to prove the murder, and we struck the witnesses as they came, and laid at their feet a mass of the most offensive corruption, and thread by thread we broke the strand with which they purposed to unite the prisoner with the body of the crime. Losing their case, they had to resort to other measures. The United States should have magnanimously abandoned the case then, but there were others besides the United States standing by, and there were others who had dreams not so sweet as Sergeant Dye's. These gentlemen wanted the verdict of a jury to cover the shedding of innocent blood on a former occasion. It was not until the first case was not proven that these new doctrines of law sprung up.

In their various twistings and turnings the prosecution have got this case in such a muddle that it is an insult to argue it before the jury. They have themselves shown Surratt's innocence, and have shown it to be a physical impossibility for Surratt to have got here. They felt the necessity of meeting this, and they now claim that his presence was not necessary here at the time of the murder. and the counsel dares the Judge to give other than such a decision as he desires, and holds up the fear what the popular voice will do. The jury dare to do right. It was an insult to the Court to dare him with the popular voice. The Court is responsible alone to God, and at the court-house door the popular voice ceases.

The District Attorney seemed to press the jury very hard that it was their duty to follow the instructions of the Court. Why did he press this so hard? Was he advised that the Court would do as he wished? The jury must give a true verdict accoding to the evidence. The District Attorney knew that the jury is to give a verdict according to the evidence, and not according to the instruction of the Court. When the jurors come to the judgment seat of God will it be any excuse for them that they brought a verdict that resulted in bloodshed, because the Judge so instructed them? The law is given you to light your pathway in the investigation. and is not mandatory upon you.

Let us deal fairly by this young man, and though the reputation of Joseph Holt should not be vindicated by the verdict of a jury for his shedding of innocent blood, let us do justice still. The propositions of law of the counsel on the other side give rise to who are the principals and who are accessories, and also as to the grade of principals. The principals in the different degrees involve different degrees in crime, and a principal in one degree cannot be a principal in another degree.

Mr. Merrick cited from Hale's Pleas of the Crown, vol. 1, page 438, and contended from this authority that he who strikes the blow is principal in the first degree, and he who stands by assisting is principal in the second degree: but if a crime is done, he who counsels, but is not present assisting, is an accessory. In support of this position, Mr. Merrick cited 1st Hale, page 612. On page 435 of the same book, it is shown who are accessories. On page 616, it is shown that that which makes an accessory before the fact is command. The principles referred to, Mr. Merrick contended, laid at the very foundation of the English law, and he did not suppose his Honor sat upon the bench to report these principles. Russell and Ryan's Crown Cases, page 22, were also cited from. Also, page 113 of the same books.

On page 249 is a case in which several parties planned the utterance of a forged order, and the actual utterer was alone held as the principal. The same principle is decided, in page 363, where it is held that persons not near enough to give aid are not principals in a crime. On page 421 it is decided that even going toward a place where a crime is being committed, but not being near enough to aid in the commission of the act, does not make a principal. What then becomes of the theory of the prosecution that if Surratt started out to aid in the murder, but did not reach here, that he is yet a principal in that murder? Is it another attempt to trick this poor boy out of life and to effect another judicial murder by setting up some law other than the common law of the land?

But the gentleman says that there are precedents in England to show that it is treason to compass the death of a ruler. Has a crown ever pressed the brow of a President? In France it is treason to imagine the death of Louis Napoleon; but is it treason to imagine the death of Andrew Johnson? If it is, then instruct your grand jury to indict Thaddeus Stevens and all his companions for treason. But this is a free country, and it is the pride of our institutions that the President is the servant of the people. Would the Corps of Legislatif dare to impeach Louis Napoleon, or even to appoint a committee of investigation? No, sir; that is a privilege of free institutions, and not an imperial privilege. There is no authority in England or France that justifies the proposition of Mr. Pierrepont, or that can sustain it.

There was another principle of law to which he desired to call the attention of the court, and that was in relation to the doubt that must be entertained to acquit a prisoner. The jury must be satisfied of guilt beyond a reasonable doubt. Suppose ten jurors, after mature consideration of the evidence, believe the prisoner innocent, the other two will listen to the convictions of these ten. He would not have the two give up their convictions. But he would ask them to study those convictions with conscientious thought. With regard to this matter of a reasonable doubt, he would read from page 654 of Roscoe on Evidence.

Take the facts of a criminal case, and if these facts are inconsistent with any hypothesis of innocence, the doubt must be given to the prisoner. In this case, if it is found that Surratt was in a conspiracy to abduct, and that conspiracy failed, and afterwards a conspiracy to murder, of which the prisoner was not a member, was formed, then the jury must acquit. Honor, Judge Wylie, has decided that a jury must be convinced beyond a reasonable and a moral certainty. There must be nothing less than a conviction and a controlling understanding, filling the full measure of the conscience, asking to be let at peace. If these principles of law be correct principles, the first inquiry is, was Surratt here on April 14, aiding and abetting the murder? If he was in a conspiracy to murder, it must be admitted that he might have been here aiding, but if it is shown that he was not here, then it is shown that he was not in the conspiracy and that he did not do that which he is charged with doing.

The burden is upon the other side to show that Surratt was here, and being here that he was aiding and abetting the murder. How do they prove that? The first witness was Sergt. Dye. Mr. Carrington said he [Mr. Merrick] had published a libel upon Dye, by offering to show that he was indicted and held to bail for passing counterfeit money. That paper came here under the broad Seal of Pennsylvania and if it was a libel it was a libel published by Pennsylvania and not by him. Dye says he sat in front of Ford's Theatre for half an hour on April 14, and heard a man call the time.

When asked, with dramatic effect, by Mr. Pierrepont, if he saw the man afterwards, he points to the prisoner and says, "I see him now!" Dye's testimony, Mr. Merrick contended, was contradicted by Mr. Ford and Mr. Gifford, for by sitting upon the platform he could not have seen Surratt as he says he saw him. Dye says he saw three men together, and that one of them was the prisoner. When summoned before the Military commission Dye swore that it was Booth who called the time, and he said another of the party was Spangler, and the other he said was the smallest. When asked why he had so sworn at the arsenal he said he only threw that in. He pitied the man as he stood before him. The calling of that time seemed to produce a deep impression on Mr. Dye.

The defence has brought the very man who called the time. Mr. Pierrepont smiles, but he cannot get over the fact. Hess says he called the time. The prosecution bring in Mr. Hess and put him beside Surratt, and the jury may judge who best answered Dye's description, Hess or Surratt. He could not have been mistaken in taking Hess for Surratt. Dye has been dreaming too freely. That same calling the time has sent one man to the Dry Tortugas, and now they would have the circumstance hang another man.

Mr. Merrick then recited Dye's testimony in relation to his interview with Mrs. Surratt on the night of the murder. Two years passed. It was a dim moonlight night. Mrs. Surratts's house fronted north, and was thrown in the shade while the moon was traversing the southern hemisphere. The house was darkened; a lady puts her head out in the darkness, and yet Dye says he identifies her. Such a story is simply absurd. If it is not perjury, it is an image created in an overwrought mind. He has thought of this and dreamed of it until his mind has become perverted, and like a frightened boy he has conjured up visions which have haunted his mind and made him see images which had no being and no reality. As in boyhood so in manhood; for the boy is father of the man.

The court then took a recess untill ten o'clock to-morrow morning.

AUGUTS 1.—The trial of John H. Surratt was resumed this morning.

Mr. Merrick resumed his address to the jury, and said that he observed a few errors in the report of his remarks yesterday, but he knew it must be necessarily somewhat ncomplete, as it did not profess to be a stenographic report. He simply made the statement in order that the counsel for the prosecution might be advised, and not be led into error in making a comparison with the official report.

Mr. Merrick then resumed the consideration of Sergeant Dye's testimony, and contended that Mr. Hess had contradicted him. Sergeant Dye also said that the lady he spoke to was of middle age, and was wrapped in a shawl. This lady, Mr. M. contended, was not Mrs. Surratt, for Mrs. Lambert, a lady whose character is not questioned, and who had no motive to speak aught but the truth, testified to holding with a soldier the identical conversation which Sergeant Dye alleges he had with Mrs. Surratt. All the features,

time, and circumstances correspond. If Dye had a conversation with Surratt, and another soldier had a similar conversation with Mrs. Lambert it is certainly a remarkable coincidence. He did not think the jury would convict the prisoner upon such testimony as that of Sergeant Dye.

The other witness who says he saw Surratt at the theatre on the day of the assassination is Mr. Rhodes, who says he was attracted by curiosity and entered the theatre, and he saw a man whom he now identifies as the prisoner. Mr. Merrick recited Mr. Rhodes' testimony. This witness, he contended, was contradicted, because it was in proof, as sworn by Raybold, that a man could not have retreated from one box to the other, as there was but one box: there was no place where the man could have retreated to. unless he came out by the door that Rhodes entered. Rhodes said that all was quiet. Lamb and others contradict him, and say a rehearsal was going on at the hour mentioned by Rhodes. Again, Rhodes swears the curtain was down, and Lamb, who was there painting all day, says the curtain was not down, and it has been shown that it was not the custom to keep the curtain down during the day, It was also shown that the doors of the theatre were locked, and that there was no admission during the day. These two witnesses, Dye and Rhodes, are the only ones that bring Surratt near the theatre, and the jury must conclude that neither are reliable.

Cushing and Coleman say they saw Surratt talk to Booth on that day, but their testimony is met by a singular circumstance, and it seems as though Providence enabled the defence to meet by direct proof what was put in evidence by the prosecution. In this instance Matthews shows that it was he who was talking to Booth, and that it was not Surratt. Grillo thinks he saw Surratt at Willard's Hotel, but he is by no means positive ; he does not swear certainly. There is no proof so difficult as of identity ; and how can the face of a man seen in a hotel two years ago casually be now positively recognized ? Features make but slight impression until they become buried in the human mind. Conversation, manner, deportment, bearing, stamp the recollection of a man upon the memory, but the features cannot make so great an impression.

David C. Reed is also relied upon, but he, Mr. Merrick contended, was contradicted at every point. Who is David C. Reed ? Does he deal out liquid fire ? Ah ! not for the money the liquid would bring, but that he might rob the victim at his faro bank. The counsel said one of the witnesses for the prosecution dealt out liquid fire. Ah! you gentlemen know the character of Reed in this community, and it is unnecessary to speak of him further. Another witness is Susan Jackson. Her testimony, when she said she saw John Surratt on that night, made an impression upon the jury; but she went too far, and it was shown that she never before gave such testimony before Captain Olcott, when she was previously examined. The Government had her testimony in the Bureau of Military Justice, and it did not correspond with the testimony given here. She lied upon this stand, and the prosecution knew it and did not check her.

This woman was contradicted by Rachel Hawkins, by Eliza Hayes, and by Susan's own husband. Rachel says that at the assassination Susan said she did not see John Surratt for two weeks. But Rachel is not the only one, for Mr. Clarvoe says she told him that she had not seen Mr. Surratt for two weeks, and there is not a man upon the jury who will not believe Mr. Clarvoe. Miss Fitzpatrick also settles this question, for she says that when Surratt was there on the 3d of April, she got him some supper, and it was then that Mrs. Surratt said to Susan, pointing to John, "this is my son; don't he look like Annie?" But there is also, beside this good angel, the bad angel of this case. Miss Fitzpatrick testifies to contradict Susan, and the fiend of the case come in also to contradict her. Weichman, the fiend, the accursed fiend, whose conscience is driven before him with the applying lash, says Surratt did not take supper with his mother on April 14. Susan Jackson's testimony was then shown to be false; but he [Mr. Merrick] believed, with a full belief and consciousness of all he was saying, that that woman was lying with the full knowledge of the United States Government. St. Marie says that Surratt admitted his presence here, but it was doubtful if the jury believed him. Why is St. Marie here to betray his friend? The jingle of the yellow earth has been the knell of many a man's honesty. What brought St. Marie here? Does he so love America that he would give up Surratt merely for that love?

But there is a voice also from the grave—a nameless grave, it is true—Mrs. Surratt says he was not there. Clarvoe asks Mrs. Surratt where John is, and she replies she had a letter

from him that day, and she had not seen him for two weeks. It is not proper to give Mrs. Surratt's declaration in evidence; but that voice comes from the grave to protect her boy! The prosecution broke the cerements of the grave, and brought Mrs. Surratt here before one word was uttered about her by the defence, and she sits beside her boy to protect him! Her spirit is here—a mother speaking for her son, and testifying in his behalf! Let gentlemen beware lest the scheme they now devise to cover a former crime drag them down yet lower and deeper!

The theory that he was here is then cast down. His living friends say he was not here, and his mother's voice comes from the grave as a last protestation for her boy, and she says he was not here, and he was not here. They got him at Montreal on the 12th, and put him upon the New York train at 3.30. They admit that on the 13th he was in Elmira; they start him from Elmira at 10 a. m. on the 13th, and they must have him here at 9 a. m. in time for Wood, the barber, to shave him.

They bring him to Williamsport, and there Montgomery ferries him across.

Mr. Bradley. Not Montgomery?

Mr. Merrick. Yes, Montgomery; for Montgomery made him; Montgomery paid and bought the ferryman: Montgomery, Conover's pet, and the prosecution's right-hand man. Conover made Montgomery, and Montgomery made Drohan, the drone, who testified here; Drohan, a backwoodsman, recognizes a particular coat. And why does not that coat figure here? Why does not Reed see the coat? Why does not Wood see it?—Wood who shaved him. dusty and travel soiled as he was? Montgomery did not do his work well, The prosecution should have waited till his partner, Conover, was out of the penitentiary.

Mr. Merrick said he thought he had shown that the testimony of Surratt's presence here was not to be relied upon, and that from its infamous character it soiled the whole case for the prosecution. A physical impossibility for Surratt to have got here. It will be remembered, also, that none of his friends saw him here; and he (Mr. Merrick) thought the alibi had been proved beyond the possibility of doubt, for his presence has been proven in Elmira by as respectable witnesses as were brought upon the stand. In reference to the belief in a witness, a juror believes a man or does not believe him according to the instincts of nature. Mr. Stewart fixes Surratt in Elmira.

The jury heard Carroll's testimony, and that witness has not been contradicted. A witness was called to contradict Carroll, but instead of contradicting, he confirms him. Mr. Atkinson and Mr. Cass testify in the manner of unmistakable truth to Surratt's presence in Elmira. Mr. Cass positively indentifies Surratt as being in Elmira on the 15th. He said he positively recognized him —not by face only, but by voice, action, deportment, and manner. Three witnesses for the defence do not swear to features, but they recognize him from action, conversation, and manner.

As to Dr. Bissell, throw his testimony out, if you choose, and throw him to the other side, where he can find congenial witnesses, and Surratt's presence in Elmira is still proven. Having then shown that Surratt was not here: that Surratt had no connection with Booth from April 7, 1865, to the present time, it is a circumstance to show he was not in the conspiracy. He was not in the conspiracy to kill, and he did not leave Montreal upon Booth's mandate.

McMillan says Surratt told him that Booth summoned him because the plan was changed. What plan? Is it shown what plan was changed? There was to be a change of plan, but is it shown what plan was changed? Mc-Millan's testimony must be taken with great allowance, for he sees the reward glittering in the distance, and he acknowledges that he is entitled to the reward if any reward is to be given. It must be remembered also in McMillan's testimony that he falsified about the receipt given to Mr. Boucher. In considering McMillan's testimony that of Cameron's must be taken with it.

Mr. Merrick read Cameron's testimony to show that McMillan was contradicted, and continued. There are certain circumstances that may justify you in believing that there was a plan to abduct, but it must be remembered that the President was not killed in a scheme to abduct. The killing showed a new conspiracy, with which the parties to the conspiracy to abduct had nothing to do.

But let us see if there was any conspiracy to be abandoned. They first formed a conspiracy in April, 1864, by three men standing upon the street corner; and then Mrs. Hudspeth finds some letters, which are again tortured into an evidence of conspiracy to murde-

by pistol, dagger, or poison; and much is made of the fact that Harold was then an apothecary's clerk, when it is shown that he never put up but one prescription. There is no evidence that Surratt then even knew Booth. Booth had at that time never been at Mrs. Surratt's house; but they say Surratt furnished the arms and put them away at "T. B." and at Surrattsville.

Now what does all that amount to? Here were a number of young men who earnestly sympathized with the South. They may have helped people across the river, and the arms may have been, therefore, their protection. There may have been a plan, even, to abduct, and if it had been attempted the men engaged in it would have been, no doubt, executed. But it might have been as an act of war. It has passed into history that there were Confederate prisoners North and Federal prisoners South who were starving, and that the North was to blame for a non-exchange of prisoners, and there might have been a wild scheme to abduct Mr. Lincoln, not to kill, but to force an exchange.

He did not blame Mr. Lincoln for the non-exchange of prisoners, and he could pass as high encomiums upon him as Mr. Carrington. But much is made, also, of the fact that Surratt owned horses; and this, it is argued, is evidence of a conspiracy. But, then, was the conspiracy to kill formed? Booth's diary settles that thing definitely, and conclusively shows that the plan was formed on that very day. Richmond had fallen, and the Confederacy was passing away. Booth with an inflamed mind, saw what he had loved passing away, and he then, alone, conceived the idea of murder.

Booth says he wrote a letter for the IN-TELLIGENCER. Where is that letter? The defence wanted to get its declaration in, but the Court ruled it out, as he thought wrongfully; for what motive could Booth have had to tell a lie at that time?

Mr. Merrick here referred to some remarks made by Mr. Pierrepont early in the trial, in which he said that the trial would set at rest reports about certain individuals, and it was promised that records would be produced. Where are those records? They were brought here once, and were withdrawn. Why was this? Did they find at the end of the record a recommendation to mercy for Mrs. Surratt which the President never saw? Would that record have shown that access was not denied to the President? Can the scene of that day ever be forgotten ? Philanthropists went to the Executive Mansion to ask a respite for Mrs. Surratt, and access was denied.

Does the conscience of the Secretary of War, or of the head of the Bureau of Military Justice now check them, or is it true that one who protested against that interview now sleeps in the waters of the Hudson, and that another blew his own brains out in Kansas ? Was there not something behind this case ?

Is it not known that in the lower House of Congress public accusations were brought against the Secretary of War, and Mr. Bingham, and others ? What has the Bureau of Military Justice to do with this case ? and yet Judge Holt takes a deep interest in it. The Bureau of Military Justice is a part of the Executive Department of the Government, and yet he has been manipulating the witnesses in his case. Why all this ? Judge Holt has certainly lost his discretion in his pursuit.

Is it not enough to try the living, or will the prosecution act the ghoul and tear the corpse from the grave and hang it also? Mrs. Surratt is here, and her presence has been felt. It is present always with Judge Holt, and he cannot bid it down, and when they come to stand before the bar of God Mrs. Surratt will there appear against Judge Holt.

A priest was put upon the stand, and he said he gave Mrs. Surratt the consolations of religion. He was not permitted to repeat what Mrs. Surratt said, tottering to the scaffold between two priests, with the world behind her and eternity before her, and her load of guilt laid at the feet of her Savior.

Why was not her declaration admitted ? Did they fear she would lie ? No: but, hardened of heart, reckless of guilt, and indifferent of justice, they would not let her voice be heard. But still it falls upon their ears ; that voice of a woman in a nameless grave, whose very body has been refused to a pleading daughter. But the District Attorney says that Surratt fled, and flight is an evidence of guilt, and it is said he deserted his mother. He did not know his mother's extremity until after she was hung, or about that time. Flight, in Surratt's case, was no confession, for, under the circumstances, Mr. Merrick argued, any man would have fled, as power had usurped the place of the courts of justice.

Three years ago there was in this city a happy household sitting beside a bright household fire. There sat a mother and a sister just budding into womanhood. and beside them a young man just reaching manhood. He would have the jury remember the changes that have come over that scene. The bright fire is extinguished ; the mother sleeps in a nameless felon's grave. The daughter, burdened and broken-hearted, drags out a wretched life, and the son is here before you, on trial for his life.

May Almighty God so guide your judgement and enlighten your convictions that the remembrance of this day and of your verdict may hereafter and forever be a sweet and pleasant recollection. I thank you, gentlemen, for your kind attention.

The court then, at 2 30 p. m., took a recess until next day at 10 o'clock,

MR. PIERREPONT'S

ADDRESS TO THE JURY.

AUGUST 3.—The trial of John H. Surratt was resumed this morning in the Criminal Court, Judge Fisher presiding.

Mr. Pierrepont addressed the jury on behalf of the prosecution, and said "Yea, all that a man hath will he give for his life." This is as true to-day as it was in the days of Job, and to secure life he will give up his liberty, resort to any measures, give up home and friends, desert father and mother, sister, and brother, and he will even committ perjury, and "jump the life that is to come to save the life that now is."

I propose to get first at facts about which there is no debate; and here let one general observation be made: That all of truth is in perfect harmony with every other truth, and every falsehood interposed dislocates it and breathes falsity in every case. No man ever violated a law of God, even in this world, that he did not get punished for it. It is so in the simplest transaction of life, as it is in the greatest. Now, let us come to one vital truth in this case. Here it is: John Harrison entered his name on April 18, 1865, in the register of the St. Lawrence Hotel, Montreal. The man is the prisoner at the bar. There is no dispute about that. After that, he passed through the hotel: he made no bill, and he fled somewhere. He fled to the house of a man named Porterfield, and then two carriages came up, and two men, both dressed alike, got into a carriage and were driven in different directions. Well, then, he was fleeing, either because he was in the conspiracy, or because he was not. He went to a priest—the priest ...·r, who

has not done his church any credit, for the Pope and Cardinal Antonelli gave up this prisoner on account of the hideousness of the crime, and Boucher will hear from the Pope before another year. Here the prisoner remained concealed. Why concealed? It was because he was innocent or because he was guilty. Which it was the jury must determine.

What was going on here at that time? The mother and other conspirators were on trial, and it was published daily to the world. There Surratt was concealed, and did not know what was going on? Boucher will hear from his Pope and bishops before one year, because the Catholic Church would never tolerate such a crime as this. Well, Surratt was concealed until September, and then taken on board a steamer and introduced as McCarty, and the steamer starts upon the sea for the Old World. He is not upon the steamer thirty minutes before he fears an American detective is on board, and he tells McMillan he has done such things as would make him [McMillan] stare. He could not keep his secret to himself, and he went behind the wheelhouse and talked to McMillan; he unburdened his mind for relief. When he got on the lone ocean he could not help telling the secret, and he told it. He arrives at Ireland. He hesitated whether he should land at Ireland or England, and after concluding first to land in England, he changed his mind and landed in Ireland. Before landing he takes tumbler after tumbler of rum and brandy until he is drunk. But in Ireland his conscience pursues him and we next find him wandering in Liverpool : and he fled again to Rome, away from his country and his kinsmen, and enlists and changes his name to Wattson. He supposes himself safe. Safe God does not allow such things to be safe. It must have been an awful hour when he saw St. Marie's face. He then goes to St. Marie and tells him about his disguise, and how he escaped, and then he heard a voice from the Vatican that the Pope's dominions had no place for him. He then makes a leap for his life and flees to Malta, but he finds no security there ; and he flees to Egypt, that ancient land where Joseph was a slave. There amid the grandest monument—there even the colossal sphynx, looking through his stony eyes, says that that darkened land can have no place for such treason and crime. And thence he could flee no further, and he is caught and brought over the long sea and up the broad river to this city of his crime, and he is here to be tried. Now this, Mr. Merrick says was the flight of an innocent man. Does it look to the jury like the flight of an innocent man ? It is a mystery that an innocent man should thus flee, and the mystery must be inquired into. But let us go back a little in time. On the 14th of April Mr. Lincoln was assassinated, and the crime sent a thrill through the civilized world. Mr. Lincoln was killed for no crime no cruelty. A few weeks before his death he spoke the memorable words of his last inaugural address. [Mr. P. read the address referred to.] This gentleman, is a trial of one of the conspirators who killed Mr. Lincoln, and it is the first trial in a court of civil jurisdiction.

At the conspiracy trial it was said that, as the President was killed in his camp, the case was one for military trial ; and it was urged that there were to many secessionists here to give a proper trial. But I always held that these matters could be intrusted to a jury of twelve honest men. Because I believe that I am here. I am not here because I affiliate with the Republican party, for I have always been opposed to that party. But if a jury could not find an honest verdict, and it was so demonstrated, then I would bid farewell to freedom. If justice cannot be done in civil courts, then let all good citizens say, let the sword write the record. This is no ordinary trial, and all the country is looking at us, and every lover of our Government will fall on his knees and pray that no such

calamity should befal the country as that a jury should not find a man guilty when the law and evidence say that he is guilty. It is claimed that the people are disloyal, and politicians are for their own purposes agitating the removal of the capital, and nothing would please them better than to be able to say, when Congress meets in November, that Washington is disloyal, and will not convict one who is proved to have been an assassin of the President. They will say ; Let us move the capital where our public officers will be protected.

Surratt is either guilty or he is not guilty. If he is not guilty, then a great wrong has been done him by the Pope, who surrendered him, and the grand jury who indicted him. I would ask a verdict only upon the evidence, and upon nothing else ; and in referring to the evidence I would not give my own conclusions, but would read this evidence. We have recently made a purchase in Russian America, and suppose two go out there on an exploring expedition, and find a baby in the forest wrapped in a blanket, the conclusion would be that it was placed there by some one, and in telling of it afterwards would not be necessary to prove that the baby had a father and mother, and that it was put there by some one. Rev. Stephen Cameron might come and swear he saw babies grow there like toadstools under a tree, or Bissell might swear he saw spiders weaving a blanket and wrapping the baby, but the jury would not believe them. It would be a fact not demanding demonstration that the baby was placed there by some one.

It is a truth that a man could not be in two places at the same time, and that need not be proven. It is known, too, that when a man is on trial for his life he has every motive to swear falsely and to make misrepresentations. On criminal trials there is no effort more frequently put forth than to prove an ALIBI, and there is nothing upon which so many mistakes may be made as upon proof of this nature, for honest witnesses think truly that they see the person charged at a time and place stated. Cases were called to show the many mistakes in proof, and the case of Webster for the murder of Parkman was referred to. It is the easiest thing in the world to prove you see an individual, but the day cannot always be positively fixed. The gentleman on the other side pretend that they can see no difference between the murder of the President and that of an ordinary man. That is not the view of statesmen; it is not the view of the Bible or of the law. It is a greater crime to murder a President, because of the consequences it tends to. All Governments are of God or of the devil, and this Government is of God. What did the civilized world think of this murder? It takes a large volume to contain the letters of condolence. It was a crime that induced all nations, even the Turk, to write in condemnation of the crime. Even the rebels thought it was a greater crime to kill the President than a vagabond.

There are a class of persons put upon the stand who are known as experts, and it is now a recognized principle that no man can successfully disguise his handwriting for any length of time, and it is a well ascertained fact that such is the case. A man's walk or talk cannot be successfully disguised, and it is a truth of general things. Each man is an expert in his own business, and in all trades and callings men are experts in particular things, and they are called on to give their opinions. It is just as true that there are experts in moral relations. A lawyer should be an expert in detecting the spurious witness from the witness who is just and true; and now let us apply these principles to the facts in the case. Men do not commit crimes without an object. We must look to see a motive where we find a thing done contrary to the course of human events. In March 1863 Mrs. Surratt was keeping a tavern in Surrattsville. The husband died in 1862, and the family had but little means. In 1864 the mother moved to Washington and opened a boarding-house. The oldest son was a rebel soldier in Texas; the youngest son was a man grown, in no employ, and he came to Washington with his mother.

Now let us see what were the sentiments of that family in 1864, and the sentiments that resulted in Mr. Lincoln's death. In March, 1863, Harold was with John Surratt at Surrattsville, and in 1864, John Surratt, Mudd, Harold, and Booth were together at the National Hotel. This was Surratt's first introduction to Booth, and I will trace this conspiracy from its beginning to its termination.

All that about the farm to be purchased was nonsense, for the purchase of the farm needed no explanation. This interview was in December, 1864, and this brings us to a more important matter, which is the testimony of Mr. Donn, the cashier of Adams

Express Company, who testifies to Surratt's employment by Adams' Express Company, his request for a leave of absence, and the refusal of the leave.

In this connection, we have a little piece of paper in Surratt's hand-writing. It is a card written by Surratt to Booth, in which he says; "I tried to get leave, and did not succeed." So he took the leave. This gentlemen [to Mr. Merrick], is no magic chain —it is a fact. Now, in this connection we come to Mr. Martin's testimony, who was on his way to get cotton out from the Confederacy, and who testified that he employed, at Port Tobacco a man named Atzerott to ferry him across the Potomac. There Mr. Martin saw Surratt. This was in January, 1864, and Martin says Surratt told him he was in Adams' Express Company, and he had leave of absence all of which the jury knows to be false, and the story was told for purposes of concealment. It is well known that Surratt had no leave of absence. Martin also testifies to a preparation of relays of horses for a large party. What was all that preparation for, and why did Surratt return to Washington at night? We now come down again to an order of dates, and there is much to give in dates. I hold here a register of the Maitby house, Baltimore. On January 21, 1864, you find Surratt and Weichman's names registered there. This is three or four days after Surratt was at Port Tobacco. What does all this mean? Nothing strange that Weichman and Surratt should have been in Baltimore, but one truth is in harmony with the other, and what truth follows next?

Let us again look at the evidence. [Weichman's testimony of the visit to Baltimore read, in which it appears that Surratt had $300 in his possession, and he went to see some one on private business, and he did not want Weichman along.] Now, who, asked Mr. Pierrepont, was that somebody? Let us read the testimony of Mrs. Bronson, who says that at that time Payne was boarding with her in Baltimore, and the visit of Surratt is explained. There is another link in that chain. Afterwards, Payne comes to Mrs. Surratt's house in Washington. This is the same Payne who assaulted Mr. Seward, and who was captured in Mrs. Surratt's house.

[Weichman's testimony again referred to, to show Surratt's intimacy with Atzerott, and that he was introduced there by Surratt

after the visit to Port Tobacco. The testimony in relation to Surratt's visit to New
York in February, to see Booth, was also
read, also the testimony as to Payne's visits
to the Surratt house.

The first time that Payne ever comes to
this house, he is shown to a private room
and given supper by order of Mrs. Surratt.
This occurs after Surratt's visit to Baltimore,
and after Payne had left Mrs. Bronson's, in
Baltimore.

[Weichman's testimony referred to as to
Payne's second visit, he represented himself
as a baptist preacher.] In this connection,
Weichman's testimony of Surratt and Payne
practicing with bowie knives was recited, as
well as the visit to the theatre on the night
Booth played PESCARA, in "The Apostate."
In commenting upon this testimony, Mr. Pierrepont said there was less than a month before
Booth enacted another drama, in which he
played assassin, traitor and murderer, as
well as apostate. Miss Honorah Fitzpatrick's
testimony relative to the visit of the conspirators at Mrs. Surratt's, and relative to the
visit at the theatre, as also the evidence in
relation to Mrs. Surratt's visit to the Herndon House, in this Mr. Pierrepont said it will
be seen Miss Fitzpatrick corroborates Weichman, and it will be shown that the Herndon
House was where John Surratt secured a room
for Weichman about this time. On "March
23, 1865," Booth telegraphs to Weichman as
follows: "Tell John to telegraph number
and street at once." Why did not Booth
telegraph to John at once? Because he
wanted to be as secret as possible, and he
wanted to send the information through a
third party. [Testimony on this point was
referred to.] Weichman showed the telegram
to John and when he asks about it, John tells
Weichman not to be so d— d inquisitive. The
number and street referred to the Herndon
House, and Surratt afterwards goes there and
secures the room that had been previously
engaged, and the name of the party for whom
the room was engaged was not mentioned.
Now the mystery is unravelled. Mrs. Surratt
goes to the Herndon House and engages the
room, and John goes there and secures it, and
that is the room to which Payne is to be
brought, and to which Booth is to communicate.

Mr. Bradley, Jr., said it was the rule of the
court not to allow counsel to be interrupted,
but he asked, if facts were misstated, whether
an opportunity would be afforded of correct-
ing the misstatements.

Judge Fisher replied affirmatively.

Mr. Pierrepont said he did not intend to
give an opportunity for correction, and for
that reason he read the testimony carefully.

The reading of Weichman's testimony was
then resumed, to show Mrs. Surratt's, second
visit to the Herndon house, when she said
she was going to see Payne; about the anger
of Mrs. Surratt when she ascertained that
Atzerott had informed him that it was Payne
who was at the Herndon House. Also, as to
the refusal of Atzerott and Payne to loan
Mrs. Surratt the horses; and with reference
to John Surratt's conversation on April 3,
1865, when he said he had been to Richmond;
the exchange of gold by Surratt at that
time, &c.

The defendant, John Surratt, was always
well supplied with money, and yet he was a
poor young man who was not in employment
and whose mother had no means. We now
come to the testimony of Brook Stabler,
the livery stable keeper. Stabler's testimony was read. In this testimony it appears that Surratt wrote to Stabler, saying
he had women on the brain. Was that so?
Had he women on the brain, and if he had
was old Brook Stabler the depositary for a
secret of love, or was this only said for a
blind? Where did Surratt get money to
carry on all these schemes and to buy horses?
He was without means and his mother was
a poor woman, as the jury had been told.
Where then did he get his money to buy
horses and to keep them at livery? He did
not get it from Adam's Express Company,
for he left there without permission. [Stab-
ler's testimony again referred to.] In this
it appears Surratt got a letter from Atzerott.
but would not show Stabler the contents;

The testimony of James Humphrey, relative to Booth's having a horse, and Surratt
becoming security for Booth, and the testimony of Fletcher, who had charge of Nailor's
stable, was read. Here it appears that Atzerott could not keep his secret, for he says to
Fletcher that, "if this thing happens to-night,
you will here of a present." Fletcher suggests he would not like to ride the horse that
night, and Atzerott replies that he is good on
a retreat. Harold that same night got a horse
at Nailor's.

Lieutenant Taffey in his testimony shows
what became of Atzerott's horse, for he found
him at Lincoln Barracks, the morning of April
15th. Another witness is Samuel Rainey,
also a livery stable keeper, and he testifies to
Surratt and booth getting horses in common

from his stable William E. Cleaver, who was a partner of Raine's, corroborates the latter. Booth brought his horse to Cleaver's stable on January 1st, 1865. The horse then brought was a dark bay, blind of one eye. He also testifies to seeing Surratt and Booth there together, and also that at one time Booth and Sam. Arnold came there together. The defence say because Cleaver has shown himself a man of passion, in a certain way, that he cannot tell the truth, I appeal to the jury, as sensible men, to say whether such a fact need necessarily prevent a man's truth —a man might be passionate in one way or the other, and yet be strictly truthful. Cleaver has gone into minute particulars, and in none has he been contradicted ; but on the contrary, he has been corroborated. On one occasion it was raining badly, and Cleaver says Surratt came aud hired a horse, and said he was going to "T. B." to a dance; but he afterwards said he was going to help some men across, but he then said in Cleaver's presence that he and Booth had bloody work to do, and that they purposed killing the President : and Surratt then said flourishing his pistol, that if Booth did not kill the President he [Surratt] would do it himself, I will have occasion to refer to Cleaver again, and show how this testimony was got out of Cleaver. The defence might heap as much abuse as they wanted to upon Mr. Ashley, but Cleaver was not to blame in this matter. He was an Englishman, and an enemy of this Government, and he did not wish to say a word ; but in the confidence of the cell, he told it to a fellow-prisoner. In some way or other a member of Congress got hold of it and informed Mr. Carrington, and Cleaver's testimony was forced out of him by power, and he did not wish to give it willingly. But now we come to an extraordinary witness in this case, John M. Lloyd, who testified in the most unwilling manner. Mr. Bradley had said he believed Lloyd was in the conspiracy, and he had said he was a drunkard. There is no doubt but that he did drink, but he was not drunk when he was on the stand, nor was he drunk when the detectives went by the morning of the murder. He kept the tavern for Mrs. Surratt, and was a most unwilling witness, and Mr. Bradley was no doubt correct when he said Lloyd was one of the conspirators. He was just the man to engage in such a conspiracy, and just the man to assist at the ...ion. He was no doubt in the con-

spiracy. But that. I contend did not make him the less truthful, nor did it give less importance to his testimony, for it was given too unwillingly, as the jury will remember. [John M. Lloyd's testimony was here read.] In commenting upon Lloyd's testimony, I reiterate the remark that he believed Mr. Bradley stated truly when he said Lloyd knew all about the conspiracy. When Surratt put the arms in his keeping, he k ew that there was mischief. He knew enough to make him guilty, and to make him liable. This witness says he met Mrs. Surratt on the Tuesday before the assassination, and he says she told him that the shooting irons were wanted that night. How did Mrs. Surratt know that her son had secreted the shooting irons in that secret room behind the joist of the house? Why did Lloyd speak of burying the shooting irons? He spoke of it as one would speak of burying a murdered corpse. Again Mrs. Surratt visited Lloyd at Surrattsville on April 14, the day of the assassination, and she handed him a package, which has been traced and proven to be a fieldglass. Mrs. Surratt also tells Lloyd to have the guns ready and two bottles of whisky, and give them to whoever should call for them that night. What will you do with this testimony, gentlemen of the jury ? Will you discard it? If so you will no doubt tell your fellow-citizens why when you come out . What was expected to be done that night, that the guns and the whisky would be needed ? The assassination occurred at ten o'clock, and at twelve Harold was at Lloyd's and the jury will remember how reluctant Lloyd was to tell that Booth was with Harold. Harold was impatient, and demanded in haste the whisky and the arms, and Lloyd strove all the time to keep Booth separated from Harold. The jury will remember the struggle to get from this witness who Harold's companion was. It will be remembered too how he persisted in not answering the question as to when he first heard of the assassination until the Court compelled him to answer, and then he drawled out that he heard it that night. He does not remember who told him, but he thought it was the man who had the broken leg, who said the President was assassinated.

Why did not Lloyd wish to talk about the assassination ?

He gives as a reason because he feared Mrs Surratt's name would be drawn in. Mrs. Surratt had gone to Lloyd in the day time, and had given orders relative to the arms and the bottle of whisky, and Lloyd had a good reason for saying that he feared Mrs. Surratt's name would be brought in. Lloyd said he did not dare to drink when he was about to go into a court to testify, because he feared he would say something he should not say. The jury saw this reluctant witness on the stand, and knew that he was not intoxicated when he testified here. Lloyd's testimony was further read to show that the prisoner and Harold were together when the arms were secreted, and that they were engaged together in the transaction.

Weichman's testimony in relation to taking the field-glass to Surratt on April 14, was read. This was the day of the murder, said Mr. Pierrepont, and Mrs. Surratt and Booth were then engaged in conversation just before they started from the House on H street for Surrattsville.

The testimony relating to the trip to Surrattsville was also read, to show that on the way to Surrattsville Mrs. Surratt expressed gratification at the removal of the pickets during the night.

The testimony of Callenback's finding the guns ; of Thompson, who testified to Harold's bringing guns to his house, saying, that he expected John Surratt, and the testimony of Morton corroborative of Thompson, were read.

At this time, Harold's excuse was that he was going to the Patuxent to shoot ducks, and it would be perceived that he and the others always had some excuse. Now we see how the guns came to Lloyd. Surratt concealed the guns. After the assassination Harold got the guns; and when Booth was killed they were taken from his possession. The defence have asked the prosecution to connect the circumstances, and this about the guns had been connected. How did Mrs. Surratt know about the guns? She was not there when Harold took them or when Surratt had them. How did she find it out on that day of the murder, when she took the glass there, that the guns and the glass would be wanted that night? How did she know of the concealment but from her son? Old Mr. Watson, who was called here by the defence, said he believed Mrs. Surratt was guilty, and he believed so yet, and he was about to say he was satisfied from the evidence, when he was stopped by Mr. Merrick.

Mrs. Surratt could not get the information from any one but her own son, a full grown man, who had secreted the guns. The opinion must be that of Mr. Watson, that all were guilty—Harold, Mrs. Surratt and all. The knowledge of secreting the guns came from none but the prisoner. Justice Piles, of Prince George, testifies that John Surratt came there to him to have some papers signed. [Pile's testimony was here read.] What these papers were we don't know, but, they mean something, or the papers would have been explained.

[The testimony of David Barry was read.] This witness brought the horses back that Surratt took to Port Tobacco, after the latter had taken Mrs. Slater down to get her across the river. Mr. Barry had two sons in the rebel army, but he told the truth and connected Surratt with the conspiracy.

Rebel though he was, he told the truth. All men of honor will tell the truth. It is but the coward who is afraid to do his duty. It is the innocent who is bold as a lion. A brave man always tells the truth, and I would be willing to submit the case to twelve brave Confederate prisoners.

We come now to the testimony of Mr. Smoot, who was a reluctant witness. Whether he was terrified by Mr. Merrick's saying he was after him with a sharp stick or not, I do not know, but he was certain the witness was either terrified or reluctant, because there was difficulty in getting him here. When we did get him on the stand he testified in a very reluctant and evasive manner. Surratt tells Mr. Smoot, in January or February, that if the Yankees knew what he was doing they would stretch his neck. What did he mean ? Did he think they would stretch his neck because he lived in Washington ? or because he was conscious of the conspiracy in which he was engaged? Why did not the counsel bring out why Surratt was fearful that his neck would be stretched ? The crime was not to be kept secret. " Out of the abundance of the heart the mouth speaketh," and Surratt realized of what he was guilty, and this realization, ever present with him, made him give utterance to the remark about stretching of his neck.

One of these witnesses has said he saw Surratt on April 3, [Weichman's testimony was again referred to.] Surratt and Weichman walked down the street, and Surratt said he was going to Montreal. It further appears from Weichman's testimony that Booth promised money to Mrs. Surratt to hire horses to go the country. On April 3, 1865,

Surratt left home at 7 o'clock. He had returned from T, B. in the afternoon. He went out with Weichman, and they parted, and there is no proof that he went in the house that night. He was not seen there by Weichman or any one else. I call attention to this to show that. Susan Jackson could not see Surratt there that night, nor were there any clothes there then to be washed, but it was afterwards. Susan Jackson says that on Friday night some clothes were left on the bed. It was on Friday night, April 14, and after nine o'clock at night. The next week Hollohan goes there and finds the clothes lying on the bed. The defence brought out that and did not know what a terrible fact they were bringing out. Weichman testifies that on April 14, when he left Surrattsville, Mrs. Surratt was anxious to get home at nine o'clock and said she wanted to meet some gentlemen at her house, but she did not say who. [Weichman's testimony as to Mrs. Surratt's remarks about the joy being turned into mourning was read.] No doubt Mrs. Surratt felt so for she had just left Lloyd. Why did she say and feel that? Because she knew what plot was to be carried into execution and she could not help saying, "All this joy will be turned into mourning." feeling an oppressive weight, she gave utterance to this remark.

Remember, this was at night, and it was nine o'clock when they arrived home. They arrived at nine o'clock, not earlier, as they did on April 3. That night while Weichman was at Surratt's, a step ascended the stairs. Mrs. Surratt was restless, and was walking up and down the room with beads in her hands, and she asked Weichman to pray for her intentions. In this Weichman is in part corroborated by Miss Fitzpatrick, who says Mrs. Surratt was walking up and down, but she did not hear her conversation with Weichman.

[Weichman's testimony of Booth's frequent visits at Mrs. Surratt's was read; also, the testimony in relation to the telegrams from Booth.❡ The telegram to McLaughlin was read. The letters written by Surratt to different parties were read, as showing that all were written by the same person. Weichman's testimony in relation to Surratt's statements was read.]

I contend that all the statements were for purposes of deception. There was no truth in the statement about the oil speculation. The oil they wanted was the blood of the murdered Lincoln. Now we come to a portion of the testimony which seems remote from this case, but which has a bearing upon it.

Mr. Pierrepont then referred to the political state of the country in 1860, and said a certain class in the South wanted Mr. Lincoln elected in order that they might rebel. Various plots were entered into and finally Mr. Lincoln was inaugurated, and then rebellion commenced. The South found a feeling in favor of the old flag, and these plots were formed for the purpose of plunging us into confusion. The first plan was to kidnap the President, but that was too complicated, and they then wanted him assassinated. The scheme of abducting was early abandoned, and this conspiracy was commenced in 1863, and the South hoped the Government would be overthrown and that they could walk into this capitol. Then what occurred? Mr. Lincoln had gone on in power, and the Government was succeeding, but there was a bitter feeling, and many thought the Government was not conducted properly. This in the South led to the belief that if Mr. Lincoln was assassinated there would be such confusion in the North as would give the South the mastery.

In 1864, as early as April, Mrs. McClernand was standing on the avenue and heard three men talking together. She heard them speak of the telescopic rifle. She heard the allusion to the wife and child of the President, and she says who those men were. Now, who was Harold? Booth said he was a boy. Booth had a sort of romantic gallantry about him, and he wanted to shield all who were connected with him. He even wanted to come out and fight all of Colonel Conger's regiment. He wanted to sell his life as dearly as possible. Now, who was Harold, and why was he brought in? He was a weak boy, and had neither courage or genius. He was a drug clerk in the store where Mr. Lincoln got his medicines, and it was supposed he could do the work with poison, and he was brought into the conspiracy. Once in, they had to keep him in. He was out of employment, and the conspirators could not discharge him—for it will be remembered that he was discharged from the drug store in 1864—and he was kept in the conspiracy until he was captured and disposed of by the Military Commission.

Upon reassembling, Mr. Pierrepont resumed and said I now come to a strange act in this dark drama; strange, though not new: so wonderful that it seems to come from beyond the veil that separates us from death. It is not new, but it is strange. All governments are of God, and for some wise purpose the great Ruler of all, by presentiments, portents, bodings, and by dreams, sends some shadowy warning of a coming dawn when a great disaster is to befal a nation. So it was in the days of Saul—when Cæsar was killed—when Brutus died at Phillippi. So was it when Christ was crucified. So was it when Harold fell at the battle of Hastings. So was it before the bloody death of Abraham Lincoln, President of the United States. In the "Life of Cæsar," by Dr. Quincy, in the "Life of Pompey," by Plutarch, is given the portents come to warn Pompey. Here it is we find how Cæsar was warned. We find it true in all cases, and never in the whole history has there been a single instance where the assassin of the head of a Government has not been brought to punishment. The assassin of a ruler never has escape,d though he has "taken the wings of the morning and fled to the uttermost parts of the earth," On the morning of April 14 Mr. Lincoln called his cabinet together.

He had reason to be thankful, but he was anxious to hear from Sherman. Grant was here, and he said Sherman was all right, but Mr. Lincoln feared, and related a dream he had had the night before—a dream which he had had previous to Chancellorsville and Stone river, and whenever a disaster had happened. The members of the Cabinet who heard that relation will never forget it. A few hours afterwards Sherman was not heard from, but the dream of Mr. Lincoln was fulfilled : a disaster had befallen the Government, and Mr. Lincoln's spirit returned to the God who gave it. The dream was fulfilled. Here, said Mr. Pierrepont, holding up a paper, is a letter which you have seen before. It is the letter found by Mrs. Benson, then Mrs. Hudspeth. Upon the letter is an endorsment, "General Dix," written in Mr.Lincoln's own hand.

Mrs. Hudspeth found the letter on November 14, and it is proven Booth was in New York at that time. [Mrs. Hudspeth's testimony read; the letters found by Mrs. Hudspeth were read.] I say these letters would show what was meant by a change of plan. At one time Payne was to kill Lincoln, at another time an Englishman was to kill him. Lastly, Mr. Booth was to kill him. The Charles Sebly letter was written by Booth,

as was proven, and the letter was written to Payne. They had cast lots as they did with Christ, and it fell to the lot of Payne to commit the deed. Mr. Lincoln had just been elected, and it was necessary to remove him. In this it appears the plan again changed, and it was stated the cup had once failed. Who is the English Harcourt who is mentioned in the letter? It was not Payne. Payne was instructed to get an introduction and listen to Mr. Lincoln's stories, and he was urged not to fail. Now let us see the contents of Payne's wife's letter to him. It is the letter of an affectionate wife who did not know her husband was in a plot to commit murder. There is truth in that letter. General Dix thought it was true, and sent the letter to President Lincoln.

Mr. Lincoln received many threatening letters, but he paid no heed to them and kept none of them. When Mr. Lincoln received these letters he went to the War Office with them and entered Secretary Stanton's private room.

Mr. Bradley, interrupting, said he hoped Mr. Pierrepont would confine himself to the evidence.

Mr. Pierrepont said the fact he now proposed to speak of was not in evidence, but it was proper for him to relate the history of this strange transaction. The letter made a deep impression on the mind of the Secretary of War, and after Mr. Lincoln's death he found the letter in the President's private drawer, and he immediately supposed it had some connection with the murder.

Mr. Bradley said that was what he objected to. The statement of the impression made upon any one.

Mr. Pierrepont said he stated the impression as part of the history of this dark transaction. These letters were dropped by Booth, and it all shows the change of plan. In 1864 it was a plan to murder ; then Payne was to get introduced, and afterwards Booth was to do the murder. It was a plan to murder from the beginning, for the plan to abduct required too many men, and they were compelled to resort to murder.

We now come to the letter addressed to Booth and found after his death at the National Hotel. It is dated South Branch Bridge, and speaks of the oil speculation. The letter is dated April 6, 1865. In this letter Booth is ordered to sink deep and see that his helpers worked. Who were Booth's helper's? We have one of them on trial now. But, after sinking his well he is told to run. Why run after he has struck oil? Why not stop and gather up? But the letter speaks of putting a poor man named Purdy out of the way. He is not satisfied with hiring a girl to charge Purdy with an outrage, but he now asks if he shall be silenced for good. What a nest of assassins have we here? Yet the counsel say we have had blood enough, and they ask a magnanimous Government to let these murderers go. The letter also speaks of Jake having funds. Jake had the funds, and he was using them in Canada; and Surratt was carrying the funds from Richmond to Montreal for Jake; and if the conspiracy had succeeded, the funds would have been divided.

[Weichman's testimony relative to what transpired at Mrs. Surratt's after the assassination, when the Government officers came, was read.] Mrs. Surratt said she expected the Government officers would search the house. Why did she expect it? Because she had seen Lloyd and told him about the guns, and she had but a short time before taken tea alone with her son. When Webster killed Dr. Parkman, he cut him up, and when told that the body had been proved, he asked at once " has all the body been found?" Who else but the murderer would have asked that question, and Mrs. Surratt said she knew the house was to be searched, because she knew what had happened.

That night it was supposed that Surratt had murdered Mr. Seward. None then doubted that Surratt was here that night; and what does Mrs. Surratt say when informed of Mr. Lincoln's murder, and Annie Surratt begins to cry? Why, she says that she believed Booth was in the hands of the Almighty. Booth seemed to have the same idea, as appears from his diary. These people had worked themselves up to such a frenzy that they supposed they were doing God's service. [The testimony of Major Smith, who was sent from Gen. Augur's to Mrs. Surratt's, was read.] It was at this time that Payne came to Mrs. Surratt's, and professed to want to get instructions to dig a ditch, and when Mrs. Surratt disclaimed all knowledge of the man. Major Smith also says he saw Susan Jackson there.

Mr. Merrick the other day asked why the prosecution did not show that Susan had said something of John Surratt on the night of the murder? The prosecution did try to bring it out, but was stopped by an objection from the defence, which was sustained. The gentle-

man must have forgotten when he spoke of this testimony not having been brought out, nor would the defence permit the fact to go in that Major Smith had made a written report. Major Smith's testimony is corroborated by that of Capt. Wirmerschercher, who says that Mrs. Surratt declared before God that she did not know Payne. She had risen from her knees, and then called God to witness that she did not know the man. Human nature is weak, and under the circumstances let us cast, if we can, a veil of charity over all this, but she did deny ever having seen Payne. [Col. Mungan's testimony was read as corroborative of Major Smith's.]

Now all this time where was John Surratt? No man can be in two places at the same time. That fact needs no proof. Surratt was somewhere. Two points are fixed. He left Montreal on the 12th, and returned on the 18th. All these things were done between the 14th and 18th, and where was John Surratt? They could tell you every hour where John Surratt was after the 18th, but they can't tell where he was between the 14th and 18th. Why not tell that? He slept somewhere, and stayed somewhere. They can give us his place for five months, and on those other days they can't tell us where he was. Why not? Why do they throw a veil of night over these six awful days. He knows where he was, and yet he does not tell us one place.

Dr. Bissell says where Surratt was, but he will be noticed hereafter. But where was Surratt? The books say they must show where the person was. Have they shown where he was, or where he staid? They won't tell us where he was, and let us see if we cant find out. I am sure where Surratt was, and. I think the jury will be sure when they heard the evidence read. The defence put Mr. Dubarry on the stand to show that there was no communication between Elmira and Washington. Mr. Bradley contended that it was a physical impossibility for Surratt to reach here. The prosecution had to prove that this was not so, and they had great difficulty in getting the railroad men here. Impediments were thrown in the way, and it was so stated, and that statement got into the papers, and after it got into the papers it had an effect, as will be shown. [Dubarry's first testimony was then read.] Mr. Dubarry told all about the schedule time, but he did not say anything about the special train, and in law a man who suppresses the truth tells as great a lie as he who tells a deliberate falsehood.

Mr. Dubarry said he did not know that any train left on April 13, and he did not know that he was in Elmira on that day. This leaves the fact without testimony bearing upon it. Mr. Dubarry said there was no record of a train running specially, but he did not know that no train had run.

We made the time perfect by producing the engineers who ran the trains. [Dubarry's testimony when called a second time was read.] We brought Surratt to the ferry, and Drohan, who ferried a man across, identified Surratt as the man. It was expected the defence would cross-examine him, but they did not. They acted wisely and well, for if they had examined him he would have brought out and clinched the fact. Mr. Dubarry was called again after it was stated in the papers that a railroad was throwing all impediments in the way. Mr. Dubarry was a witness for the defence, but we called him, and when Mr. Dubarry's memory was refreshed he told all he knew, and he then recollected he was in Elmira on the 12th and 13th. Mr Dubarry, on this second turn, testifies that the train leaving Elmira on the 13th would reach Baltimore at 7.25 —and the gentleman's physical impossibility vanishes into thin air. All physical impossibilities vanish when they are opposed to truth. Now Mr. Koontz testifies that the train got here that morning at ten o'clock.

Mr. Bradley. Now get him to the barber-shop and have him shaved by nine o'clock.

Mr. Pierrepont. We will get him to the barber-shop and have him shaved without a quiver. We will give him such a clean shave that he will never want another.

Mr. Pierrepont then resumed and examined the testimony of Mr. Strayer, who ran the special train on April 13, and he illustrated the route travelled by a map fixed upon the wall. In coming down, Strayer meets Rogers going up, and they have a conversation about Mr Dubarry. Mr. Rogers, who was going up, corroborates Strayer and says he met him at Troy, twenty-five miles south of Williamsport. Mr. Glines, who had charge of the ferry, testified to the running of construction trains on April 13, and Mr. Hepburn, the trainmaster, testifies to the same effect. [The testimony of the railroad men was read. Drohan's testimony read, relative to the ferrying of Surratt across the river at Williamsport.] Drohan's face did not look like that of a man who told a lie. and they offered no evidence to show that he ever did tell a lie.

How did the defence treat that witness? Mr. Bradley says to him : " That's all ; get down from that stand ; we want no more of you." Mr. Carrington calls that acting. I do not know whether it was or not, but it is certain they now have Surratt upon a train which could bring him to Washington. Their witnesses did not come here willingly, but they were brought here, and they told what they knew, and their testimony will stand the test of truth when we all stand befor the bar of God.

Now we come to Mr. Wood's testimony. Mr. Wood was put upon the stand early in the trial, and the defence could have found out all about him if they had desired to do so. They probably did find out who he was, but they did not attempt to question his character. This witness identified the prisoner positively. He says the prisoner was dirty and travel-soiled, and he was, because he had just come from Baltimore. The jury saw the witness on the stand, and they know his appearance was that of a man who told the truth. He went into minute particulars, and gave a correct account. We have now got rid of all the physical impossibilities, and now come to the moral of the case.

We now come to the testimony of Judge Olin, a member of this court, in reference to the appearance of the box when examined by him. [Judge Olin's testimony read.] Now, gentleman, that examination showed that the bar was put there just shortly before the act was done. It is one of the little circumstances going to confirm the testimony of Mr. Rhodes. The shavings must have been left on the floor just a short time, because the box had previously been swept, cleaned, and garnished to receive the head of the nation. [Cleaver's testimony relative to meeting Surratt on the street on April 14 was read.] Cleaver knew Surratt, and he cannot be mistaken: either he told the truth or he committed wilful perjury. He could not be mistaken.

Now how did the Government get hold of this testimony? He did not give it willingly. He gave a reason on the stand, that he was inclined to shield Surratt. Cleaver was an Englishman, and an enemy of this Goverment, and he wanted to shield Surratt. He would never have told of this unless Conover had told on him. The subject was forced out of Cleaver, much against his will, by Mr. Ashley, a member of Congress and a member of the Judiciary Committee. [Mr. Pierrepont here read further from Cleaver's testimony.] Cleaver gave this information in confidence to his fellow prisoner Conover, and Conover told it to Ashley. He was a friend to Surratt, and did not wish to implicate him. Referring to Mr. Reed's testimony, I find that Reed said he was as sure of seeing Surratt as he was of standing on the witness stand.

Mr. Merrick asked where that testimony was found.

Mr. Pierrepont said Reed had testified to it, and it is here [taking up a book of the conspiracy trial.]

Mr. Merrick. Not there, sir. You must speak of the testimony in this case.

Judge Fisher said Mr. Pierrepont could speak of anything brought out on this trial.

Mr. Pierrepont I contend that Reed's testimony was plain and to the point, and must be believed, also the testimony of B. W. Vanderpool, who, he said, a member of the "Lone Star Club" of which Booth was also a member, and he had an opportunity of knowing Booth. He swears to seeing Booth and the prisoner together in the concert saloon on the afternoon of the day of the assassination. He does not say there was any performances going on there. He simply says he saw one woman dancing. He could not be mistaken, and he was positive he saw Surratt. Now, how did they attempt to discredit Vanderpool? Did they do it by showing he did not go to the concert hall, or that he did not go to the Paymaster's office? Not at all. But they attempted to discredit him by showing there was no performances at a place called Metropolitan Hall, on D street. Nothing was said about D street or about an afternoon performance. They asked about all the halls on the north side of the avenue and in D street, but they did not say a word about Teutonia Hall, which is at the south side of Pennsylvania avenue. Vanderpool said it was along there some place, but he could not recollect the name. Teutonia Hall is the only one on Pennsylvania avenue, and it was there Vanderpool went, and there he saw Surratt. A witness called by the defence themselves says there was a rehearsal at Teutonia Hall, and that there were round

tables there, and in this Vanderpool is corroborated.

I now refer to the testimony of John Lee, who swears he recognized Surratt on April 14, and he says Surratt had then no goatee. This is in harmony with Wood's testimony, and there is no testimony here that is not in harmony with all other testimony, because it is all true. Again, Grillo swears to seeing Surratt. He is not positive, but he thinks the prisoner is the man. He had walked up to Willard's with Harold, and there he saw Surratt.

Mr. Coleman testifies that on that afternoon of April 14 he saw Booth in conversation with a man whom he at this trial thinks was the prisoner at the bar. [Taltanil's testimony was here read.] This testimony I contend, confirms Sergeant Dye relative to the lights in front of the theatre. The testimony of Susan Jackson was referred to, and Mr. Pierrepont argued that simple-minded people were more apt to tell the truth and to give a clearer statement than the more educated; and it is well known that a plain, simple story cannot be embarrassed by any cross-examination.

[Susan Jackson's testimony read.] Susan says on Friday of the assassination she took some of John Surratt's clothes to wash, and she is corroborated by Hollahan, who afterwards found Surratt's clothes cleanly washed on the bed. Did this woman make up this story about the clothes, or did counsel tell her thus to testify? No; but it dropped from her plain and simple, as all truth drops out. She then saw John Surratt and had a conversation as to who he looked like. It occurred on April 14, and not upon April 2, as counsel for defence attempted to show. It was in proof that on April 2 Surratt left the house before seven o'clock, and did not return that night, and the time Susan Jackson testifies was 9 o'clock. Surratt left on April 2, and returned April 14. When asked if she was examined elsewhere, Susan Jackson said she was, and it was attempted to show that she had been examined and the counsel for defence would not permit it to be brought out. The witness is positive it was the Friday night, Mr. Surratt came from the country, and the night of the assassination that she saw Surratt. In all the cross-examination she insisted upon the same thing, and she could not be embarrassed in telling her simple story. There were persons in that house on Friday night who knew whether Surratt was there or not, and why were they not put upon the stand?

But this testimony is not all as to Surratt's presence here, for Mr. Heleton, a clerk in the Land Office, saw him in front of Ford's Theatre. And this brings us to the testimony of Sergeant Dye. He was one of the earliest witnesses in this case, and yet he has not been impeached. It is true something was said about his passing counterfeit money. He did not know whether the counsel knew of the whole record. He hoped they did not; but he had the record, which shows that the charge against Dye was erroneous, and that it was dismissed by the prosecuting attorney of Philadelphia as soon as he heard the circumstances. Here is that record [holding up a piece of paper], and here is the affidavit of the very man who preferred the charge against Dye. He hoped the counsel for the defence did not know of this record, or they would not have done such injustice as had been done to a brave soldier.

Mr. Merrick said they had not seen the record.

Mr. Pierrepont said he knew they had not.

Mr. Merrick said when he said the defence would impeach Dye, that record was not in existence; it was obtained afterwards: and the District Attorney of Philadelphia had dismissed the case.

Mr. Pierrepont said he knew the gentleman did not know of the record, or they would not have done Dye injustice.

[Dye's testimony was here read.]

In commenting upon Dye's testimony, it was no wonder Surratt should have a pallid face that night, because their great deed was about to be committed. Why should Mrs. Surratt, as Dye was passing, ask what was going on down town, unless she had known what it was intended should be done? It was an evidence of guilt, for up in that neighborhood the night was quiet, and no one seemed to have heard of the assassination, for Dye first gave the information to the policeman. Wherever you find witnesses not situated alike, and they tell the same thing, you may be sure the story is made up, for no two men hear or see exactly alike; but as in this case, where all tends to the same end, the testimony varies a little. The witnesses are more to be relied on. Now we have come to this point: that three men see Booth and Surratt before the theatre; Booth goes into the drinking-house and takes a drink, when the last time is called, and then goes in and kills the President, who is seeking relaxation from his public duties. It was the very day when he was with General Grant and his Cabinet, and when he was devising the best ways of leniency to heal the people who had been conquered. Mr. Lincoln had but few moments of relaxation, and he sometimes went to the theatre. His great pleasure was to visit the hospitals and the sick soldiers, and this night, when he was sitting beside his wife in the theatre, is selected for this bloody act.

But counsel say we have had blood enough, and they say that a man connected with the plot should be allowed to escape. Is it not time that we put a stop to this murder and assassination? No jury has ever yet passed upon this great crime, but the civilized world has condemned it, and Turks, Infidels, Greeks Arabs, Christians, and Mahommedans—all nations, from sea to sea and from pole to pole —send here their letters of condolence and their words of condemnation of this atrocious crime; and yet counsel say this murder is no more than that of an ordinary man. The murder has been committed, and Booth and Harold flee to the home of Mrs. Surratt, and get the arms prepared for them and left there, and with which they flee. After Mr. Seward had been assassinated, or almost assassinated, it was supposed Surratt did it; but it is now well settled that it was Payne, and after his crime he rushed back to the house of Mrs. Surratt. No jury has yet passed upon the case, but you are going to do it now, and your country, your friends and the world look on to see how that duty will be discharged.

Mr. Pierrepont then spoke of Surratt's flight, and argued that the horse seen by Mr. Ramsdell was the one hired by Atzerott, and that it was ridden away by John H. Surratt. Ramsdell says the man riding the horse was suspicious and nervous. This was just as he appeared upon the steamer, when he was fearful of an American detective clutching him. This horse has never been found, and all the other horses that have appeared in the case have been found.

Mr. Bradley said there was no evidence of that fact.

Mr. Pierrepont insisted that there was evidence of it. The horse has never been found, but the man who rode him has been found. Where did that man go to? We hear of him next on the Burlington boat, then at the depot where the handkerchief was found; then he is recognized by Hobart as having been on the railroad train. [Testimony of Blinn and Hobart read.] Blinn found the handkerchief, and Hobart carried the man on. This was on the 17th, and while Hollahan was in Washington, and before he had got the handkerchief which the defence claims was lost, Hobart, the conductor, corroborates Blinn as to the arrival of the boat. Upon the train Surratt pretends to be a laboring man, just as Payne pretended when he went to Mrs. Surratt's, after he had done his bloody work, and the jury will remember that Surratt told St. Marie that he escaped in disguise. The witness Chapin corroborates Blinn as to the finding of the handkerchief, for he saw the handkerchief the Wednesday afterwards. He saw the handkerchief before Hollohan had any chance to lose his.

On reassembling, Mr. Hobart had shown that the train on which Surratt was, reached Montreal at 9.45, but Surratt did not continue on that train, but left at St. Alban's and went in another direction, and did not reach Montreal until some time afterwards. John Surratt was here in the city of Washington on the night of April 3, and he is registered in St. Lawrence Hall at 10 a. m. on the 6th of April. He could certainly come from Montreal here in the same time that he could go from here to that place. My friends, physical fact is all out of the way again. He wanted to put on the toggery of an Englishman. He left St. Alban's at once, and the next we hear of him he turns up at Montreal, where he registers his name on the hotel books.

Mr. Pierrepont here read from the testimony to the point, and remarked that the prisoner then went across the country and was secreted in Porterfield's house. It was claimed that he was all this time in Elmira. Will they tell why he fled and secreted himself from observation? He read from the history of Cain and Abel, and the curse of the Almighty upon the former, making him a fugitive on the earth. He also read from the testimony of St. Marie, as to the manner of Surratt's getting away from Washington, and the hard time he had of it. Disguised as an Englishman, with a scarf on his shoulder, thus did he escape, and attempted to put off his broken English on Hobart. It has always been said truth is stranger than fiction; the attempt of the defence to prove that Dye was lying, and by the testimony of Gifford to show that Dye was not on that platform, was a dead failure. They also brought Hess to

show that he was calling the time, and was the person whom Dye had heard call the time [He here read from the testimony of Hess, covering his part in the play of that evening.] One lie generates another, till a thousand lies are told, and one cannot tell the difference between one lie and another. I am not afraid of a liar on the witness stand. Hess, in speaking of the time of night, said he was wanted in a few minutes, and immediately went back to the stage. Yet, on cross-examination, he admitted that he was not required until after the play was over. This is all fiction. To show that Dye and Cooper were not on the platform, Hess said if they had been there Gifford would have made them get off.

Mr. Pierrepont here read from the Bible concerning the bearing of false witness, and saying that false testimony never agrees. It cannot get together nor keep that way. The testimony of Dye and Cooper was adverted, to concerning their passing the house of Mrs. Surratt, and the attempt of the defence to contradict it, by the testimony of a Dutchman who was in a house in another street. This man was sitting on the steps, and his testimony was brought to show that the conversation, as related by Dye, did not take place. They did not place his wife on the stand. If they had she would have stated that she put her husband to bed that night, and that previously he had taken a quantity of lager. They also brought Mrs. Lambert to the stand, who said she came out on the porch first, and that afterwards she went to the window and that a great many were passing by. The Dutchman said no one passed. Mrs. Lambert says it was between 11 and 12 o'clock when she talked with the soldier. She meant to be truthful and stated positively the hour. The President was murdered at five or ten minutes after ten o'clock, and by the time Mrs. Lambert was talking with the soldier at her window, Dye and Cooper were at home in their camps.

There was another physical impossibility attempted to be proved by the counsel, and that was the question of getting Surratt from Montreal to Elmira, and going over it all they finally brought him there at 8 o'clock at night on the 13th. Before that they had him there all the time, talking with the people on the day of the 13th. The Government did not try to fix him in Elmira; they had him all the time in Washington.

Mr. Bradley here interposed, saying the

prosecution brought Surratt down the road from Albany. and the defence did not think it necessary to advert to the Ogdensburg road.

Mr. Pierrepont, resuming, said the prosecution put Surratt on no train; they found him in Elmira and brought him to Washington.

Mr. Pierrepont here read from the testimony to show how long Surratt was at St. Lawrence Hall on the 18th, and said there was evidence to show what time he reached there. The fact was, he was at Elmira, and came to Washington, reaching here on 14th. He read from the testimony of Boucher, who first saw the prisoner in St. Laboise. Why did he come to Boucher's house and go by the name of Charles Armstrong? What occasion was there for it? A few days before he registered as John Harrison. If he was innocent, why hide from public view and go under an assumed name? This man Boucher secretes him, and months after Surratt was in Rome, and the head of the church which Boucher so outrageously villifies gave him up, even before he was demanded by the United States authorities. Neither the Pope nor any of that noble Church tolerated that infamous crime, and the shame which Boucher has brought upon his Church will be wiped out by that noble Church itself. Surratt left Boucher's house about the last of July, and then went to the house of La Pierre. Why did he do this? All those who had been arrested had been tried. Surratt knew where his mother was, and he, an innocent man, lies there concealed!

Would not any honest person, if he heard of a charge pending against him, go before the authorities and give himself up, and invite investigation into his alleged crime? Yet when peace has been restored he does not appear, but in disguise goes on board the Peruvian and flies to Rome—a strange land, whose language he understood not. Why did he fly to Egypt? Was he an innocent man? He is not innocent. Boucher should have been wise, and stayed away as Lapierre did. I have been informed, since I have been speaking, that Lapierre has already been punished by his Church.

Mr. Pierrepont continued to read from Boucher's testimony. The learned counsel called him Father Boucher. The jury saw Father Boucher. The speaker thought he never should confess to Father Boucher. There is something wrong about him. He would not long be a reproach to the Church.

They will soon take the jury might be so

Mr. Pierrepont her mony of McMillan, a the history of all crim at some time. Somet times by flight, and s statements. Upon of the testimony befor pont said the prisone over the world to quences of his crime, t had now been broug trial, and it rested wit he was innocent or gui of God it had been jurors to decide upon whether this was a e mitted, or whether if

I am now nearly d 1 would pass to the proved by the defen as the weakest 1 hav in a court of justice. to be-true. There mistakes had grown

The testimony of C witness only relied house as to the date Elmira, and that Ca reference to any oth record. The testimon that Stewart could was in the store on month, and that he of those dates it wa

The testimony of at the store, could on ratt's visit by the ent taken to pay the exp to New York, and it of that partner that S which was either the I can find no fault for I believe they te

The testimony of worthy of belief. Bi ness who testified Surratt in Elmira on of Bissell's testimony was not a word of t mony of Mr. Wetm York, goes to show in Elmira on the 14 was in witnesses of was consulted there Eaton, the counsel in and also shows that Bissell's character had been very much canvassed, and that his reputation was very bad.

Witness after witness followed to show that whenever Bissell went from place to place he bore a blasted name amongst all who knew him. They all gave him the worst reputation, I have ever heard given of a man in a court of justice. I can see through his horny eyes a stream of lies generating perjury in his brain, like flies in a rotten carcass. There was no word of truth in what he said.

Gentlemen, I am now through. I had no expectations of keeping you so long. I cannot express my feelings of gratitude for your kind attention. I have never seen men listen so long and so well. This is a matter affecting us all. You may pass into military rule and have all crimes tried, but you, nor I, nor our children, will have no more protection. Government is for the benefit of society. We have had rivers of bloodshed in this land. If you in your rides have passed back of the Soldier's Home you have seen a city of the dead. Five thousand braves sleep there, their graves watered by the tears of mothers and dear ones.

Think you from their mouldering flesh no plants will spring, no forests will grow? Think you that their souls would not come if they thought a plotter of the assassination was to go free. What did they fight for? What would the Pope of Rome say, who gave up the prisoner before any demand was made, if you say "not guilty." But the blood runs cold at the thought, and there is not an honorable rebel in the land who would not utter his curse at such an act. I would not take the blood of any creature unless he had violated the laws of my country. It is in the Executive power to make whatever adjustment of any punishment for any crime he may see fit. With that we have nothing to do. I have only to say when this man is found guilty honest men will say so. In this case he is proved guilty. I know who is guilty.

I will appeal to any lawyer in the land to say if there was ever a case found with such a demonstration of facts. If there is a man of you who has a doubt in this case, if you will go before your God together on bended knees I know that God will give you light, and I shall say that your verdict is right, whatever it may be, and then if you so feel, having done your duty to the end, you may join with those who see by faith that justice reigns with mercy's life.

JUDGE FISHER'S

CHARGE TO THE JURY.

GENTLEMEN OF THE JURY: "Whoso shed-deth man's blood, by man shall his blood be shed." So spake the Almighty to his servant Noah, when the great deluge had receded and the ark had safely rested upon the holy sum-mit of Mount Ararat. This is God's own law, and its wisdom is acknowledged by all civilized nations. Now and then we meet with sentimental philosophers who think themselves wise above what is written, and who deem it their duty to lift up their voices in condemnation of this fiat of Jehovah, and although they have made but few thorough converts to their pernicious doctrines, they not unfrequently succeed in creating in the minds of honest and tender-hearted people a vitiated sentimentalism which leads them too often to shut their ears to the stern voice of justice, and listen only to the gentle, kindly whisperings of mercy, forgetting that mercy to the guilty is injustice to the innocent.— With such sentimentality you have as jurors, nothing to do. It is no matter of yours to inquire whether the prisoner at the bar is a proper subject of Executive clemency, if you believe him guilty of participating in the crime with which he stands charged before you, but simply to determine his guilt or innocence.

When the dark clouds of war which for four years had lowered in our national horizon had began to lift, and the sun of peace was about to gladden us again with its benign rays; when the main army of the rebels who fol-lowed the traitor Lee in his retreat from Richmond had been overpowered, and had surrendered to the military hero of the age and the army under Johnston was in vain flying from impending capture; when our city was radiant with illuminations in honor of the downfall of the stronghold of a most wicked and atrocious rebellion: when the hearts of all loyal men were leaping and dancing to the merry peans of victory, and when the eyes of all lovers of peace throughout the land were eagerly looking to him whose great heart had never cherished the feeling of malice for even an enemy, and abounded in love and charity for all, in the hope that ere another year should have passed away the hands which had lifted up against each other would again be clasped in friendship and brotherly love, and States dissevered should be again united in harmonious relations—on the fourteenth day of April, 1865, the Executive head of this great nation, the Commander-in-Chief of your army and navy, by the most foul and wicked conspiracy, the record of which has ever stained the pages of history, was stricken down at the hands of the assassin, John Wilkes Booth, in the metropolis of the Re-public, and under the very shadow of the Capitol.

Historians and text writers may treat of the heinousness of the crime of imagining the death of a weak or a wicked king, or of a wise and benignant monarch, but you know, gentlemen, as well as you know that you exist, that to murder the duly elected Pres-ident of the most powerful people on earth is not less atrocious in its character than to com-pass the death of a king or an emperor, albeit he may have sprung from the strong loins of the people, who have made him their representative head, and may have no royal blood coursing through his veins. You may be told that it is a crime surpassingly heinous to take or to compass the life of him who was born to inherit a throne simply because he may be the king of an enslaved people but that to take the life of a President of a free republic is an offence of no greater magnitude than to murder the veriest vagabond that walks your streets; but an American jury will only believe this doctrine when the people have become so demoralized and corrupt, so devoid of the love of liberty and patriotic feeling, as to prefer to have a king and ruler foisted upon them by the accident of birth or fortunate adventure rather than have the making of their own selection of him who is to execute their laws, and for the time being to stand as the representative head of their collective sovereignty.

It is a mistake to suppose that a free people in any country will ever consider it a more heinous crime to kill a being, or even desire his death, than it is to assassinate a President. It is no avail to tell you that to surround the life of a President of a republic with safe-guards as sacred and powerful as those which in monarchies are thrown about a king, as you have been told in the argument, is a modern idea entertained only by those whose eyes have been dazzled by visions of stars and garters, and who are desirous of changing our free institutions for a monarchical form of government. On the contrary, they only can be opposed to guarding with sacred vigilence the life of a President of a free people, who are themselves prepared to submit to the rule of a despot. Why should the people be less proud or less regardful of the life of a ruler selected by themselves from among themselves than they would be of the life of him who claimed to rule over them of his own right ? When this question can be sensibly answered, I shall be willing to admit that the life of a President is less worth the preserving than that of king, and that to destroy the life of a President is a crime of less atrocity than to merely desire the death of a prince ; but not till then, nor do I believe will you,

One of the conspirators who took the life of the President, Abraham Lincoln, on the 14th day of April, 1862, he who fired the fatal shot, in his flight from the scene of the murder was overtaken by the swift vengeance of the Almighty and at the hands of his pursuers. Others, charged as co-conspirators in this enormous crime, were tried two years ago by a military commission. Some of them were condemned to expiate their guilt upon the gallows, and others doomed to suffer imprisonment for life on the Dry Tortugas. You have been told, gentlemen, in the argument of this case, that those who were tried before that military commission, and hung upon its findings, were themselves the victims of a base and disgraceful conspiracy to murder. Brave, gallant, and honest soldiers of their country have been held up before you as inhuman butchers of innocent men.

It has been said in support of this denunciation that the Supreme Court of the United States have, in the case of Milligan, declared that the military court which tried Harold and others for the murder of Abraham Lincoln was an illegal tribunal, organized without law, without right, and without warrant in the Constitution—a mere convocation of military men, having no right to try the cause committed to them by President Johnson. And it has been said that it was convoked not to try but to condemn. In my humble judgment, the Supreme Court has made no such decision. If so, why have not the prisoners now confined upon the Dry Tortugas for complicity in the greatest crime of the age been released from their confinement ? They have sympathizing friends enough to have applied any such decision in the direction of their discharge, and they would not have remained there a week after the decision had been made to the effect that they were unlawfully restrained of their liberty.

If I understand the decision in Milligan's case aright, it went upon the ground that the commission which tried Milligan was not organized in obedience to the act of Congress providing for the punishment of such crimes as he was charged with committing, and the opinion of the majority of the court was based upon the ground that no hostile foot had ever pressed the soil of Indiana at the time when he was arraigned before a military tribunal there, and that therefore the tribunal which condemned him for acts of treason committed in that State had no authority to try him notwithstanding the whole nation was involved in the most terrible struggle for its life. The majority opinion being thus predicated upon a possession of historic truth, we could not, perhaps, have looked for a more rightful decision.

Unprepared, however, as all loyal hearts were for such an announcement, the American people would be even yet more astounded to have it declared by any court in this contry that the Commander-in-Chief of the army and navy, the President of the United States, has not the power, in time of war, to institute a military commission for the purpose of trying a gang of spies and traitors who have found their way within the entrenched encampments of the nation's capital to take the life of the chief of the army and navy; to assassinate all the heads of the executive departments in the interest of the pretended government with which the Federal Government was engaged in war.

They who maintain such a diction profess to defend it upon the ground that no such power is delegated by the Constitution as they did who could find no warrant there to coerce seceding States into submission to the Federal authority. But the day has passed by when honest statesmen will longer, if they ever did, regard the sovereignty of the Federal Union as possessing no other powers save those expressly enumerated in its Constitution.

The Government of the United States was doubtless created by the adoption of the Constitution. But when it had once been spoken into being, it stood upon the same level with other nations, and was clothed with all the powers incident to an independent sovereignty under the laws of nature and of nations, and among them was the power, in time of war or of great public emergency, to arrest and inflict upon spies and traitors the most summary punishment, whenever and wherever the strong hand of military justice can be laid upon them,

It is a power incident to the right and duty of self-preservation, and ought to be exercised, just as the individual owes it to himself to strike down the assassin who is feeling for his heart-string, without waiting to lose his own life, in order that the courts of justice may at their leisure proceed to try the felon according to the formulas of the law and the Constitution. The right of self-defence needs not to be inscribed upon parchments, either for individuals or for sovereign States. The Almighty imprinted right and duty upon the hearts and minds of men, long before he wrote the decalogue upon the tables of stone.

To say that this Government has not the power in time of war to exercise this great duty of self-preservation for want of warrant in the Constitution, is to condemn the action of the Government in acquiring from France and Spain, and Mexico and Russia, territory lying far beyond the limits of the original thirteen States, because such power of acquisition is not provided for by the Constitution. Both these powers are but the incidents of sovereignty, requiring no warrant in written governmental characters. They are derived from the common law of nations and are coexistent with sovereignty. But with this military commission, gentleman, you have no concern at this time: whether it was a legal or an illegal tribunal is not the matter upon which you are now called to decide.

The oath that you have taken requires that you shall "well and truly try, and true deliverance make between the United States of America and John H. Surratt, the prisoner at the bar, whom you have in charge, and a true verdict give according to the evidence." the prisoner stands before you indicted for the murder of Abraham Lincoln, on the 14th day of April, 1865, in this city. About the time, and place, and manner of the death of your late President no controversy has been made in the case. If there had been, your recollection of a nation in tears, and of a whole civilized world in mourning, would have revived your memory of the sad and terrible fact. The only question, therefore, for you to determine is, whether the prisoner at the bar participated with John Wilkes Booth and the others named in the indictment, or either or any of then in this diabolical crime.

If from all the evidence in the case, your minds shall have been convinced, beyond a reasonable doubt growing out of that evidence, that the prisoner did co-operate with them ; if that shall have produced a moral conviction in your minds that the prisoner did participate in the conspiracy to murder, or in a plot to do some unlawful act which resulted in this foul murder, no considerations as to the legality or illegality of the tribunal which tried the prisoner's mother, no feelings of sympathy for other members of the family, no consideration of his youth, or that other lives have already been forfeited for this crime should for a single moment tempt you to step aside from the plain pathway of duty. If, however, upon a full and careful consideration of the whole testimony, uninfluenced in the slightest degree by prejudice or bias of what-over character, the moral conviction of the prisoner's guilt shall not have been impressed upon your minds, but you shall still entertain an honest and unbiased reasonable doubt fastening itself upon your judgments, and suggesting that all the credible proofs pointing in the direction of the prisoner's guilt may be strictly true and may be still consistent with some hypothesis of innocence which you can construe from the whole credible evidence in the cause, you will give him the benefit of such doubt. It is my duty, however, gentlemen, to say to you that this doubt, to the benefit of which the prisoner is entitled, must not be a mere speculative or capricious one, prompted by passion or prejudice, or pity, or feeling of any kind, save the desire in your hearts to do exact and equal justice, by rendering a verdict in accordance with the facts.

It must not be a vague suggestion that, after all, the prisoner may not be guilty. It must not be the mere shadow which the angel wing of mercy may momentarily cast upon your mental vision, but it must be such a doubt as the voice of justice shall whisper in your ears. If the testimony shall convince your understanding of the guilty participation of the prisoner with Booth or others in this crime, such conviction is the moral certainty required by the law, and it excludes the idea of reasonable doubt.

The indictment in this case charges the prisoner with being engaged in a conspiracy with John Wilkes Booth and others to effect the murder of President Lincoln, and with having succeeded in the accomplishment of that atrocious crime. It has been argued by the counsel for the prosecution , that to take the life of the President of the United States is a crime so heinous in its character that each of the conspirators is responsible for the act of each of his co-conspirators, committed in furtherance of the conspiracy, so long as he continues to be a member of that conspiracy, and that he can only be relieved of criminal responsibility by repenting, abandoning, and renouncing his connection with the conspiracy, and countermanding any orders he may have given in relation to it.

On the other hand, it is contended by the counsel for the defence that the indictment no where charges a conspiracy to kill or the killing of the President of the United States, but simply charges a conspiracy to kill or the killing of Abraham Lincoln, the indi-

vidual ; that inasmuch as there is no allegation in the indictment showing that Abraham Lincoln, at the time of the murder, was President of the United States, but simply avers the killing of an individual, the case is to be governed solely by the same principles of law which are applicable to ordinary murder, and cannot be regarded by you as being in any degree more heinous in its character ; that even admitting that to take the life of the President of the United States is a more heinous crime than the murder of an individual in a private station, yet, for the want of an allegation in the indictment of the fact of the Presidency, you cannot, no matter what the evidence may be as to the killing of the President, and all the heads of departments, and the Vice President, in your consideration of this case and in making up your verdict, regard it as a crime standing on the same footing in its atrocity with the crime of treason or conspiring the death of a king.

They argue that although by the common law of England to compass the death of a king is a crime so heinous in its character to admit of no accessories before the fact, yet the law of murder is different in England and here, and that in cases of murder, he who counsels, aids or commands another to commit murder, without being present to render material aid in its commission, can only be proceeded against as an accessory before the fact, and not as a principal, as in this case. You are told that it must both be alleged in the indictment and proved by the evidence, or you cannot consider the killing of a President, or the conspiracy to murder him and all the chief officers of the Government, for the purpose of bringing anarchy and confusion in the nation, and thus to favor the cause of the rebellion. But there are some things of which courts and juries will take judicial notice.

One of the elements of the definition of murder is "the killing of a reasonable creature." It is never either alleged in the indictment nor proved in the evidence that the subject of the crime is a human being. It is not necessary, because it is one of those things that are presumed to be taken judicial cognizance of. It is not alleged in the present indictment that Abraham Lincoln was a reasonable creature, nor has any proof been adduced to show it ; and yet we take judicial cognizance of the fact. So we may take judicial cognizance of the fact that at the time of the murder he was President of the United States, because it is something known to every man, woman, and child in the country capable of knowing anything : and taking such judicial cognizance of it, it need neither be alleged in the indictment nor proved by witnesses.

It is true, as stated by the counsel for the defence, that it has been laid down by Sir Matthew Hale, in his work entitled "Pleas of the Crown," that although treason is so heinous in its charater as to admit of no accessories before the fact, but that its heinous character makes all principals who in any way contributed to its commission, yet that murder, and other felonies not being so heinous in their character, aiders and abettors are to be proceeded against only as accessories before the fact. When, however, he comes to treat of misdemeanors, a lower grade of crime than felonies, he tells us that they will not admit of accessories before the fact, because of their want of character sufficiently heinous.

Later writers have generally followed the law as laid down by Hale, and many decisions have been founded upon that authority. the writers and judges seeming contented with his reasons, or indisposed to depart from the principles laid down by him: but I confess the reasons are not very satisfactory to my mind. I have never been able yet to discover any sound reason why he who originates the plan of murder, but employs another or others as his agent or agents to perpetrate the crime, is not equally guilty with the perpetrator of it.

If I, actuated by the malice of a depraved and wicked heart, conceive the purpose of murdering him whom I suppose to be my enemy, but lacking the opportunity or courage to carry my purpose into execution, hire another person who wilfully executes my wicked design for me, common sense and the common conscience of mankind, which, after all, seldom fails to direct us to the principles of the law, "which has been defined to be the perfection of reason or common sense," would seem to dictate that I cannot be less guilty than the agent whom I had employed, upon the well-known principle of law that he who does an act by another does it by himself, a principle which has been recognized by the Supreme Court of the United States in the case of Gooding vs. The United States, 12 Wheaton, page 460, as applicable to criminal as well as civil cases; a principle recognized in more ancient and higher authority than even the Supreme Court of the United States, or than Lord Hale, or any other writer upon the law to whom we are accustomed to look for principle or precedents.

There are two cases which now occur to me. Probably others might be found reported in the Book of highest authority known among Christian nations, decided by a Judge from whose decision there can be no appeal, and before whose solemn tribunal all Judges and jurors will, in the great day, have their verdicts and judgment passed in review. Man cannot make better law than God, nor can he better expound or administer the law. One of these cases is that of Naboth and Ahab, contained in the first chapter of the first book of kings, Naboth, the Israelite, was the owner of a vineyard hard by the palace of Ahab, king of Samaria, which had excited the cupidity of the latter, who offered to purchase it with money or to give in exchage for it another vineyard. But Naboth was unwilling to part with it, because it was the inheritance of his father. This excited the wrath and displeasure of king Ahab and his Queen Jezebel, who conspired together to effect the death of Naboth, and they succeeded by having witnesses suborned to swear against him as a blasphemer, that he might be stoned to death by the elders and the nobles of his city.

The plan was laid by Jezebel; the motive to the murder was Ahab's cupidity, and he lent his wife his signet ring with which to send the letters which she sent to the elders and nobles whom she employed as the agents to consummate the wicked plot. Two sons of Belial, we are told, were the perjured witnesses who proved the blasphemy on Naboth, and this effected his death. Ahab, profiting by the crime, took possession of the vineyard of Naboth. "The word of the Lord came to Elisha the Tishbite, saying; Arise! Go down to meet Ahab, King of Israel, which is in Samaria; behold he is in the vineyard of Naboth, whither he has gone down to possess it, and thou shalt speak unto him, saying; Thus saith the Lord, hast thou killed and also taken possession? In the place where dogs licked the blood of Naboth shall dogs lick thy blood, even thine. And it came to pass that dogs licked up the blood of Ahab, according to the judgment which God had decreed against him."

The other case to which I have alluded is that of David and Uriah, recorded in the 11th chapter of 2d Samuel. Uriah, a subject of King David, was a brave and gallant soldier in the army of Joab, which was engaged in war with the Ammonites. His wife, Bathsheba, was comely in person, and very beautiful to look upon, and King David coveted her. In order to effect his wicked purpose he sent a letter to Joab, his chief captain, even by the hand of Uriah himself, saying, " Set ye Uriah in the forefront of the hottest battle, and return ye from him, that he may be smitten and die." Joab obeyed the behest of his king, and Uriah, the Hittite, was slain. But the Lord sent his prophet Nathan unto David, saying, " Thou art the man who did this evil thing. Thou hast killed Uriah, the Hittite, with the sword, or hast slain him with the sword of the children of Ammon."

This judgment of the Lord was not that David was accessory to this murder, but was guilty as the principal because he procured the murder to be done. It was a judgement to the effect that who does an act by another does it himself, whether it be a civil or a criminal act. The counsel for the prisoner at the bar in this case contend that he was not in the city of Washington or near enough to the scene of the murder to have taken part in it by rendering material aid to Booth, the actual assassin who fired the fatal shot, and that the evidence adduced on the part of the Government as well as that of the defence shows such to have been the fact.

This is what is termed in the law an "alibi," a Latin word for elsewhere. This is a line of defence always held in little favor by the courts and juries, not only because it is one which common sense teaches us may be most easily supported by perjury, but because it is one involving identity of time, as to which mistakes are very easily made, so that it is by no means difficult to support this plea frequently, and especially after the lapse of months or years, by the testimony of honest and truthful witnesses, who, on account of the great liability of the human mind, particularly when influenced by the promptings of pity or sympathy, to be mistaken as to the precise time, in reference either to days or hours. The past experience of crime teaches us that in the days

of notorious public depredations upon society, it was a very common device to gallop upon fleet horses straight across the country, and by appearing before credible witnesses shortly after the commission of a robbery, or other crime, to obtain the testimony of such witnesses, and thus secure an acquittal by an alibi.

We have an instance of the honest fallibility of the human memory in respect to the identity of time under the promptings of pity, or friendship, or sympathy, in the case of the Commonwealth of Massachusetts against Webster, for the killing of Dr. Parkman, some eighteen years ago, in which several witnesses of respectability swore so positively, and yet so honestly, to facts placing it beyond the pale of possibility that Dr. Webster could have been present at the scene of the murder, that the general sense of the community seemed in doubt as to whether Littlefield, an important witness for the prosecution, was not in fact the real murderer of Parkman, and yet, after the verdict of the jury had been rendered, and the sentence of law pronounced, the prisoner, Webster, who knew better than any other mortal, made full confession of his guilt.

If it were true that hard ridings across the country in olden times furnished facilities for criminals to establish the defence of an alibi, how much greater facilities for that purpose are furnished at the present day by the power and speed of steam, by which space and time have become almost annihilated? I have already said that this plea has always been regarded with extreme suspicion, and yet when once clearly established to the satisfaction of the jury it constitutes the most complete defence. But an honest and sensible jury cannot fail to regard it with suspicion, unless it shall be so clearly established as to satisfy them of the prisoner's absence from the scene of the crime. The suspicion which attaches to this plea has passed into a proverb among the people, as well as with courts and juries, and is it true that an unsuccessful attempt to establish an alibi is always a circumstance of great weight against a prisoner, because a resort to that kind of defence implies an admission of the truth of the relevancy of the facts alleged against him, and the correctness of the inference drawn from them

In this connection I may also observe that when once a conspiracy to commit a crime shall have been proved on the party who is on his trial for an act done in pursuance of that conspiracy: he having been connected with it, if the evidence shall satisfy the minds of the jury that he was present, either constructively or actually—that is to say, either at the scene of the crime, in person, or near enough to give any or the slightest support or encouragement in the actual perpetration of it, or if he be remote from the scene for the purpose of aiding it, and in performance of the part of the plan assigned to him—he is equally guilty with his co-conspirators, who actually perpetrate the crime.

You have been told, gentlemen, by the counsel for the defence, in a manner not very respectful, certainly by no means complimentary to the Court, that you are the judges of the law as well as the facts in criminal cases, and that you have the right to disregard the instructions of the Court in matters of law: and they tell you that their exposition of the law, and the weight of character they possess, may be more safely relied upon than the instructions which may be given you by the Court. The weight of character of a prisoner's counsel would be a very variable, and not unfrequently very unsafe criterion by which the jury should judge as to the law of the case. Perhaps they would have you regard the court as sitting upon the bench merely to discharge the duty of preserving order in the court-room, which, probably, the crier of the Court, or the bailiff, might be disposed to regard as an usurpation of his prerogative.

If the jury entirely disregards the judge's instructions as to the law of a case, I confess I see but little left than that for him to perform. It is true, gentlemen, that you have the power, and in cases where your consciences are satisfied that the instructions of the Court are dictated not by an honest desire to enlighten the jury as to the true state of the law, but by corrupt and wicked motives, you may have had the right to disregard the instructions purposely intended to mislead you. But to claim that the jury are better judges of what the law may be than the court, is about as reasonable as to assert that a plain farmer or merchant may be taken fresh from his plough or his counter, and be more capable of navigating and manœuvring a steam frigate, or to lead your armies to certain victory, than your Admiral or your General-in-Chief.

In my opinion, you have just the same right to disregard the evidence of the witnesses who stand before you unimpeached in any matter respecting the facts involved in the cause, as you have to disregard what the Court may say to you, under an official oath, as to the law that may apply to the facts. A jury have the power, if they choose to exercise it, after having assumed the obligation of an oath, to say that they will neither believe the judge nor the witnesses, but decide the law and facts according to their own caprice or the confidence which they may repose in the counsel upon either side. But such is not the purpose for which juries were instituted, and they have no right so to act. When the witnesses in the cause have testified before you as to the facts, it is then the office of the judge, under his official oath, to testify to you in the spirit of truth, according to the best of his knowledge and ability, as to what is the law which may be applicable to those facts; and an honest jury will disregard neither the testimony of the witnesses nor the instructions of the judge, unless they are satisfied that corrupt motives have actuated them. They will leave the party to his legitimate redress—a writ of error to the Appellate Court.

Much stress has also been laid by the counsel for the defence upon a fact which they assert, that during the progress of this trial more than one hundred and fifty exceptions have been taken to the ruling of the Court concerning the admissibility of evidence. If they have found themselves under the necessity of calculating the number of these exceptions, and parading them before you with a view of having you to render a verdict according to irrelevant evidence not before you, rather than according to the testimony which you have heard, I have no disposition to criticise their taste, but leave them to present their case in their own way. At the same time, I feel it to be my duty to remark to you that, if the counsel will be so bold as to present propositions to the Court which every tyro in the profession ought to know are untenable, it does not necessarily follow that the judge must always be so weak as to sustain them. It has heretofore been supposed that exceptions to the ruling of a judge at Nisi Prius were intended to be passed in review before the Appellate Courts.

I have never before known them to be neatly calculated and presented to the jury in the way of arguments. In reference to these matters. I may observe that perhaps I owed it to the dignity of the bench to have interrupted counsel in their conduct of the case in this particular; but in a cause involving the life of a prisoner upon the one hand, and the vindication of the outraged justice of a nation in mourning upon the other, I deemed it my duty to cast not an atom in the one scale or the other which might by any possibility tend to prejudice either side of the issue. I can now direct your attention in a general way, only, to the evidence.

It would be impossible for me to review it in detail without taxing your patience which has already been nearly exhausted. I have already said that the counsel for the defence rely upon an alibi to acquit the prisoner. They also have endeavored to destroy the credibility of nearly if not all of the material witnesses whose testimony has tended to connect the prisoner with the body of the crime, either by contradicting them by other witnesses on points material to the issue, or by attacking their character for credibility. Whether they have succeeded in destroying the credibility of any one or more of them you are to determine.

On the other hand the prosecution rely for a conviction on the evidence which they have spread before you, tending to show the malice of the prisoner toward the Federal Government, and especially toward the deceased, Abraham Lincoln, for a long time prior to the murder; his frequent communications and intercourse, private, confidential and mysterious, with Booth and the other conspirators, personally and by letters; his interest manifested in providing quarters at the Herndon House for Payne, who attempted to assassinate Secretary Seward; his procurement of arms for aiding the escape of Booth and Harold, and the concealment of them at Surrattsville shortly prior to the assassination of the President; his fabrication of false accounts and contradictory statements as to the object of his movements; his expressions used to Smoot, shortly before the assassination of the President, that if the Yankees knew what he was doing, or was about to do, they would stretch his neck for him; his fixing of the wooden bar against the door of the President's box at the theatre; his presence here in the city on the day of the murder; his being in company with Booth and McLaughlin at the barber's on that day; his appearance in front of Ford's Theatre on the night of the murder; his excited and suspicious manner while there, and his calling out the time to Booth and the other men with him two or three times, shortly before the fatal shot was fired by Booth, as the signal for action; his alleged activity in the management of the entire conspiracy planned for the fatal evening of the 14th of April; his flight from the city on the morning of the 15th of April, as soon as it was possible for him to leave; his swift haste to get into Canada; his abandonment of his mother and family; his concealment of himself in Canada at the house of the rebel sympathizers, Boucher and La-Pierre; his disguise of his person by the coloring of his hair; the changing of his dress and wearing spectacles; his flight from Canada under an assumed name and disguised personal appearance; his free and voluntary confessions to Dr. McMillan on board the steamer Peruvian; his constant apprehension of the United States detectives even on the British steamer and on British soil; his flight from England to Rome, and entering the Papal service; his confession to St. Marie while there as to the manner of his escape from Washington immediately after the murder; his failure to prove to you where he ate and slept during the time when he left Montreal on the 12th of April till he returned on the 18th of the same month, and his flight from Rome to Egypt. All these matters are presented for your careful and candid consideration.

You are to weigh them all, and then make up your verdict. In giving these matters your attention, you will not fail to remember that flight from the scene of crime, the fabrication of false accounts and contradictory statements, the concealment of instruments of violence, are all circumstances strongly indicative of guilt. You will further bear in mind that a confession of crime, when freely and fairly made, the body of the crime being proved, which is in this case the fact of murder, is one of the surest proofs of guilt, because it is the testimony of the Omniscient speaking through the conscience of the culprit. You will not either forget that circumstantial evidence carries with it the highest degree of moral certainty. These are well-settled rules of law, to which it is my duty to invite your attention.

From the observations which I have addressed to you, you will infer:

FIRST. That a conspiracy formed in time of war to take the life of the President and Vice President of the Republic, and the heads of the executive departments, for the purpose of aiding the enemies of the Federal Government by throwing it into anarchy and confusion, to treason, as heinous and hurtful to the people of this country as the compassing the death of the King or Queen of Great Britain is to the subject of that realm.

SECOND, That every person engaged in such conspiracy, as long as he continues a member of it, is responsible not only for the act of treason, but for any murder or less crime which may flow from it.

THIRD. That the Government may waive the charge of treason against any or all the conspirators and proceed against them for the smaller crime of murder, included in the greater crime of treason.

FOURTH. That under an indictment for a murder, resulting from the prosecution of such conspiracy, evidence of the entire scope of the conspiracy may be considered in estimating the heinous character of the offence laid in the indictment.

FIFTH. That it was not necessary to aver in the indictment the fact that Abraham Lincoln, the victim of the murder, was at the time of its commission President of the United States, or to prove it in order to allow the jury to take that fact into the account in determining the heinous character of the crime, it being a fore fact of which the courts will take judicial cognizance.

SIXTH. That he who does an act by another does it by himself, and is responsible for its consequences, in criminal as well as in civil cases.

SEVENTH. That although an ALIBI, when clearly established, forms a complete and unanswerable defence, the mere absence from the immediate scene of a crime resulting from a conspiracy unrepented of and unabandoned by the party, it will not avail him if he were at some other place assigned him, performing his part in that conspiracy.

EIGHT. That this plea is, unless clearly made out, always regarded with suspicion, and a circumstance weighing against him who attempts it, because it implies an admission of the truth of the facts alleged against him and the correctness of the inference drawn from them.

NINTH. That flight from the scene of the crime, the fabrication of false accounts, the concealment of instruments of violence, are circumstances indicating guilt.

TENTH. Although a confession in the slightest degree tainted with the promise of favor, or by duress or fear, is not admitted as evidence against him who makes it, yet, if made freely and voluntarily, is one of the surest proofs of guilt.

As to the credibility of the witnesses, you are to be the exclusive judge, You see them face to face; you know whether they are confirmed or unsupported or contradicted by other witnesses of credit and other circumstances. You are to judge whether their testimony has been impeached, and are to consider every matter which will tend to shed any light upon the question as to what has been truthfully or falsely deposed by any witnesses.

You will diligently collate and compare, and carefully weigh and consider all the testimony in the cause on both sides. You will not disregard or reject the testimony of any witness unless you shall be satisfied that he has been shown to be unworthy of credence by reason of his want of character for truth, his contradicting himself, or being flatly contradicted by others of better credit, or by dishonesty of purpose manifested by his conduct and manner in testifying before you.

In conclusion, you will take the case with the honest purpose to do justice to the United States and to the defendant, bearing in mind that it is the office of the law to secure the punishment of the guilty and the protection of the innocent. If John H. Surratt, in the honest and intelligent convictions of your judgment and consciences, is not guilty, so pronounce by your verdict, thus giving a lesson of assurance that a court of justice is the asylum of innocence.

On the contrary, if guilty, pronounce him guilty, and thus, by your verdict, furnish a guarantee of protection to the inteded victims of guilt, and a testimonial to the country and the world that the District of Columbia, set apart by the Constitution of the United States as the theatre for the exercise of Federal power, gives the judicial guarantees essential to the protection of the persons of the public servants, commissioned by the people of the nation to do their work, safe and sacred from the presence of unpunished assassins within its borders.

Mr. Bradley said that he understood it was not necessary for the defendant's to reduce their exceptions to writing and have them signed by the Court before the jury retired, but that it could be done afterwards.

Judge Fisher replied in the affirmative.

Mr. Carrington then handed the indictment to Mr. Tood, the foreman of the jury.

Mr. Tood asked if the jury could have a copy of the record containing the testimony.

Judge Fisher replied that it was not customary to allow the jury to have the written evidence.

Mr. Bradley said, so far as the defence was concerned, they were perfectly willing to allow the jury to have a copy of the record.

Mr. Carrington said he must adhere to the established rule of practice, and he therefore deemed it to be his duty to object to the jury having a copy of the record.

Judge Fisher said we must act the same in this case as in other cases, and directed the case to be given to the jury.

Mr. Middleton, the clerk, then administered the following oath to the bailiffs, Messrs. Wm L. Roos and Robert Hughes.

"You shall take this jury to some convenient room, and keep them apart by themselves; you shall not suffer any person to speak to them, neither shall you speak to them yourselves, unless it be to ask them if they have agreed upon a verdict, without the permission of the court."

The bailiffs took charge of the jury, and they retired to their room at twenty-eight minutes before twelve o'clock.

WAITING FOR THE VERDICT.

2 35 p. m.—The jury has now been out three hours. The spectators, male and female, remain in the court room, and seem determined to sit it out.

A bailiff has just appeared with a message for the judge, but its purport has not transpired.

3.30 p. m.—Judge Fisher has gone home, to be absent two hours; whether he has information that the jury will not speedily agree has not transpired.

3. 50 p. m.—The spectators have got tired, and many have left the room. Among the rumors now flying about is one that the jury stands 10 to 2.

4. 10 p. m.—The prisoner has been taken from the room, and his removal was the signal for the departure of a large number of the spectators.

6.30 p. m.—Judge Fisher again entered the court-room and took his seat upon the bench, but as nothing was heard from the jury he again left.

9 30 p. m.—Bedding has been brought into the court-house, and taken to the jury-room, an indication that there is no prospect of an agreement to-night at least.

The crowd in the court-room hangs on, and not a few are fast asleep in their chairs. There being no gas fixtures in the court-room, it is dimly lighted up with candles.

10 p. m.—Judge Fisher again took his position on the bench, and was informed by a bailiff that there was no prospect of an agreement. The Judge then stated that he would go home. He did not order a recess, but it was understood that he would not be here to receive a verdict until to-morrow morning. Some of the jurors are comfortably disposed upon pallets, and others are striving to convince others to their views.

THE LAST DAY.

CLOSE OF SURRATT'S TRIAL.

UTTER INABILITY TO AGREE.

How They Were Divided.

JUDGE FISHER DISCHARGES THE JURY.

He Dismisses Mr. Bradley from the Bar.

ALL CLASSES INTENSELY EXCITED.

Mr. BRADLEY Challenges JUDGE FISHER

WASHINGTON Aug. 10.—At 12 30 Deputy marshal Philips came into the court room and stationed the officers. This was a signal for a rush on the part of the crowd that had been patiently waiting outside, and they quickly filled up the space outside the bar. A number were admitted inside the bar. Attorney Carrington was in the court room at the time, and Mr. Bradley, Jr., one of the counsel for the prisoner, came in a moment afterwards. Mr. Bradley, Sr., and Mr. Merrick subsequently entered the room, they having been sent for. There was a decided commotion in the court room, and it was whispered about, "The jury has agreed," "They are going to discharge the jury," "They can't agree, and have asked to be discharged," &c., &c.

At one o'clock the prisoner was brought into the court room and assigned the seat occupied by him during the trial beside his counsel. He came into court smiling, and seemed to be in good spirits, as he chatted with his counsel, and looked around among the crowd present.

Mr. Merrick made an allusion to a report that an attempt would be made at a rescue, whereat the prisoner seemed to be much amused.

At five minutes past one Judge Fisher resumed his seat upon the bench.

Mr. Malloy, the Crier, called the court to order, and Marshall Phillips was directed to bring the jury down. By this time the room was much crowded. The jury was brought in at eight minutes past one, and by direction of Judge Fisher the names of the jurors were called.

Mr. Middleton, the clerk, addressing the jury, said ; —" Gentlemen of the jury, have you agreed upon your verdict?"

Mr. Todd—We have not been able to agree.

Judge Fisher—I have received the following from the jury ;—

To the Hon. George P. Fisher of the Criminal Court :—Sir :—The jury in the case of the United States vs. John H. Surratt, most respectfully state that they stand precisely now as when they first balloted upon entering the room—nearly equally divided —and they are firmly convinced that they cannot possibly make a verdict. We deem it our duty to the court, to the country, and in view of the condition of our private affairs and the situation of our families, and in view of the fact that the health of several of our number is becoming seriously impaired under the protracted confinement, to make this statement, and to ask your Honor to dismiss us at once.

Most respectfully submitted.

W. B. Todd,	James Y. Davis,
Robert Ball,	C. Alexander,
J. Russell Barr,	Wm. McLean,
Thomas Berry,	Benjamin F. Morsell,
George A. Bohrer,	B. E. Gittings,
C. G. Schneider,	W. W. Birth,

After the letter had been read, Judge Fisher asked if anything was to be said on either side, why the jury was not to be discharged.

Mr. Bradley said the prisoner did not consent, and if there was any discharge, it would be against the protest of the prisoner.

Mr. Carrington said he would leave the whole matter to the court.

Judge Fisher said he had already received two or three notes of a similar tenor to the one read. If there was any possibility of

the jury agreeing, he would not object to keeping them for a reasonable time. But as he was informed they could not possibly agree, he would discharge them.

The jury was accordingly discharged at ten minutes past one o'clock, and immediately left the court room.

Judge Fisher then immediately read the following :—

I have now a very unpleasant duty to discharge, but one which I cannot forego. On the 2d day of July last during the progress of the trial of John H. Surratt for the murder of Abraham Lincoln, immediately after the court had taken a recess until the following morning, as the Presiding Justice was descending from the bench, Joseph H. Bradley, Esq., accosted him in a rude and insulting manner, charging the Judge with having offered him (Mr. Bradley) a series of insults from the bench from the commencement of the trial. The Judge disclaimed any intention whatever of passing any insult, and assured Mr. Bradley that he entertained for him no other feelings but those of respect. Mr. Bradley, so far from accepting this explanation of disclaimer, threatened the Judge with personal chastisement.

As he understood, no court can administer justice, or live, if its judges are to be threatened with personal violence on all occasions whenever the irrascibillity of counsel may be excited by an imaginary insult. The offence of Mr. Bradley is one which even his years will not palliate. It cannot be overlooked nor go unpunished as a contempt of court. It is therefore ordered that his name be stricken from the rolls of attorneys practising at this court.

Mr. Bradley immediately rose to his feet and asked if the court had adjourned.

Judge Fisher—It has not, sir.

Mr. Bradley—Then, sir, in the presence of the court and this assembly, I hereby pronounce the statement just made by the Judge as utterly false in every particular.

Judge Fisher, interrupting—Crier, adjourn the court.

Mr. Malloy (the Crier)—The court is now adjourned.

Mr. Bradley—Well, then, I will say now—

Judge Fisher (rising to leave the bench)— You can say what you please, sir, and make a speech to the crowd, if you like.

Mr. Bradley you have no authority to dismiss me from the bar. That must be the act of three of the judges of the Supreme Court.

Judge Fisher said—Very well, Mr. Bradley, you can make the proper appeal. He then left the room, followed by a large crowd of persons.

Immediately after leaving the court room, Judge Fisher proceeded to the street and entered a car for the purpose of proceeding up town. He was followed closely by Mr. Bradley, who entered the car, and stepping up to Judge Fisher, handed him a note.

Judge Fisher took the note, rose to his feet, opened it, and began to read it, and Mr. Bradley turned and left the car, around which an excited crowd had gathered. It is understood that the note was a challenge. Several policemen sprang into the car, and Officer McHenry stepped to the side of Mr. Bradley, and kept in this position while he remained in the car.

By this time the street was blocked up, at least a thousand persons surrounding the car. Mr. Bradley was pushing his way out, when the friends of Judge Fisher cried, "Wait and get your answer: you'll get one." Judge Fisher rose and moved toward the door, when Mr. Bradley turned, half pushed back by the excited crowd. The movement looked to those in the street like a collision, and the cry of "He's going to shoot" caused the spectators to fall back.

The police dispersed the crowd and ordered the car to move on. A good many of Surratt's friends were armed, and it looked for a few moments as if an outbreak were certain. Two gentlemen, friends of Judge Fisher, were armed and remained by his side throughout.

It was not until the car had moved away from the tumult that Judge Fisher read Mr. Bradley's note, which was dated August 6, four days previous to its delivery, and stated in effect that on the occasion of the altercation between Judge Fisher and Mr. Bradley, on the 2d of July, Judge Fisher had stated that he was sick and could be found when wanted, or words to that effect. The epistle went on to give the writer's (Bradley's) ideas of honor, the satisfaction due a gentleman, &c., and in conclusion the writer expressed a hope that Judge Fisher would arrange a time to meet him outside the District limits, where the mutual difference might be satisfactorily settled, and they might avoid the odium which might be occasioned by any controversy here or in public.

Leaving the car, Mr. Bradley passed through the crowd and entered his office, and was followed by several friends belonging to the bar. A large crowd immediately gathered on the corner in front of his office. After remaining in his office a few moments Mr. Bradley came out, arm-in-arm with his brother, Charles Bradley, Esq., of the National Bank of the Republic, and proceeded down Louisiana avenue, followed by a crowd of friends and curious persons, who excitedly discussed the proceedings which had just transpired.

In the meantime, Judge Fisher resumed his seat in the car, and continued his perusal of the note, while the car moved off. A number of his personal friends had entered the car, and a great deal of apprehension was manifested of a personal encounter between the Judge and the deposed lawyer.

The order of Judge Fisher dismissing Mr. Bradley has created the most intense excitement among all classes, but the police are preserving order. The members of the bar generally are bitter in their denunciations of the Judge, and have called a meeting to be held on Monday morning. They seem to make common cause against the Judge, who, they openly declare, has disgraced himself by using his official power to resent a personal insult. Surratt was remanded to the custody of the Marshal, and returned to jail.

There is good authority for stating that the jury disagreed on the question of the absence of Surratt from Washington at the time of the assassination of the late President, and that they were entirely agreed upon this point, that had he been indicted for conspiracy, he would have been convicted immediately on retiring to their room.

The following fact as to the nativity of the jurors may not be uninteresting to the public:—

W. B. Todd, born December 3, 1809, at Newburyport, Mass.

Robert Ball, born April 30, 1827, at Alexandria, D. C.

J. Russell Barr, born January 7, 1812, in Northumberland county, Pa.

Thomas Berry, born February 10, 1816, at New York city.

George A. Bohrer, born January 1, 1816, at Georgetown, D. C.

Christian S. Schneider, born June 12, 1831, at Wurtemburg, Germany.

James Y. Davis, born July 30, 1819, at Northumberland county, Va.

Columbus Alexandria, born September 15, 1815, at Alexandria, Va.

William McLean, born December 1, 1820, at Kilmarnock, Scotland.

Benjamin F. Morsell, born January 30, 1821, at Prince George county, Md.

Benjamin Gettings, born December 31, 1808, at Montgomery county, Md.

William W. Berth, born January 11, 1803, at Washington, D. C.

It is said by gentlemen who have seen the communication handed by Mr. Bradley to Judge Fisher to-day, that it first refers to the affair in the court room between Judge Fisher and Mr. Bradley, early in July last, during the progress of the Surratt trial, and quotes the expression attributed to Judge Fisher, to the effect that he (Mr. Bradley) knew where the Judge lived, and that the latter would receive a communication from him at any time. It then states that the writer could give but one interpretation to that declartion by Judge Fisher, and refering to the misunderstanding between them, it suggested that Judge Fisher should appoint as early a day as conveinent to meet Mr. Bradley outside the District, for the purpose of settling their difficulty.

Mr. Bradley further suggested in his communication that if they met within the District they might be interfered with.

The letter is dated July 6, at about the date of the previous difficulty, but was reserved autil the conclusion of this trial.

During the retirement of the jury, seventy-two hours, they remained as follows on the verdict:—

FOR CONVICTION.

Mr. Todd,   Mr. Schneider,
Mr. Barr,   Mr. McLean.

FOR ACQUITAL.

Mr. Davis,   Mr. Alexander,
Mr. Berry,   Mr. Morsell,
Mr. Ball,   Mr. Gettings,
Mr. Bohrer,   Mr. Berth.

FEELINGS OF THE PRISONER.

Surratt was very much depressed at the result, and remarked to his brother that he would have preferred any verdict to going through another trial with the consequent long imprisonment and suspense. Owing to the rumors of impending trouble, the prisoner was ironed and taken back to jail by a heavy guard.

THE NEXT TRIAL

Will take place at the December term of the Criminal Court, Chief Justice Carter presiding.

AN INDICTMENT PROBABLE.

It is contemplated to have Mr. Bradley indicted under an act of Congress which prohibits any one, under penalty of five years imprisonment at hard labor, from writing or sending a challenge to any one in this District to fight a duel without its limits.